LOVE
&
REGRETS

A NOVEL

Sheryl Mallory-Johnson

To Sherry,
may this story touch
your heart.
Enjoy!
4/12

PUBLISHED BY WANASOMA BOOKS

First printing: December, 2011

ISBN #: 978-0-9822085-2-6

Library of Congress Control Number: 2011939414

PRINTED IN THE UNITED STATES OF AMERICA

Cover by Marion Designs

All WANASOMA titles are available at special discounts for bulk purchases for sales promotion, premiums, fund-raising, educational, or institutional use.

ACKNOWLEGMENTS

It is said that no writer writes a book alone. This couldn't be truer than in my case. I have so many individuals to acknowledge I hardly know where to begin. Yet, I must start somewhere.

I thank God primarily. He is the agent of all my success, the source of my power and the benefactor of my blessings.

From the bottom of my heart, I thank my magnificent husband, Rudolph A. Johnson III, for supporting my passion and allowing me to play for a living. I must also acknowledge my children, Rudolph A. Johnson IV and daughter, Mallory T. Johnson. You are the wind beneath my wings.

To my extended family, including my mom, mother-in-law, siblings, cousins, aunties, nieces and nephews, you have encouraged me in ways you'll never know or understand and I thank, thank, thank you!

A special shout out to my brother-in-law, Rashad Johnson and his "boys" for the ongoing debates that led to great material for this book. This includes my cousin and Oakland Raiders Offensive Lineman, Khalif Barnes. He and Bret Maxie, retired New Orleans Saints turned NFL Coach, were an open window to the life of a professional athlete.

Also, thank you so much, Andrea Dixon, for your detailed knowledge of event planning. In addition, I thank Precious Hubbard and LaMar Hasbrouck for their encouraging feedback during the initial development of this story.

I especially thank my friends, readers and cheer squad, Alice Kennedy and Cynthia Keeve, along with my primary editor and life-long friend, Karen Zinn-Amos. It cannot and should not be taken for granted when people take the time out of their own lives to contribute to yours. Thank you for your invaluable gift to not only my life, but this book.

OTHER BOOKS BY AUTHOR

Sense of Love

L.A. Summer: Friends Til the Blood End (YA)

LOVE
&
REGRETS

Thin Line From Crazy

Carmen Hill-Dougherty swiped her employee-parking pass and entered the lot of the five-star Tower West Hotel. The first person she saw and didn't want to see was Kendall. He was maneuvering his monstrous motorcycle in circles, searching for a parking space. Carmen quickly parked in her space designated for the senior sales manager.

"You need me to help you carry something, boss?" Kendall said, catching her on the run. What he could do for her, quite honestly, was stay the hell away from her, Carmen thought.

"If you want to help, get started catering to the needs of one of our most important clients of the year," Carmen told him.

"My department assistant days are done. I have my own events to cater to, you know?" Kendall said as if annoyed by her order.

Carmen knew damn well he had been promoted to an associate sales manager, and whom did he have to thank for it? She did the hiring and firing in the department and now wished she could forget the day Kendall walked into the hotel and into her life a year ago. Only she knew Kendall's qualifications for the job had little to do with why she hired him, and more to do with his ability to make her smile when there wasn't a smile left in her. A good-looking Dominican man who spoke fluent Spanish would add a refreshing change and extra color to the office aesthetics, Carmen had thought on a conscious level. On the lowest level of consciousness, Carmen was prompted to hire Kendall for other reasons.

The time frame was chiseled into Carmen's mind like phrasing on a gravestone. It was sometime around her thirtieth birthday, not hard to forget when she did more crying than celebrating. In the middle of her life, while she was humming along, she ran into a brick wall. It sprang up out of thin air and cast a shadow over everything she loved. She never felt so vacant and discontented, so unchallenged and unaccomplished. She thought of finishing her bachelor degree, changing careers, joining the black ski club, taking up sewing, scrapbooking, winemaking, enlisting in the army and shipping off to another country. Some days she hoped for an earthquake to put some excitement back into her life. Then along came Kendall, Mr. Excitement himself.

"Every associate is on deck for this event, Kendall. You are not an exception." Carmen's eyes were as cold and crisp as her tone.

"For you, I'll do anything." Everything Kendall said had hidden meaning, signified by a wink of his brow and ogling eyes. He back peddled so Carmen wouldn't knock him aside as she pressed onward. He then took a bow and gestured for her to proceed into the hotel ahead of him. Being a public nuisance had become a game to him, to see how far he could push her over the edge, she supposed.

Hoping to lose Kendall, Carmen trucked past Madeline, the new department assistant who took Kendall's old job, nodding a terse hello along the way. Ignoring the curious stares of her other three associate sales managers, Carmen closed herself inside her roomy office and let out a weighty sigh, dropping into her office chair like her workday had ended, not started. A minute to calm her quaking nerves after colliding with Kendall was the most Carmen could afford. For the next eight hours, every other minute was consumed with things to do. Thank goodness her anxiety had lowered enough to manage this zoo of an event today, Carmen thought as she buttoned the blazer of her pinstriped pants suit.

Recalling the importance of today's banquet, Carmen hopped up and got to work, hoping Kendall was busy doing the job she hired him to do.

Eight hours of work turned out to be ten, and the day had turned to night by the time Carmen walked toward her car in the parking lot. Picking up DJ from Momma Corrine's and going to bed were the only two things on her mind. Work was worse than a zoo today. Certain clients were straight from hell and this one was no exception. But could she blame the client? Had she been paying closer attention to this event along the way, it wouldn't have been turned upside down. With forty-five minutes to spare before the event took place, they were able to properly reset the banquet room of four hundred seats and switch out the color scheme without a minute to spare. Bottom line, the meeting planner screwed up on their end, and she had to step in and get the job done right, if it meant enlisting an entire crew. Carmen would love to blame the calamity on Kendall and give herself an excuse to fire him. To her misfortune, Kendall was the best damn associate on the job and seemed out to prove to her he could be a hardworking husband if she gave him half a chance.

"Ms. Centerfold!" Kendall called out, his heavy Dominican accent slicing through the evening air so distinctly Carmen was sure everyone in the parking lot heard him. Initially the term of endearment Kendall started, because in his opinion she had the body of a Playboy Bunny and the face too, flattered her. What thirty-something mother of one wouldn't feel complimented being compared to a centerfold beauty? The fact that she was flattered, however, only served to remind Carmen she had suffered from temporary insanity.

Kendall chuckled at the glower on her face, his bright smile outshining the night-lights, his energy much too high after a hard day's work. It reminded Carmen that Kendall had the stamina of most twenty-five year olds, in and out of bed.

"Please do not call me that!" Carmen snapped, abandoning her professional conduct.

"Can I call you Ms. Beautiful?"

"What do you want, Kendall?"

"You know what I want." He winked his brow.

"You know my answer without me having to tell you, again."

"Answer this for me," Kendall said. "How much longer will it take me to be a manager like you?"

"It's based on seniority, meaning you haven't worked for the company long enough, and should feel lucky you promoted as quickly as you did in this industry. It took me three years to promote from a department assistant to sales associate. You beat the world record."

"Want to know what my dead dad told me once? The top is never far from my head."

Carmen grunted and made it safely to her car. She would have driven off if Kendall hadn't posted himself in front of her car door. He feathered his fingers against hers and motioned a kiss, making Carmen go cold outside and hot within. Then he put on that exotic smile of his; one that would have moved her in the wrong spot if she wasn't in her right mind. To maintain control, Carmen gave Kendall the hardest, coldest stare she could muster, which told him if he didn't get the hell out of her way, he was bordering termination.

The minute she got the chance, Carmen flew into her car and out of the parking lot.

Fifteen minutes later, the time it took to get from LAX to Culver City, Carmen whipped her Acura sedan into Momma

Corrine's driveway and slammed on the brakes, feeling as if an invisible force was pulling her away from reality. The same force thrust her out of the car, causing her hurried walk. This panic attack had Kendall's name written all over it. Wanting to get home to relax as fast as she could, Carmen practically ran to the door.

Dana appeared at the door in jeans, heeled boots and a belted tunic top; her sandy colored sister-locks hanging wild and loose.

"Sorry to rush you," Dana said. "I'm on my way out with *Omar*." Dana rolled her eyes. "I fed DJ for you. Come on in, Carmen. I have a few minutes."

Carmen didn't step a foot in Momma Corrine's house or past the laminated wood panel that separated the small foyer from the living room. When her anxiety escalated to this degree, life became dreamlike, making her feel as plastic as a bowl of fake fruit. She wasn't up to putting on pretenses tonight, and surely not up to socializing with her sister-in-law.

Lately, Carmen had been avoiding her in-laws as much as possible. When she could look them in the eyes without being reminded of the real reason her husband walked out on her, Carmen would love to spend a day helping Momma Corrine in the garden or hanging out with Dana, shopping and talking like old times. Thankfully, DJ came running into her arms, sparing her the added guilt.

"That's okay, Dana. I need to get home." Carmen grabbed DJ's backpack from Dana's hand, ready to fly down the porch steps.

Dana's eyes peered into hers like they appeared off-centered. "Are you okay?" Dana said.

"Yes. I'm fine. Why?"

"I planned to stay out of it, and probably should. It's really not my business... but what's up with you and Devon?"

"Ask your brother," Carmen said curtly.

"I will, when he returns my phone calls."

"I really have to go, Dana."

Dana caught Carmen by the hand before she could run off. "Carmen, whatever happens between you and Devon, we'll always be sisters. I hope you know that."

"I know, Dana. Thanks, for everything, okay?" Carmen hurried away.

To get to Downey from Culver City, Carmen took the 105 East, a thirty-minute stretch without traffic. Her nerves were crawling as if a million ants were scurrying beneath her skin. She controlled her increased heart rate and shortness of breath by using a deep breathing technique, counting to five and slowly exhaling. Regardless, she felt turned inside out; each whisper of wind seemingly agitating her nerve endings, and raising her anxiety. She prayed to God these sudden attacks would go away. One minute she felt cold, the next hot; a minute later, without warning, her oxygen was cut off, causing her breath to short out. How the hell had she developed a condition called "panic attacks?" She couldn't explain them to anyone. Who could imagine being in a windowless, airless room constricted from all four sides, with your body being the room, and your mind screaming to get out. It was a mental imprisonment she wouldn't wish on anyone. If Carmen could peel out of her own skin and set herself free, she would. The most she could do was roll down her car window for air and pray she didn't have an accident.

Halfway home, Carmen's heart rate had found a stable rhythm and her nerves were no longer on the run. Her mind, however, never gave her a moment's peace, chasing one thought after another: What if Devon found out she was contemplating a move back to DC? The last thing she needed or could handle was a custody battle. And based on her brief conversation with a divorce attorney, no judge in the state of California would let her cross state lines as long as the father had joint custody. Besides, knowing Devon, he would fight her with every dime he had for his son. She would be imprisoned in L.A. until DJ turned eighteen. And for the next fifteen of those eighteen years, she'd be tortured by the guilt of causing her own pain.

It had to be a family curse that caused her marriage to fall apart. Her sister's marriage didn't last, and her own parents' marriage finally caved in to their bickering and unhappiness after so long. Her grandparents' marriage, by a miracle, surpassed the forty-year mark.

"Just because you crossed the finish line, doesn't mean you've won the race, Carmen. Put more energy into staying married than you put into getting married, and don't be fool enough to think you're the only woman in the running. There's always someone waiting in the wings, ready to take your gold."

Her grandmother's advice came while Carmen was being laced with a string of pearls that had passed from neckline to neckline on every blushing bride in her family. Carmen was beginning to think the pearls were cursed. It wasn't as if she hadn't run a good race, always looking over her shoulder, and never letting the dust settle under her feet, only to find out it wasn't another woman she had to watch out for, but another man.

At that, Carmen's thoughts returned to Devon, compelling her to do what she was sure to regret. The urge was like an itch in the bend in her back she couldn't reach. However inconceivable, she had to scratch it. Knowing she shouldn't, Carmen did it anyway.

Devon answered on the first ring, as if expecting her random calls to make his life as miserable as he made hers.

"It's me," she admitted slowly. "You need to take your son to your mother's house in the morning?" It was the quickest lie

Carmen could come up with for calling Devon today. Yesterday was another story.

"If I didn't have something to do, I wouldn't mind," Devon said.

"You're not the only one, Devon."

"Do you really need me to take him, Carmen?"

"If I didn't, I wouldn't have called you."

"Did you call for any other reason?"

The real reason Carmen called pressed on her heart with the weight of an elephant. Her throat grew so dry and scratchy she groped for her bottled water in the passengers seat and knocked it back like the glass of wine she could use.

Clearly fed up, Devon said, "I'm hanging up."

Carmen hung up first, in Devon's face, and tossed her cell phone beneath the dashboard to keep from throwing it out of the window. If her itch to call Devon returned before arriving home, she couldn't reach it.

At home, Carmen lugged DJ by the hand into the house. He was crying about something Carmen didn't have the patience to figure out. He was cranky and sleepy, and for a three-year-old that meant the world revolved around his needs. Her needs were put on hold or didn't exist in his little mind. Times like this took everything in Carmen to hold herself together. The higher her anxiety climbed the crankier DJ became. His energy played off hers like a bad note.

Earlier that week, Carmen hadn't felt like listening to the daycare provider's daily run down of DJ's ongoing tantrums. She didn't need the woman telling her what her natural motherly instincts knew better than anyone. DJ missed his daddy. Well, so did she dammit! And what could she do about it? She couldn't fall out, crying and screaming over it like a three-year-old, now could she? Though, there were times when Carmen wanted to do just that.

Carmen carried DJ, kicking and screaming, to his bedroom. "When you're ready to act like a big boy, you can come out," she told him and closed the door.

The screaming and crying kept up while Carmen undressed down to her panties and bra, and started filling the tub with warm water and bubbles. The faster she could get DJ bathed and ready for bed the quicker she could calm her nerves. She slipped on a warm robe and walked next door to DJ's room where she found him stretched out on the floor, sleeping peacefully. She shook her head and changed DJ out of his clothes and into his pajamas, then put him to bed, kissing his cheeks along the way.

"Sweet dreams, mommy's big boy." Carmen turned on the night light and left the room quietly.

In the kitchen, Carmen poured herself a glass of wine and gulped back a mouthful, then another. Her thoughts returned to Devon and how lonely she was without him. The first day Devon left, Carmen felt a sense of needed freedom, predicting Devon to return in a heartbeat. A week slowly went by before she saw Devon again, when he returned to pack up the last of his clothes. Carmen was crazy that day, demanding he tell her why he was leaving her and where the hell he thought he was going.

"You know why," Devon kept saying, his eyes so caked with hurt and pain Carmen had to look away. Reality set in two weeks later when Devon hadn't returned, but instead had set up a visitation plan to spend time with his son. It had been five weeks and some days since Devon moved out, five weeks!

How could he up and leave her as easily as her parents upped and divorced? What happened to through sickness and health, until death do us part and all that bullshit? The wine goblet in Carmen's hand went flying into a kitchen cabinet before she knew it, cracking the stained glass into a million spider veins. *Forget Devon, this house and everything in it!* She screamed silently. The Travertine floors, Berber carpet, two-head shower, his and hers marble vanities, speckled kitchen granite, whatever upgrades she and Devon could afford was in their house. And for what?

Carmen stormed out of the kitchen, deciding to deal with the mess she made later. Her cell phone rang before she could step into the bathtub. Knowing who it was, she answered without delay.

"Damn you, Kendall! It's over. Do you understand? Stop calling me!" Carmen hung up and turned off her phone. Once she climbed into the whirling white bubbles and sank to the bottom, her anxiety slowly gave way.

Every Girl's Nightmare

On a normal day Tempest Perry wouldn't dare walk out of church during Pastor Lacey's rousing sermon, with the entire congregation on its feet giving the Lord His praise. Today was anything but normal for Tempest. She slid discreetly from the pews and fled New Jerusalem Church before Mother Washington wished everyone a blessed day. At the rate she was moving, she could use Mother Washington's blessing. Her long legs trotted in three-inch stilettos toward the parking lot with her chiffon sun dress floating against a light wind. Anxiety cloaked her like a creeping plant, making her all nerves. She dropped her keys and fumbled for the car lock, praying her ride back to Fox Hills would take the usual twenty minutes instead of thirty or forty. On a lazy Sunday, Los Angeles traffic could easily slow her down.

Barreling out of the lot in her cherry Mustang, Tempest cut a sharp right and got caught at the first light she approached. "Come on, come on," she murmured. The light, thankfully, turned green. Tempest sped forward, getting caught behind a slow moving truck.

"The devil is a liar!" She cut to the next lane, accelerating to an illegal speed; all the while angry with herself for going to church on an important day like today. Anyone who knew her knew worshipping was the most important part of her life. But if anyone knew, Jesus knew Sterling was too.

Tempest first met Sterling two years ago at a pool party in L.A.'s sumptuous View Heights community. If love at first sight was possible, she and Sterling experienced it firsthand. From across the bustling yard their eyes met and never parted. Tempest could recall the feeling that came over her. Running to the bathroom to revive her make-up was her first impulse. Her skin dampened and her heart, she was sure, stopped beating momentarily. There were enough fine men at the party that night for Tempest to choose from, and no shortage with their eyes on her in the gold metallic bikini she wore, radiant against her mahogany skin. But no man, past or present, captivated Tempest's eyes and heart more than Sterling. When she and Sterling were close enough to speak, they couldn't stop talking. They eventually ventured away from the party and sat in Sterling's then Nissan truck, where they kept up their conversation until the party concluded, listened to what became 'their song,' and closed the night with their first kiss. The fact that a few years later Sterling would be an NFL rising star wouldn't have mattered to Tempest. From then until now, she loved Sterling and would forever. Now she was counting down the months to her wedding day.

Tempest picked up speed. Peripherally, she saw cars falling back on the highway as hers dashed forward. She concentrated on the exit signs ahead as if willing herself home was possible. Going eighty miles an hour sure wasn't getting her there fast enough. As she rounded a sharp bend, feeling the wheels of her car grip the blacktop unstably, she caught sight of a police car parked alongside the road. Her heart came to an instant standstill. She didn't have time to get a speeding ticket. *Please, Jesus*.

By the grace of God Tempest arrived home not a second too late to see Sterling.

Now Tempest sat on her sofa, devastated, sick to her stomach, and tasting the salt of her tears. Everything she knew about her life moments ago felt surreal. Did what happened really happen, or had she never awakened from a nightmare?

She retraced her steps in her mind. It was Sunday morning. That, Tempest was certain of, recalling Pastor Lacey's rousing sermon this morning and how she raced out of church, forsaking God for Sterling. She had rushed into her one-bedroom condo, tossed her handbag on the sofa, slipped off her stilettos, and turned on the TV, opting for the 42-inch flat screen in the living room, with high definition to better see and hear Sterling. The NFL pre-game special hadn't started. A commercial gave her time to raid the refrigerator. Too nervous to digest anything of sustenance, she poured herself a shot glass of orange juice. After gulping down her breakfast, she stood before the television with her hands steepled in prayer.

Sterling's name floated across the screen in bold letters: *STERLING   ALEXANDER...STERLING   ALEXANDER... STERLING ALEXANDER*. Clips played of Sterling charging up the field for the tackle. One after another, the clips highlighted Sterling's aggressiveness, quickness and determination to tackle his opponent. Tempest squealed, clapped, and cheered as she had in high school.

The sports commentator appeared in the studio, a black man wearing a bright colored suit. Seated across from him, Sterling wore an Armani ensemble, tan with four buttons, and a royal blue dress shirt opened sexily at the collar. Tempest couldn't have been more proud of herself. Apparel design was her profession, the main reason Sterling called her from Minneapolis and had her FedEx his wear. Working at Nordstrom's, the leading apparel store in the country, had paid off. Sterling's pretty dark skin glowed in the color combination she selected for him. His hair was freshly cut, his pencil beard and mustache perfectly lined, and the two-carat studs in his ears sparkled. New money couldn't have looked better than her man did, Tempest thought.

"At six-four, two hundred and forty pounds," the commentator said, "defensive linebacker Sterling Alexander led the Spartans in a thirty/twenty-one victory against the Panthers last week with two interceptions, five tackles, and two sacks. Fresh off the bench, filling the hole left by starter David Banks, who was injured in the preseason, Sterling took advantage of this career opportunity by giving Spartans fans a taste of his fearless aggression." The commentator turned to Sterling.

"Last season, you could only dream of signing as an undrafted free agent for the Spartans. Now, your persistence has paid off. Do you see your story as an inspiration to other aspiring athletes hoping to make it in the pro league?"

"I don't know if I'm an inspiration," Sterling answered in his bass voice. "I've stayed focused on my goal, worked hard... been a team player. I hope that inspires anybody out there looking to be successful at whatever they do. Mostly, though, I think you have to be hungry for it, live for the opportunity. When it comes, be ready."

"Tell 'em, boo!" Tempest cheered.

"You're like the Cinder-fella of the league, an NFL fairytale story come true. At twenty-five, this is only your second season when other players are veterans. So, what's your story, Sterling?"

Tempest recounted Sterling's unconventional story along with him. How he played for two years at a junior college, earned a starting position and a full scholarship as a walk-on at USC, and the number of years he walked on and off fields, praying to get signed. When Sterling's chance finally came, Tempest was by his side, helping him celebrate.

Sterling didn't sign a twenty-five million dollar contract over five years like the top ball players. His was a six hundred thousand dollar, two-year deal in which he'd received a two hundred thousand dollar signing bonus. If Sterling made the lineup next season, however, he could renegotiate for a small fortune. Tempest had every intention of being at Sterling's side—before what happened, happened.

The camera zoomed in for a close-up of the commentator, so close Tempest made out the deep pores on his golden brown skin. "Born and raised in South Central Los Angeles, Sterling says he's starting to adjust to the Minnesota climate and the people. He even hopes to one day win over the hearts of Minnesota Spartans fans...." Aiming at the stands, the camera panned the cheering crowd. In a split second, Tempest caught sight of her. Not her face, but her hair—long, brown spirals with blonde highlights. Her heart died when the commentator said, "Looks like Cinder-fella has already won the heart of one beautiful Spartans fan."

Tempest couldn't remember a scene or remark more. She went deaf, blind and cold to the bone. Silence came down on her like darkness, along with a torrent of tears.

In the middle of her catastrophe, the phone rang. Tempest could only imagine who was calling, any one of the million people she told to watch Sterling's first televised interview. Determined to hide from her embarrassment and shame, she allowed the service to answer on her behalf. She should've known her sister, Charlene, would be the first to call, only to say, "I told your ass Sterling wasn't about nothing!" Charlene spread negativity as if her life depended on it. If Tempest called anyone back today, it definitely wouldn't be Charlene. It wasn't that she didn't love her sister, but she could only take Charlene in small doses most days.

The phone rang again. Again, Tempest let the service answer. This time Nadine, her oldest sister, was the caller. "Temp, are you okay? Pick up," Nadine said. She was trained to be rational and understanding at times like this. As an attorney, before she became a stay-at-home mom, Nadine was highly sought after to iron out messy divorce cases. Tempest called Nadine whenever she needed a calming confidant. When she could manage to move from the sofa, she would call Nadine back.

There was no end to the ringing. Message after message rang with shock and disbelief. Her baby sister, Salia, was "tripping out!" Her mother said, "Don't believe everything you see on that idiot box, Tempest." Her father called it "media sensationalism," and her girlfriend Yasmine cursed into the recorder as if delivering her fury directly to Sterling. If anyone else called, including her cousin, Dana, Tempest didn't want to hear their interpretation of what may or may not have happened. She ripped the phone plug from the wall and turned off her cell phone.

What came next didn't take Tempest by surprise. Her feet were in motion the instant her heart plunged to her stomach. Bowed over the toilet, she threw up her devastating upset. With each thought of Sterling with another woman came another gag. Legs weak and trembling, she rinsed her mouth, pausing before the vanity mirror at the sight of her swelling eyes. Not only was she questioning her future with Sterling, old insecurities that hadn't crossed her mind since high school resurfaced to mock her. Back then, she wished for lighter skin than mahogany; her eyes she wished weren't slanted as a Siamese cat's. She hated, too, that her cheekbones sat high up on her face, and her plump lips, in her opinion, sure weren't *vogue*. The question of her own beauty fell to the back of Tempest's mind when her classmates voted her "Most Likely to Be a Super Model." Yet, here she was at age twenty-six, feeling as she did back in high school—not pretty enough, especially for an NFL star like Sterling.

AN HOUR INTO HER CRYING, Tempest's sisters arrived at her door. The three of them—Nadine, Charlene, and Salia—marched in like paramedics on an emergency call. Before Tempest could object, her sisters were buzzing around her condo worse than flies out to annoy her. A family like hers was a blessing and a curse. She could count on her family being there when she needed them, never feeling alone in the world, and never having a holiday, birthday, or special occasion go by without her family to share it with her. That was the blessing. The curse was times like today when she could do without family. How had she become the one sister everyone treated as if she were a weak and wounded sparrow that couldn't fly on her own? Could she help it that she was highly sensitive, that seeing a dead animal on the side of the road brought tears to her eyes; that commercials about starving kids in Third World countries made her want to become a missionary and heal the planet. Her problem was her heart was too big—so big that it absorbed everything around her. Maybe if she had less of a heart, she would kick her sisters out of her house.

To keep her mind busy and off of their insensitive conversation about Sterling, Tempest walked about tidying up, choking back her desire to tell Charlene to take her feet off of her sofa with shoes on. Made of superior Italian leather, that sofa was the rarest crimson color she could find in a sectional, let alone pay for without Sterling's help. She hadn't owned the sofa or rented her condo long enough to enjoy them, and Charlene was already coming in tearing things up.

"Eat something, Tempest. You'll feel better," Nadine said.

"No thanks. I'm too sick."

"I'd be sick too if my man was messing with a white girl and I found out about it on TV," Charlene said.

"She wasn't white," Salia said.

"She looked white to me," Charlene shot back.

"If God hates anything worse than ugly, it's ignorance, especially when people with some intelligence should know better," Nadine said.

"Quit acting holy because you went to church today, Nadine. Any other time you'd have something to say about Sterling's cheatin' ass."

"I would not. It's not my place to say. I'm here to support Tempest, not to make her feel worse than she already does. Don't mess with me this morning, Charlene." Nadine dared Charlene with her eyes to push her. She was the oldest, close to forty, and never let any of them forget it by treating them like her children. She was sitting at the bar counter ravishing a glazed donut, bursting out the seams of her church dress. Nadine swore that before she had the last of her four children and blew up to a size twelve, she was a size one like Salia. She arrived this morning bearing Starbucks and donuts as if they were celebrating a freakin' holiday. Never mind that her fiancé might be cheating on her.

"I'm with Charlene," Salia chimed in. "Sterling is put out of the family."

"Both of you need to think before you speak. Tempest loves Sterling, and so do I! He's already my brother-in-law, wedding or no wedding." Nadine gave Tempest a wink and a smile.

Charlene frowned. "Sterling ain't none of my damn brother, not after dogging my baby sister out on worldwide TV."

"It wasn't worldwide, Charlene," Nadine corrected.

"Everybody in the world saw it, didn't they?" Charlene said.

Tempest's throat tightened and her nerves prickled as if an acupuncturist had poked her with a million needles. Still, she kept silent, knowing that it wasn't her sisters getting to her as much as waiting for Sterling to return her call. For the next few hours, Sterling would be on a field, in the throes of a brutal football game. The game was blacked out in California. Even if it wasn't, Tempest couldn't bring herself to watch, haunted by visions of that chick cheering for him in the stands. The most she could do right now was bide time, replaying Sterling's interview in her mind, convincing herself that the camera had played a trick on her, a cruel one. When she called Sterling earlier, she left him a brief message, saying only that she watched his interview and that she was proud of him. The last thing she would do was accuse Sterling of cheating without giving him the benefit of the doubt.

Tempest walked toward Charlene. "Can you move your feet please?" she asked politely.

You would've thought she asked Charlene to scrub the toilet the way Charlene looked at her. "It's not hurting you, is it?"

"Fine. Leave them there, Charlene," Tempest said, avoiding the confrontation Charlene was hoping for. She straightened the stack of *Cosmopolitan* magazines on her nest of end tables and walked away. If there is a crazy person in every family, Charlene won the crown "the crazy one" in their family. Charlene was also the prettiest Perry sister and tallest, closer to six feet than Tempest. She looked most like their father, with the same Hershey chocolate skin and pouted lips. It didn't help that Charlene had a domineering personality to go along with her overbearing presence. She had charged through the door bolder than a red-haired bull, talking about Sterling worse than if he were the dirt on the bottom of her shoes. Guilt aside, Sterling was the man Tempest loved. The least Charlene could do was give Sterling that respect.

Ignoring Charlene, Tempest moved to the dining area. She couldn't understand for the life of her why Salia waited until she sat at her dining table to take out her braids. Fake hair of any kind made Tempest's skin crawl.

"You're missing the bag, Salia. Hair is everywhere."

"Can somebody help me? I can't do this all by myself," Salia whined. She was the baby of the family, just shy of nineteen, and a freshman at Cal State Long Beach studying to be a pediatrician someday.

"I put 'em in, I'm not takin' 'em out," Charlene ranted over Salia's request. They called Salia "Chicken Little" because of her yellow skin and petite frame, different from anyone else in their family.

"I'll help you," Nadine said.

It took hours to unravel the million individual braids in Salia's hair, and hours later her sisters hadn't budged and Sterling hadn't returned her call. After vacuuming up the hair Salia left behind, Tempest walked to the kitchen and washed the dishes her sisters dirtied with the pizza they ordered during an afternoon pay-per-view movie. All eyes were back on her. She guessed her sisters expected her to say something since she smacked her lips and cleared her throat to much of what was said throughout the day.

"Tempest, are you okay?" Nadine said carefully.

"Where do you think you're going?" Charlene asked. Without a reply, Tempest closed herself in her bedroom, curled under her satin robe, and let her tears flow.

She wasn't as Pollyannaish as people thought she was. She predicted chicks would come crawling out of the woodworks, like roaches scampering for a slice of pie, the minute Sterling went pro. No matter what happened or didn't, she wasn't going to dwell on negativity. To replace her negative thoughts with positive ones, Tempest reminisced on the weekend she and Sterling flew to Vegas to celebrate their "first date" anniversary. Sterling spared no expense on luxury that weekend, renting a penthouse suite with sprawling windows that stared into the face of Vegas from every angle. The trip was unforgettable from beginning to end, the most romantic proposal for marriage any woman could dream of and a comforting thought in the face of the doubt around her.

"It feels like I've been with you my whole life, Tee," Sterling had said. "I never thought I'd be saying this at this time in my life. Maybe when I got older, had ten seasons under my belt; you know, got my play out, I'd be ready and the right girl would be there waiting for me. But God called an audible on me, switched up the play. I don't have time to second-guess His call. I have to make the adjustment, go for the win. You know what I'm saying, baby?"

"Yes," Tempest said, not following his line of reasoning.

"I want to be, Tee."

"You want to be what?"

"I want to be with you for the rest of my life." Sterling then reached into his pocket and presented her with a beautiful ring that glimmered, along with the Vegas lights, right before her eyes. Tempest's heart responded first, fluttering rapidly. Even recalling that night still seized her heart and breath. "Will you be my wife?" he'd said.

Every girl, Tempest believed, dreamed of that day, in the perfect place, at the perfect time, with the perfect man. She didn't have to say yes. Sterling knew her answer to his proposal when she threw her arms around his broad shoulders, wrapped her legs around his sturdy waist, and trampled him to the floor. They didn't come up for air for hours.

The ringing landline brought Tempest back to an imperfect world, where love had its deceptions. She dived for the phone on the nightstand, hitting her bare foot on the bed's iron casting. It hurt like heck, but she didn't care. The pain and her upset stomach could take a backseat until she heard Sterling's voice.

"Sterling!" Tempest said. "No, I don't have time to do a survey. Thank you."

After hanging up, Tempest attacked her computer, logging into *Cheaptickets.com*. She didn't care how much of a dent it put in her bank account, she booked the first flight she could find to Minneapolis/St. Paul. If the truth didn't come to her, she would find it.

First Person Singular

$\mathscr{D}$ana Dougherty was about to be irresponsible, careless, and rash for the first time in her life. She reasoned that other women went as far and blamed the slip-up on faulty birth control. "It just happened," she would tell everyone. At least she would have a baby to show for a relationship that amounted to nothing more than a headache.

In three years Omar had promised her nothing, but in Dana's mind he promised everything that he never made good on. She fell in love with Omar, not for any good reason she could recall, other than that his sleepy eyes captured hers when she walked into Subway. That he gave her a footlong sub on the house with his number written in balance due. Not to mention, when she called him weeks later, he remembered everything about her, from her sister locks, the freckles sprayed across her slight nose, down to her silver butterfly toe ring. But of all the men she could have fallen in love with, why had she fallen for a type C personality whose ambition, at age twenty-eight, stopped at being single for the rest of his life.

Last night, when Omar called, Dana knew his motive. Desperation laced his voice, presumably because he hadn't had sex in the time they had been apart. But loneliness on a Saturday night and Omar's skillful way of manipulating her won out. She quickly gave into his game, agreeing to a date and thinking that maybe he had matured since she dumped him two months ago.

Dana soon discovered Omar hadn't matured much when he insisted on keeping their date a surprise. A surprise date with Omar meant one or two things: a movie or a quick meal at a three star restaurant. Then, it was off to his parents' house where they would make passionate love. That is, when his parents weren't home or his mother wasn't lurking about. When Omar drove toward the city of Gardena, passing the familiar discount supermarket, rows of flat-roof apartments, and fading businesses, Dana didn't have to guess where they were headed—to his parents' house; what a big surprise.

The mood was ideal for making love last night too, with a moon in full bloom and Omar's parents motoring across the country in their house on wheels. However, Dana wouldn't allow Omar to manipulate her that easily. Throughout the night, she kept her legs shut, unmoved by Omar's persistence to take off her clothes. Her impenetrable armor came off and nature took over when she awakened snuggled next to Omar's warm body just moments ago, hearing the birds twitter, an owl coo, and bathed in the peace of Sunday morning. It was then that her thoughts of "accidental" pregnancy popped up.

"You sure you want to do this?" Omar said.

A cold sweat washed over Dana. For a moment she wondered if Omar had picked her plan out of her head. Likely, he wondered if she was sure about having sex with him. Even if she wasn't sure, without sex she couldn't get pregnant. If Dana was sure of anything, she was sure she wanted a baby by Omar. She welcomed him into her arms and between her thighs, giving her future completely to chance.   There was no talk of protection, not on Dana's part anyway. Unknown to Omar, she came off birth control weeks ago.

Omar entered her eagerly.

"Wait!" Dana said, before he could go an inch deeper. Omar's lustful expression turned to disappointment.

"You're changing your mind?" he said.

Dana had changed her mind and hated herself for living her life much like she drove a car, always traveling the speed limit and within the strict boundaries of two white lines. If she was going to have a baby, a proposal and a ring would have to come first.

"You have something?" she said.

Now Omar was grinning down at her. "I thought you were on something?"

"I'm not, and even if I was, I'm not having risky sex with someone I'm no longer in a committed relationship with."

"I have one, somewhere. Don't move. I'll be right back." He was back in bed before Dana could change her mind again.

Within minutes, Dana's absolute love for Omar was rekindled. She loved the feel of Omar's skin, as close to hers as her own, the way he clung to her tighter than ever, as if afraid he might lose her again. She loved, too, his dusty brown skin, lips that stayed moist and ready to kiss, and the sexy way his lids drooped over his eyes as they gaped into hers.

"You like that?" Omar chanted, driving home his point. Dana didn't like it. She loved it! And Omar too! But loving him was one thing, and saying she loved him was another. Other than her insuppressible moans and groans, Dana kept her sentiments silent. Before long, a titillating rush of euphoria caused her to lose her breath and have to gasp to catch it. She held onto her orgasm like a fond memory she never wanted to forget, sinking deeper into Omar's embrace and wishing she could lay in his arms forever. Her common sense reminded her not to count on it. Omar always found a way of wrecking "forever."

"I miss us having sex," he said. There went Dana's exhilaration.

Tasting an old bitterness in her mouth, she replied, "Is that all we had, *sex*? Sounds like a dirty word."

"I miss that good, juicy stuff then." This, Omar found funny.

"I'm not laughing."

"I'm just playing with you. You're too serious."

"One, you play too much and two, I'm not *that* serious," Dana retorted, although she did sometimes question her serious nature. She wanted to laugh and frolic with Omar as if they were on a honeymoon of no return, but that simply wasn't the case, and would likely never be with Omar. Moreover, somebody had to be serious in the relationship. God knows Omar wasn't serious enough.

"Does this mean we're back together?" he said.

"Since when has there been a *we* in this relationship?"

Omar laughed. "What're you talking about now?"

"My second graders would know what I'm talking about without me having to repeat myself, Omar."

"Explain it to me like I'm a kindergartener then."

Dana pulled herself out of his arms and propped herself up on both elbows. "Well…." She spoke at a snail's pace, as if talking to her second graders who sometimes didn't get the simplest answer to an easy problem. "In this relationship, there's *you* and there's *me,* but if there were *we,* I would know by now."

"You and I will always be we. You should know that by now. You got the upper hand in the relationship. I'm just along for the ride."

"Whatever, Omar. Talking to you is like talking to myself, only I listen."

"You're confusing. First you say I need to grow up, then I need my own spot, then I play too much. Now, I don't listen. Which one is it?"

"Take your pick."

"What do you want from me? Tell me. I wanna know." He said this as if she hadn't told him time after time.

"I want you to take me home." Her abrasiveness made Omar sit up and spread his arms.

"What did I do wrong this time?"

"Not one thing." Dana swung her legs to the side of the bed, ignoring his bewilderment. She found her clothes and began to dress. Omar hopped up and walked up to her, gently cupping his warm hands around her neck. His thumbs caressed her cheeks. His cinnamon hued eyes held her face as if he was admiring her every feature. When he pressed his moist lips against hers, the room spun against her will.

"I love making love to you. Is that better?" he said.

Now that the effects of her orgasm had worn off, Dana wrestled over her decision to make love to Omar in the first place, least of all contemplate what she was sure to regret nine months after the fact. Her burning desire to marry Omar and to have his baby had turned into burning anger, mostly for setting herself up for disappointment. Again she had allowed herself to be Omar's play toy—not worthy of marriage, not worthy of his absolute love, only worthy of good sex and a smack on the ass. And he hadn't fed her before he screwed her this time.

"Take me home, Omar," Dana said adamantly.

HOME FOR DANA WAS ACROSS town. She lived with her mother in a pink stucco house on Braddock Street, tucked away in the quaint neighborhood of Culver City. The houses on Braddock were built sometime pre-central air and heat, possibly before World War II. Every time Dana walked into the house she asked herself the same question—why had she moved out of her centrally heated studio apartment, and in with her mother to begin with? Moving back home at age twenty-six was not in her plans. Her sleeping space was reduced to the corner of her mother's office/sewing/guest room. She favored it over the more spacious den her mother offered. Living comfortably was precisely what Dana didn't want. It would be different if her mother lived in the house where she grew up, but Corrine moved to a neighborhood designed for empty nesters. She had been enjoying her own empty nest ever since Dana and her brother left for college.

Dana's original thought for moving back home was to save money. By now, she should have substantial savings for a down payment on her first home, or shack, whichever she could afford on a teacher's salary in L.A.'s outrageous real estate market. She hadn't saved much, nor had she progressed beyond her paranoia of not qualifying for a home loan. This is where Omar came into the picture; two incomes were better than one and would afford her and Omar a nice first home to start a family. Now, the idea sounded more ridiculous to Dana than the idea that she actually believed it for so long. She had been married without the benefit of a wedding and now divorced without anything to show for it.

Without stopping, Dana headed to her small corner of the three-bedroom house. Before she could cure her hunger pangs or scrub Omar's masculine scent off her body in a long, hot bath, her cell phone rang. Sure it was Omar calling, Dana ignored the call. In the closet she lived out of were unpacked boxes. After rummaging through one box after another, she found a pair of jogging shorts and her favorite Spelman sweatshirt that Alonzo Jones bought for her—another regrettable relationship in her life and a waste of her time. Alonzo was a business major at Morehouse. She gave him two years of her life to prove his intentions, which he never proved.

She could sure *pick 'em,* couldn't she?

Bathed, dressed, and on her way to the kitchen, Dana ran into Devon, who used his key to let himself into the house. Although

Dana couldn't be happier to see her brother, it wasn't happiness that showed on her face.

"Where's Mom?" Devon said.

"I couldn't tell you."

"She told me the pilot's out again."

"So fix it."

"Are you getting smart with me, kid?" Devon said, being playfully antagonistic, a trait of his that hadn't changed from their childhood. Dana glared crossly at her brother, who was four years older than she, and at five foot ten, stood six inches taller. Dana never believed those who said that Devon and she favored their mother. Other than their copper-coated complexions, Devon undoubtedly looked more like their father, based on pictures Dana had seen of her father after his death. Devon's strong brow, composed expression, and receding hairline, which he recently shaved bald to conceal, mirrored their father's features. Her brother was what her friends over the years called "fine." His looks drove them to ditch her company in exchange for his whenever they stayed nights at her house.

"You mind moving?" Dana said.

"Move me."

"You know I will, Devon."

Devon gave her his wide, slow grin and said, "You have something you want to say to me?"

"Since you asked, yes, I have a lot to say. Why are you divorcing Carmen? Now I hear you have a girlfriend. What's up with you, Devon?"

"A *girlfriend*?" Devon shook his head. "Is that what mom told you? You know how she gets things twisted. I don't have a girlfriend. Let's get that straight first. And who said anything about a divorce? Carmen and I are separated, and that's her fault, not mine."

"You leave her and it's *her* fault?"

"Listen to me for a minute, Dana, will you?" Devon looked at her as if making a plea for his life. "Here's the situation with Carmen. I can't do anything right in her eyes lately. Like the other day, she called and asked me to pick up DJ. What did I say? 'I'm with a client. I'll call you back.' That wasn't good enough. She started crying and carrying on, saying I never loved her or my son. I had a client right in front of me! That's what I'm talking about. She's crazy."

"How do you expect her to act, Devon? She probably thinks you're never coming back."

Devon scratched his chin. "I had my reasons for leaving."

"What reason do you have for leaving DJ?" Dana said. "He's hurting most in this. Have you noticed the change in him? Well, I have. He really misses you."

"I see my son every chance I get."

"He needs you at home, not seeing him when you get a chance."

Devon walked down the hallway. Dana followed like a car too close on his tail. She couldn't miss her brother's broad shoulders and muscle-packed thighs that had made him one of the top outfielders in the high school baseball league. He gave up baseball and his dream to play in the major league after a severe knee injury; the long-term damage expressing itself in his wide-leg strut that dipped slightly to the right when he walked.

"And by the way," Dana said, "when were you going to tell me where you live now or do I have to find that out from mom too?"

"You could've as easily called and asked me."

Dana poked her brother in the chest. "Nice try. I called you three or four times and left messages."

Devon kneeled before the wall heater. "You're right. My fault. I'm staying at Calvin's place if you need to find me."

"*Calvin's*! Is that what this is about, reliving the single life? The grass isn't greener on the other side, Devon. Let me be the first to tell you."

"What?" Devon said, looking up as though dust had gotten into his eyes.

"There's a good reason why club hopping *Calvin* has never been married and doesn't want to be," Dana said, knowing more about Devon's best friend than Devon was on to. She and Calvin had a one-time fling, one that Dana had never shared with anyone, especially her brother who had a "hands-off" rule when it came to his sister. In short, Calvin was a single woman's nightmare.

Devon stood and wiped the dust from his hands onto his khaki pants. "I'm your brother, Dana. When has clubbing been my thing? I don't even like to dance."

"Because you can't," Dana teased. She and Devon both had a laugh. Not only did Devon not dance, but he was as straight laced as they come. Devon had never gotten a speeding ticket, never been arrested, never been a smoker or a big drinker. Before graduating from college, he was well on his way to being the white-collar conservative guy he was now, with the perfect persona of a successful insurance broker. At the time their father died, Devon was thirteen years old and she was eight. Dana vividly remembered how the structure of their family changed. As a working single mother, Corrine couldn't raise two kids alone, forcing Devon to become Dana's secondary overseer. He was the male figure she looked to for validation, the father that put her boyfriends through a litmus test, and the pestering brother who taunted her until she cried uncle. Nevertheless, Devon always did his best to shore up the household in the absence of their father. Dana loved her brother like no other man alive, but at the moment she was staring into the eyes of a man she couldn't respect for walking out on his wife, leaving Carmen part of a growing statistic—a black, single mother.

"You said you had your reasons for leaving Carmen, you never said what reason."

"Put it this way, I'm not the one trying to live the single life." Devon hiked up his brow. Dana took a step closer.

"What do you mean? What's going on?" She didn't know why she whispered, maybe because of the suggestive tone in Devon's voice.

"I'll have to tell you about it another time," he said.

Was she that jaded not to have noticed the hurt in her brother's eyes before? She was the serious one in the family. Devon was easy going and full of life. Today, Devon looked as if someone or something drained the life out of him.

Dana bribed Devon into staying with a plate of leftovers. They sat in the den, where Devon stuffed himself on barbeque chicken as though he hadn't had a decent meal since he left home. Without adding the two cents strangling her throat to be heard, Dana merely listened while Devon painted a picture of a Carmen she couldn't imagine. More shocking than hearing about Carmen's body piercing and tattoos was hearing that Carmen was coming home extra late from work, drinking more and acting like someone her brother didn't know. Dana held her tongue up to the point when Devon said Carmen forgot to pick up DJ from daycare more than a few times.

"How can a mother forget her child!"

Devon ignored Dana's sudden outburst and continued. "Did mom tell you Carmen is seeing a psychologist?"

"She needs to," Dana said under her breath.

"For a thirties crisis she's having. Do women have a thirty crisis?"

"I'm having one at twenty-six, so it's possible." Dana honestly didn't care what Carmen's excuse was for her behavior. She was married to her brother and was the mother of her only nephew, whom she loved like the child she longed to have. Devon didn't say what he suspected Carmen was up to. Whatever his speculation, Dana let Devon cleanse his mind without adding her suspicions.

"I do everything I can for Carmen," he went on. "I'm not the perfect husband, by no means, but I'm not like a few no good ones I can name. What should I have done, Dana, stood by and let her treat me like a stranger in my own house?" Devon shook his head. "I don't know anymore. Maybe I took it over the top by leaving."

"Sounds to me like you're ready to go back. It's not the worst thing that can happen, Devon." Dana said this casually. She couldn't *tell* her brother what to do, never could. She had to persuade him into thinking reuniting with Carmen was his bright idea.

"I'm not making any promises," Devon said and gave Dana a warm embrace before he left. "Tell mom the pilot is back on."

When Devon left Tempest called. Detail for detail, Tempest relayed the story of what happened during Sterling's first NFL pre-game special, sounding like she swallowed shards of glass. The whole story didn't come as a shock to Dana. She suspected the minute Sterling went pro, gold diggers would pick him from the field like cotton. What burned Dana's neck most was that Sterling had humiliated Tempest on national TV! Now she didn't feel bad for missing Sterling's interview this morning, screwing around with Omar.

"Tell me something, Temp. Was this chick black or white?" Tempest huffed at Dana's question. "I'm only asking."

"You think it's true too, don't you, Dana? Like Charlene and everybody else." Dana sat on the daybed and measured her response to Tempest's question, pressing her lips together not to say what was on her mind. The last thing Tempest needed to hear was her honest opinion, which could be brutal if she didn't think before responding. Brutality, of any kind, Tempest couldn't handle. It was best to offer Tempest the remote possibility, however doubtful, that Sterling wasn't a typical professional athlete she didn't respect.

"I'm sure it's media hype," Dana said.

"That's what daddy said, girl! I would know if Sterling was cheating on me, wouldn't I? I mean, I was in Minneapolis three weeks ago. Sterling wasn't acting like he had committed a crime or anything…." Tempest paused as if reflecting on something pertinent. "And at the games, I've never seen any chicks staring me down. You know I'm always on the lookout for that when I'm there. But you think it's true, don't you, Dana? Be honest with me. I'm not as weak and fragile as my family treats me."

Dana often wondered, particularly now that Tempest was ignoring the obvious, if they would have become best friends if their mothers weren't God-sisters. They call each other "play cousins," but the word play drew no distinction from real. They were cousins, blood or not, and polar opposites, living in different worlds, and seeing vastly different pictures when looking at the same canvas. Tempest lived in fantasy land, sifting through neurons to control negative information to her brain; sort of like a miner panning for gold in a cesspool. She, on the other hand, lived in reality and recognized crap for what it was. Sterling was knee deep in it. Dana could smell it from L.A.

"I wish I had an answer for you, Temp. You know Sterling better than anyone. What did he have to say?"

"I'm waiting for his call now. Can you believe Charlene called Sterling every name in the book without giving him the benefit of the doubt? She's here now, getting on my nerves. Nadine and Salia are here too. Can you come over? I need outside support."

"I would, but I'm babysitting DJ again. If you're up to it, we can go out to dinner, my treat. Call me when they leave."

"My sisters won't leave unless I put them out, girl," Tempest whispered. Dana laughed, knowing she wouldn't be any more help to Tempest than Charlene if she joined the Perry sisters' powwow today. All men were in the dog house with her; Sterling now added to her list just below Omar.

Dana finally went to the kitchen to eat. While munching on a power bar, she stared through the garden window wondering where Corrine might be. Her mother was usually doing what she often did in the backyard on Sunday mornings, fussing over her small vegetable garden of collard greens, tomatoes, carrots, cucumbers, and some form of squash. There was never a dull moment in Corrine's life. A one-woman show since her husband died, if Corrine wasn't starting an industrious project around the house, she was traveling with friends, running marathons, or back in school, this time for her Ph.D. through an on-line degree mill to tack onto her master's degree in education.

Her mother seemed to hold the key to happiness. Deciding never to remarry after her father died was probably more productive than her approach to happiness—waiting to be married with children.

Unexpected Guests

Tempest's hurry to get to Minneapolis had her so preoccupied that her thoughts couldn't connect with anything Dana was saying over the noisy chatter of TGIF, let alone connect to her own actions, consumed with the time, her flight, and how surprised Sterling would be to see her. She had never been this impulsive, and definitely had never arrived on Sterling's doorstep unannounced. Packing was another thing she needed to do, not having the chance earlier with her sisters buzzing around her place for hours. She finally kicked them out by lying about her dinner plans with Dana that she hadn't intended to commit to. She wasn't committed to dinner with Dana now. Her mind was everywhere but on their conversation and she hadn't touched a crumb on her plate.

Dana said something about being between lives—the life she once had and the life she anticipated she would have by now. "…a starter home, and a husband and six babies in the making." That got Tempest's attention.

"You want six kids, girl!"

"How many times have I told you?"

"You're going to be like the old woman who lived in a shoe."

Dana smiled. "I love kids."

"I love those little rugrats too, enough to have *one*, girl. Sterling knows not to ask me for a baby more."

Dana went on to say something else that Tempest half heard behind her thoughts that stayed on Sterling. After talking to him earlier, her stomach settled, somewhat. She never found the courage to question him about the interview. Besides, Sterling volunteered the whole story, and as she thought, there wasn't much of a story to tell, not one that would make headline news. The chick they flashed was Sterling's teammate's sister who needed extra game tickets, which Sterling left at 'Will Call.' End of story. With her whole heart, Tempest believed Sterling and would have cancelled her trip if seeing him wouldn't do her heart and stomach some good.

"I'm sorry, Dana, but I have to go," Tempest said, cutting Dana off. She was ready to see Sterling that instant if she could.

"We just sat down."

"You know my stomach," Tempest lied.

"You go. I think I'll stay."

"By yourself?"

"Yes, by myself."

"Are you sure?"

"I'm positive."

"I hate seeing people eat alone. They look so…lonely."

"It'll make good practice since it looks like I'll be by myself for a long time."

"Stop it, Dana. You will not."

"I may even treat myself to one of these delicious-looking desserts."

"Let me pay the bill for you, please, Dana."

"You're not going to pay the bill, Temp. I don't need you to feel sorry for me."

"Let me do something."

"You can leave. That's what you can do." Dana twiddled her fingers, waving Tempest off. If Sterling weren't her priority, Tempest would stay and be the dumping ground Dana obviously needed. But Sterling took precedent over everything in her life.

"Okay. I'm leaving." Tempest stood.

"One more thing before you go," Dana said.

Tempest withheld a sigh and sat on the edge of her seat. Not to be rude, she subtly checked the time on her cell phone. *Eight thirty!* That left her with little time to pack if she was going to have any window before her flight departed. "What is it, girl?"

"Devon left Carmen. Did I tell you?"

"Nooooo! That is so sad, Dana," Tempest said with bated breath. Hearing about the breakup of any relationship was the last thing Tempest wanted to hear today. Dana may as well have told her someone died; the news couldn't be more devastating.

"Why would any man leave Carmen?" Tempest went on. "Anybody with eyes would call her pretty. Take it from me, not every woman has the face to pull off a razor cut like hers, unless they're Halle, girl. Devon can't get any closer to Halle than Carmen. Plus, she's a fierce dresser."

"Only the fashion police would know," Dana mocked. When Dana opened her mouth to say more, Tempest didn't give her the chance.

"I need to get out of here. We'll talk later. Pray for Devon and Carmen, Dana." Tempest kissed Dana's cheek and fled the restaurant. During the drive home, the knot in her stomach had elevated to her throat. She couldn't hold back her tears. She had to see Sterling.

FROM THE WINDOW SEAT OF the airplane, Tempest admired the blueprint of Minneapolis. The view from above was mesmerizing, a patchwork of velvety green lawns, sculptured gardens parading autumn in bloom, and teal lakes radiating under a dawning sun. Tempest's love for the city was intertwined with her love for Sterling, a passion she didn't have for Minneapolis/

St. Paul before Sterling made his home here. Nevertheless, she hated the thought of living in Twin City after she and Sterling married. Shoveling snow, wearing too heavy clothes, and living so many miles away from her family wasn't her idea of living. Furthermore, her warm blood couldn't bear the cold growing up in a state where summer days lingered through fall, winter, and spring. And if she had to shovel snow, why not shovel it in New York, Chicago, DC or a fashion conscious avant-garde city. Those were Tempest's thoughts before she learned that Minnesota was ahead of the times when it came to fashion trends. In Bloomington, not too far from Minneapolis, was the Mall of America, the largest mall in the U.S, with 520 stores. Whenever Tempest found the time during her visits, Mall of America was her playground.

Eager to land, Tempest struggled to sit idle during the four-hour flight, acting as fidgety as the toddler behind her. Her sketchpad and art pencils kept her hands and mind busy. Earning a B.A. of fine arts in fashion marketing and design from American InterContinental University had taught her everything she knew about pattern making, sketching and illustration. She had loved fashion since childhood, spending much of her playtime sketching designs, and using up tree loads of paper around the house. If she wasn't sketching a design, she was usually sewing one, trying her hand at various patterns and becoming known for creating her own fashion trends. Tonight, she sketched a rough design for her clothing line; a breezy top saturated in striking spring colors, and a pair of studded pocket, boot cut jeans. Someday her line would be *Bebe Coutour's* fiercest competition.

"Please prepare for landing," the flight attendant announced in no time. The airplane pushed against the wind, tilted its nose, and descended from the sky. Tempest found her purse beneath the seat. The queasiness in her stomach was gone; her jitters were not. She wasn't here to catch Sterling cheating, she reminded herself. She was here to prove his innocence.

Following a short ride from the airport in a rented Toyota, Tempest had the key to Sterling's luxury brick townhouse in her hand and was opening his etched-glass front door. Cautiously, she turned the key, calling out Sterling's name as she entered. When she didn't get a reply, she shoved the door open and barged in like her name was already on the deed. Heart hammering, she froze in the foyer, listening for a sign of life, laughter, God forbid she should hear any moaning and groaning. A laugh burst through Tempest's lips at the idea. Sterling was never home at this time of morning, unless he had skipped a day at practice, which would take an act of God.

The house was quiet enough to hear the faucet dripping in the kitchen. Tempest's shoulders relaxed. As always, she changed into comfortable clothes and started cleaning up whatever dishes, shoes, and clothes Sterling left lying around. Not that she was looking for anything, she really wasn't; but she didn't come across any evidence that another woman had been there besides her. There was no lone earring, bras, thongs, or anything a skuzzy might leave behind.

Tempest made her way around the house, sprinkling Carpet Fresh along the way and vacuuming up behind it. If she hadn't talked Sterling into renting furniture, she would be vacuuming an empty shell. For now, Sterling was conserving his money and refused to spend it on certain things like furniture, adequate towels, proper dishes and whatnot—things she couldn't live without. He was happy standing at the bar to eat, lying on the floor to watch TV and play video games, and sleeping on a mattress without a bed frame. Tempest talked him into renting full bedroom suites for each of the two bedrooms, a leather sofa set for the living room, and a dining table with matching barstools. When he signed his new contract, Sterling told her she could go crazy decorating their mansion. He didn't have to tell her twice. She planned to.

After washing the dirty laundry piled on Sterling's closet floor, eating the sandwich she had scraped together, and catching up on her soaps she rarely had a chance to watch, Tempest drove to the shopping center to pass time.

It was close to dark when Tempest returned to Sterling's house. She thought for sure he would be home. She stood on the rooftop getaway of Sterling's townhouse, with her hands jammed deep into the pockets of his suede winter jacket, waiting for Sterling's black SUV to turn the corner. When it finally did, Tempest planned to fly down the stairs and surprise him at the front door with a juicy kiss.

Another ten minutes went by. Tempest was ready to ditch her plans. Despite the miserable cold, she stayed put. The view was eye-catching enough to hold her attention. From where she stood on the balcony, she had a direct view of Lake Calhoun, a clear view of the illuminated skyline, and could see the evening traffic building at the stoplight on Lake Street.

While Tempest enjoyed the view, she thought about Linda, the store manager at Nordy's. Maybe she should have told Linda about her plans to catch a red eye out last night. Linda wouldn't appreciate one of her top managers skipping town without adequate notice, not while they were in the process of accepting applications for the holiday season, their busiest time of the year. Tempest reasoned that Mondays and Tuesdays weren't too busy. And besides, she had rarely missed work in the five years she worked for Nordy's. It shouldn't be a big deal if she called in sick for a few days. She would be back to work by Wednesday morning if everything went well tonight. Tempest was sure that it would.

When the headlights of what looked like an SUV pointed in her direction, Tempest's pulse pumped double time. As the headlights approached, she realized it wasn't Sterling's black Cadillac Escalade but a white Beemer X5. It slowed in front of Sterling's condo. Tempest didn't think much of it until the X5 parked in Sterling's driveway.

Before the doorbell rang a second time, Tempest had flown down the stairs leading to the living room. When she yanked open the front door, the chick drew back.

"Oh. Hi," the chick said.

"Hi," Tempest said.

"You're Tempest, Sterling's fiancé', right?" Her question quieted Tempest's thumping heart. It was good to know Sterling wasn't out here hiding their engagement.

"Yes, can I help you?" Tempest said in her professional voice. The chick plastered on a smile and stuck her hand out to shake. Her hand was as cold as Tempest's.

"I wanted to give Sterling this." She handed Tempest a box. "It's nothing," she practically swore. "A small token of my appreciation to thank him for the tickets." The chick laughed. "I'm sorry. I should introduce myself, shouldn't I? I'm Diamond. Sterling and my brother, Mark, are teammates. Sterling was nice enough to give me extra game tickets for a few of my friends." Diamond's fixed smile disappeared. She pressed her hand over her heart and tilted her head. "I hope that was okay."

Tempest's heart hit an air pocket, dropping 100 feet. She knew the chick looked familiar. She couldn't miss those dark ringlets and blonde highlights. This chick was undeniably the "beautiful Spartans fan" they flashed during Sterling's interview.

Putting on a disingenuous smile, Tempest replied, "I don't mind. Too bad they lost."

"Miserably," Diamond said and laughed. She stuck her cold hand out again. "Nice meeting you, Tempest."

"You too." Tempest flipped her silky tresses to one side of her shoulder and smiled with confidence. Her eyes zoomed right in on Diamond's noticeable flaws. The bridge of Diamond's nose started above her close-set eyes and humped in the middle. Her slender lips had no sex appeal, and her stature looked dumpy in contrast to her own statuesque one. "Cute," was how Tempest branded Diamond, giving her credit for having one glamour girl quality—hazel eyes that could win her a full-page spread in Cosmo. Otherwise, Tempest had upset her stomach pointlessly. On top of that, she couldn't wait to tell Charlene and Dana that Diamond was clearly not a white chick, but a black one. Although Tempest didn't care if Diamond were red, green or purple with polka dots. She was a woman, possibly after her man.

"I'll tell Sterling that you stopped by," Tempest said politely.

"Thanks."

Tempest watched Diamond hurry to her X5 and didn't close the door until the car's tail lights vanished up the dark road. She stepped down into the sunken living room and sat on the couch nearest the fireplace. The gift was in her hands, gleaming in black and gold wrapping paper—Minnesota Spartans colors. A chill washed over Tempest as if a window flew open in the room.

Ten minutes later she heard the front door open and ran toward it. "Surprise!" Tempest yelled when Sterling walked in. He drew back with a clenched fist.

"You almost caught one between the eyes, girl," he said. Tempest laughed and threw her arms around Sterling's football neck. He wrapped one strong arm around her waist and stared at her like she was the sun, the stars, the moon, and the seven phenomenal wonders of the world.

"What're you doing here?" he said through his smile.

"I couldn't sleep without you tonight," Tempest lied. Sterling smothered her lips in his, happy to see her for whatever the reason. A draft of cold air blew in through the open door. Using the heel of his size fourteen tennis shoe, Sterling slammed it shut and tossed aside his sports bag. Tempest followed him into the bedroom and watched him strip out of his fleece warm-up suit and skin-tight Under Armour. He threw his Spartans beanie on the bed and came out of his shoes, barely pausing as he headed for the shower. Sterling was the most beautiful man alive to Tempest. From his broad nose to his large luscious lips that stole attention from his big brown eyes, right down to his silky black skin. His serious athletic body and bowed legs only enhanced his beauty. As he walked, the set of dice, totaling seven, and the phrase *'Can't lose'* quivered on his left shoulder blade. It was one of the six tattoos decorating Sterling's upper body. The cursive 'T' tattooed across his heart in her honor proved Sterling's love for her was eternal.

"Haaaaa…" Sterling sang out in a deep laugh that echoed off the blue tiled walls. "I know what's up. You came to stake claim on your boy. Who've you been listening to? *Charlene?"*

"You think you know everything, Sterling. I have my own mind, you know?"

"I know you, Tee."

"Then you should know that the last person I'd listen to is Charlene." Tempest opened the shower door. The strong smell of bar soap burned her nose.

"You're listening to somebody. Tell whoever's got your head twisted, I'm out here grinding. That's all I have time for."

Tempest laughed off the truth. "Are you happy to see me?"

"I'm always happy to see you. You should've told me you were coming, though. I almost laid you out."

Tempest was caught in a daze, watching the white soap suds roll down Sterling's naked body, fighting back her desire to step into the shower with him. Sterling smirked, his look half wishful and half disbelieving, almost as if irritated that she would get his hopes up.

"Can you close the door, baby? My nuts are frozen," he said. Tempest moved as far away from Sterling and her immoral thoughts as possible. Standing near the sink, she rearranged his assortment of expensive colognes, afraid to look at him when he stepped onto the bath rug and yanked a lush bath towel off the nearby rack. He then handed her the bottle of lotion and asked her to rub it on. Tempest massaged the creamy substance into his shoulders with both hands, taking extra care to work the knots out of his tense muscles by kneading her thumbs beneath his shoulder blades, and sliding her fingers slowly up his spine. She then gave his neck and shoulders the same attention and affection.

"Thanks, baby. That felt good," was Sterling's brisk reply, having the restraint not to act on the noticeable erection bulging beneath the towel wrapped around his waist.

Troubled by his self-control, Tempest followed him to the connecting bedroom. When had Sterling not tried to talk her out of her clothes when he got aroused? While he slipped on his gym shorts, Tempest stretched out on the king-sized bed, wishing she could read his mind. She had the window to his heart and she knew Sterling as well as he knew her. Today she couldn't see past his furrowed brow that told her more than sore muscles had him uptight.

To loosen Sterling up and set a warmer mood, Tempest lit the apple spice candles she bought earlier, which glowed on the fireplace mantel. She then started a cozy fire and dimmed the recessed living room lights. After, she prepared his favorite meal. Sterling was like a big kid, sitting at the counter, waiting for his plate. She handed him seven crispy tacos.

"I love you for this, baby. I needed a home-cooked meal. Where's my Spanish rice, though, with corn in it? You know how I like it."

"You're spoiled, Sterling. You need a maid and a cook," Tempest teased, though she loved spoiling him.

"I have a maid and a cook, and you're about to get *paid.*" He pulled her onto his lap and smacked her on the lips. "I'm on the lineup next season, baby."

"You are? How do you know? I mean, they told you?"

"I don't want to jinx myself, but I'm thinking, hoping, praying…if Banks stays down—not that I'm wishing dude bad luck or anything—but I don't know, baby. Things are looking up."

"You should be on the lineup, boo. You're the best tackle in the league."

"Don't underestimate the competition. Banks be doing damage out there, bringing the *heat.* He's pretty banged up, though. I heard a career-ending injury possibly."

"That is so terrible, Sterling. Isn't he married?"

"Wife, four kids, close to hanging up his cleats." Sterling shook his head. Tempest curled into Sterling's arms and laid her head on his shoulder.

"I don't know what I'd do if something happened to you."

"That's the nature of the sport I'm in. If I worried about getting hurt, I couldn't do my job every week." Sterling was so right. The most they could do was stay prayerful, knowing only God had the power to protect Sterling from a career-ending injury.

After they ate, an unusual empty space stood between them, one that never existed before. The gap stretched as wide as the Pacific and covered every square mile that stood between them. Sterling must have sensed it too. He suddenly pulled her into his arms again, only to stare at her as if he lost his train of thought. He then pecked her on the forehead and walked away. Tempest trailed him, her mind worried with questions she would never find the courage to ask.

On a Monday night, Sterling always watched the game; the New York Giants and the Cleveland Browns were playing. Stretching out on the floor, Sterling propped one of the sofa pillows under his chin. To be close to him, to feel his love, to close the gap between them, Tempest lay on the floor next to Sterling. They watched the game in absolute silence. After, they went to bed. This was always awkward for them both, sleeping together. The only intimacy between them was a hug and a kiss goodnight. Some nights they cuddled, talking into the night about their wedding plans. Other nights they couldn't keep their hands off of each other. Tonight Sterling slept like a baby. Tempest didn't sleep at all. She thought of Diamond's visit and the gift Diamond left for Sterling. It was now tucked away in her suitcase, prepared for a flight back to California. Sterling would never see Diamond's gift if she could help it. Giving it to him would be as suicidal as cutting out her heart and handing it over to another woman.

When Will It End?

If Carmen wasn't off work today, she would have found a reason to take the day off. Two things had her stressed out: someone finding out about her relationship with Kendall and losing her job as a result. It seemed Kendall was doing his best to make sure both happened.

What worried Carmen most was raising further suspicion among a few already raised brows, Lillian's to be specific. The young, cutesy sales associate had her eye on Kendall and wasn't shy about letting everyone in the office in on her little crush. If Kendall so much as whispered a word to Carmen, Lillian's ears came to a point. Carmen swore the girl had the senses of a canine.

It helped that her bi-weekly therapy session with Dr. Jessup was today. She needed to talk down her anxiety. With DJ in pre-school and her appointment with Dr. Jessup set for two o'clock, Carmen found peace on the backyard deck in the meantime, happy not to be on anyone's schedule but her own at the moment. The mass of swirling Jacuzzi bubbles and vibrating jets relaxed her, but didn't quiet her mind. Dr. Jessup warned her about over thinking. According to the good doctor, thinking too much would only flare up her condition. "Try to look on the bright side of things, Carmen," said Dr. Jessup once. Carmen was trying. She really was. Maybe if she had taken the anti-anxiety pills Dr. Jessup prescribed, she wouldn't be thinking, but rather floating on one of the white fluffy clouds in the sky. At Dr. Jessup's insistence, she sampled the seemingly innocuous-looking white pills following her first visit with Dr. Jessup and slept so hard that night it scared the shit out of her. She didn't need Devon accusing her of child neglect coupled with everything else, should they divorce. It was wise that she handle her condition prescription-free, though the Jacuzzi and glass of wine wasn't much of a substitute. At that, Carmen stepped out of the jetting water, dried off, warmed herself in a swimsuit cover-up and headed back into the house to call her sister, Tan. She was tired of talking to herself.

By eleven o'clock in the morning, Carmen was on her second glass of wine for breakfast. She needed it. Talking to Tan didn't help her look on the bright side of things. Tan had orchestrated her life in Maryland before she could get there. She and DJ were moving in with her, Tan said, which would be perfect, because the twins, Conrad and Cameron, would make great playmates for DJ. In truth, she and DJ would fill the void in Tan's life and take up the space in Tan's four-bedroom house that Carl, Tan's ex-husband, left behind. Tan hated living alone and was always moving somebody in to keep her company. Tan's last houseguest was a long lost cousin who needed a temporary place to live. It took Tan six months to get their cousin out of the house. With that came Tan's bitching and moaning whenever they talked.

Carmen grabbed another bottle from the wine rack, turned on relaxing R&B Soul cable music and took respite at the cushioned bay window seat off the kitchen nook, where she nursed her wine and watched the big white clouds in the sky clear way for the sun.

Carmen thought about the past seven years of her life, living on the west coast and loving days like today, when the sun overtook the city and the wind was perfectly slight. The District of Columbia this time of year, too, couldn't be beat. If she moved home, she could look forward to a true fall season, when vibrant foliage brightened the city and the air was cool, crisp and clean. *Though snow would be nicer*, she thought. She missed winter seasons where people had a reason to stay indoors and do nothing but think.

Besides, moving back home to DC would be a welcome change to this life. At least there, she had a mother dying for her to return home and a best friend for a sister, one she could talk to face-to-face versus on the phone daily.

When the phone rang, Carmen let it. It was only Tan calling back to reconstruct her life (If only her sister knew why her life needed reconstructing). Hell, if anyone knew, for that matter, she wouldn't be able to show her face in public. Only Dr. Jessup had gotten that deep into her psyche. Devon suspected, but he couldn't put a finger on it, and she turned a finger back on him whenever he tried. If she was acting strange, it was his fault—his job, his friends and the attention he gave to this or that and not her. Even the television was a source of blame. Devon kept his eyes on it more than on her, she accused. Carmen thought of everything she could to deflect the blame from her.

Now that the phone stopped ringing, the doorbell started up. Carmen took her time answering it, sure that it was her neighbor returning to take her order for the Girl Scout peanuts she promised to purchase from the woman's daughter. Without verifying, Carmen opened the door.

"Ms. Centerfold," Kendall said, confirming it wasn't Carmen's imagination. Kendall was undeniably at her house, standing on her porch!

"What the hell are you doing here?" Carmen said, finding her voice.

"I took a sick day to be with you." Kendall invited himself into her house and took a seat on her living room sofa. "If you want me to leave, you'll have to call the law to move me."

"Damn you, Kendall!" Carmen slammed the door shut. She rarely talked to her neighbors, but she had a good mind to close every open blind in the house for fear someone would see Kendall and presume the elicit. For her own safety, Carmen stayed close to the front door, tightening the belt to her cover-up, even if the sheer white fabric couldn't keep Kendall's lusting eyes from seeing she had little on underneath.

"Before I put you out, how did you find out where I live?" she said.

Kendall admitted, with a shameless smile, that he followed her home one night.

"Are you crazy? What if my husband was home!" Carmen's emotions were having a head-on collision. She was furious as ever at Kendall, yet stimulated by what being alone with him would result in.

"It's you that drives me crazy."

"Look, Kendall, it's over between us. How many times do I have to tell you?"

"Do you believe it is over, Carmen? The eyes talk, not the mouth. Your eyes tell me you don't." Carmen could only swallow the lump in her throat and look away from him, unsure of what she believed. She hoped like hell it was over between them, and was going to do her damndest to make sure Kendall understood.

"As your *boss*, I'm ordering you to get the hell out of my house and get back to work!" She opened the door. "Get out, Kendall!"

"This is your doing, Carmen. You see my eyes. I'm a man who can't sleep nights, you know that." Curling his lips up in that closed mouth sexy smile of his, Kendall sauntered over to her, his feline-like stroll slow and purposely. "What is it you're wearing under that thing there?"

"Don't come near me, Kendall. I can't lose my job after losing everything else." Carmen's voice was whispery and weak. Even she wasn't persuaded by her order.

"I promise not to tell a soul." He closed the door. "Let me see all of you."

Kendall hadn't laid a hand on her, and Carmen could feel his brawny hands exploring her body like the new world, his mouth ravishing hers; feel him lifting her powerfully off of her feet and plunging deep inside her. Her breathing intensified, her legs weakened, until she thought she would spread them in defeat. Wearing a bikini only made her hypersexual; the skimpy fabric being defenseless against Kendall's bedroom eyes that stripped her of struggle like a lion would his feast for the day. Regardless, Carmen needed to put a stop to this affair, to find within her yearning body the strength to resist Kendall. She threw her hands out and shoved him back.

"I'm married! You fool! Do you understand? You don't, do you? Why should I expect you to? You're a *boy*, Kendall, with nothing to lose and nothing invested, not even your own damn house!"

"Don't talk to me that way, Carmen. It's you that does not understand." Kendall pointed to himself, practically beating his own chest. "When I was a *boy*, I provided for my family after my father's death so my sister would not have to trade sexual favors for her schooling. I put food on my family's table to eat. In my country a man isn't a man because of his age, Carmen. A man is a man because of what his experiences have taught him. *Boys* like me can teach a woman like you things you have never learned."

Carmen understood Kendall's overstated manhood had more to do with his upbringing than his age. Growing up poor in the barrios of Santo Domingo had left its mark on him, both good and bad. He told her the extreme details of his childhood, how he got caught up in a large drug ring selling heroin to feed his family; how he slept outside his house with a gun at his waist to protect his family because the police were too afraid to enter his community, and how his large family lived in a two-bedroom cement house with a roof that leaked in the winter and walls that sweat in the summer. Carmen's heart went out to Kendall for his troubled upbringing at one time but had since hardened. What Kendall failed to understand was their slight age difference was a minor factor compared to the enormity of obstructions that stood between them.

Yet, Carmen's arguments and excuses were no match against Kendall's seductive power over her. At six foot one, Kendall stood a good foot above her head; his good looks so polarizing a magnifying glass couldn't capture his lush skin, gold and ruddy as a Caribbean sunset, more vividly than her own eyes. His strong jaw line, mass of curly black hair atop his head and laying softly around his heart-shaped mouth weakened Carmen. He had her nailed to the door with his hands above her head, his legs spread wide so that she couldn't get around him or escape his black catlike eyes.

"Do I look like a boy to you, Carmen?" Kendall untied the string securing her cover-up. "Do I?" He slid the cover-up down her shoulders and dipped his tongue into the hollow of her shoulder blade, striking her like lightning. "Let me make love to you. After, if you want me to leave your house, look me in my eyes like a woman and tell me to go," he said.

Before Carmen could break away, Kendall suspended her against the door, his tongue sweeping over hers impatiently; his hot and heavy breaths filling her ears like the night cries of the jungle. Carmen couldn't keep her legs from wrapping desperately around Kendall's waist. Her back came to a steep bend from struggle and desire. Her chest heaved as her breathing synchronized with his. She then felt herself being carried across the room and falling back on a hard surface that served as a ready mattress. Kendall's brawny hands ripped off the skimpy fabric she wore. He started between her toes and snaked his tongue up her thigh. That was only the beginning of her ecstasy to come.

Kendall and Carmen now lay on the floor of her walk-in closet in the master bedroom. How could she have let this happen again? A terrifying vision of Devon walking in and finding her and Kendall's naked sweaty bodies sprinkled with carpet fragments flashed in her mind, setting off a heat wave inside of her.

"Let me up, Kendall! I have an appointment I can't miss." Carmen fought to free herself. Kendall held her hostage, pressing his body firmly against hers and pinning her hands over her head.

"This house is too big for you; I should move in and keep you company."

" That'll never happen, so wipe the thought out of your mind. Now move!"

"Do you know that in my country a man can marry a woman at sixteen without permission?"

"Do you know in some countries I can be executed for cheating on my husband?"

"With me you wouldn't have to cheat. Your life would be much better."

"I don't want a better life, Kendall. I had a good life before you complicated it."

"You like to tell me lies."

"You can't accept the truth."

"The truth is not what you hear but what you feel. I feel you can't live without me."

Carmen laughed. "Get over yourself, Kendall."

"You are a cold woman, Carmen, do you know that?" Carmen was being cold. If not, she and Kendall would never cool down. She was already heating up again feeling Kendall's manhood pressed between her thighs. "I know how to warm up a woman like you," Kendall said and suckled her neck in a way that brought a groan to her lips.

"Stop!" Carmen said. She wrestled herself free and hurried to shower, slamming the shower door in his face. "If you come near me again, I'll fire you!" Carmen yelled over the shower water. Kendall laughed, but took her serious enough not to join her in the glass enclosed shower, its two heads ideal for what Kendall had in mind.

"*DO YOU LOVE YOUR HUSBAND, Carmen?*" Dr. Jessup's question played repeatedly in Carmen's mind as she rode the elevator from the fourth floor of the six-story office building. She walked out into a sun that shocked her tearful eyes, and shaded them with her hand to see clearer. With the question still playing back, Carmen couldn't remember where she parked her car. She walked about aimlessly.

How could she answer Dr. Jessup honestly after what could best be described as a pre-therapy sex session between Kendall and her? The encounter took them from the dining table, to the soft mattress of her guest room, and ended on the Berber carpet lining her walk-in closet before she finally dressed for her appointment to see Dr. Jessup.

The bed she and Devon slept in as husband and wife was off limits. Carmen made that clear. But really, what difference did it make? She hadn't been woman enough to look Kendall in the eyes and tell him to get out of her house after they had sex throughout it. She let him fry up her bacon, scramble up her eggs, and whip up a stack of pancakes, and didn't mumble a word when he served her breakfast in bed, the heated syrup and whipped cream serving as devices for his next spectacular sex act. When Kendall finally left her house, he strutted out like a man who had marked his territory.

Then Dr. Jessup hits her with the question of the day. *"Do you love your husband?"*

"More than anything," Carmen finally said, wiping her eyes dry with the tissue Dr. Jessup handed her. Dr. Jessup was always handy—handy with tissue, handy with a cup of water to wash down a lump in her throat, and handy with advice Carmen sometimes didn't want to hear.

"My advice, Carmen, is that you let go of your guilt. What happened is unchangeable by definition. It's up to you to close this chapter in your life by choosing the love you have for your husband over... let's call it lust for this other man."

Letting go of her guilt wouldn't be as easy as Dr. Jessup made it sound. More than the affair, Carmen felt guilty for betraying her and Devon's friendship. They had been best friends before anything else. Back in college, she would never have predicted her relationship with Devon would come to an end. Devon was a homesick freshman at Norfolk State, unsure of himself and his major. She was sure of her plans to one day be a hotel interior designer, a career track she chose in her sophomore year, after a summer working as a hostess for a Virginia Beach hotel. Her career aspirations sidetracked when she got a call from her mother announcing her decision to divorce her father. For Carmen, the earth had shattered beneath her feet, leaving her feeling lost and uncertain of her future.

Eventually, she dropped out of college short of thirty credits needed to graduate with a degree in fine arts, found a decent-paying job in the hotel industry, and rented her own apartment.

In those days, her independence meant everything to her, and certainly didn't cause her the kind of anxiety she lived with these days. She cooked for herself and kept an apartment any man wouldn't want to leave. Through it all, Devon was the rock she leaned on, the comfort she could count on, her knight in shining armor. His friendship never faltered while she gave herself to other more desirable men. It was during the period Devon had a girlfriend, one Carmen was sure he would someday marry, that she realized her undeniable love for Devon.

So how could choosing her love for Devon over Kendall be complicated? Her affair with Kendall had nothing to do with love or friendship. Her overactive sex drive was the problem. It had taken over her life until lust and love had fused, one seemingly unsatisfied without the other. Each time she tried to end her affair with Kendall, the more aggressive he became; their untamed sexual exploits leading them to beach fronts in the dark of the night, parking lots in broad daylight, parks, hotels, and now the sacredness of her home.

When would it end?

Carmen found her car and passed it by. The park bench overlooking a rolling sea of green grass adjacent to the building looked inviting. She hurried across the busy street and sat among the palm trees and a flock of fluttering birds, thinking over more of Dr. Jessup's handy advice.

"Make a choice, Carmen, but whatever choice you make, live with it guilt-free. Can you do that for me and for yourself?" Carmen could only say that she would try since the choice wasn't exactly hers. She was powerless to whether or not Devon returned home and powerless to Kendall. But if Carmen had the choice to make, her love for Devon would win out. She couldn't imagine a life with Kendall. He awakened a part of her that was better left in slumber, her impulsive, invincible, daring side that

she hadn't known since adolescence. The two of them combined was as explosive as hot oil to water. Devon, however, brought out her precautious, vulnerable, rational side that enjoyed regularity and peace of mind.

"What's your greatest fear, Carmen?" Dr. Jessup once asked her. The question was so obvious Carmen thought it was a trick one. She had any number of fears, but if after three months of seeing Dr. Jessup, the woman didn't know her greatest one, Carmen had wasted her time talking until she was blue in the face. The mere thought of her greatest fear had her so paralyzed she sat on the couch in Dr. Jessup's office, twiddling her thumbs. Finally, she was able to speak the word softly. "Divorcing."

"Do you see the paradox?" said Dr. Jessup. Carmen did see the paradox, and for the life of her couldn't understand why she was working harder to achieve her greatest fear than to avoid it. But if Dr. Jessup knew so much, why couldn't she pinpoint the source of her fear? *That's up to you to figure out, Carmen,* Dr. Jessup would likely say to her question. *No shit,* Carmen thought to herself. Whatever the source of her fears, she was caught in the eye of a tornado, whirling out of control.

Carmen dug her cell phone out of her handbag and called Devon, taking Dr. Jessup's final advice of the day. *"Call your husband, Carmen; this time for the right reason.* Here goes nothing. The lump in Carmen's throat was already cutting off her airways before Devon picked up. Maybe today, with Kendall's scent fresh on her body, wasn't the best day for honesty and transparency. Carmen hung up before Devon answered. Her call to her husband would have to wait for a better day.

Another Kinda Brother

*O*n her primary colored classroom, where mature mollies, swordfish, and Harlequin Rasboras swam in the dome-shaped aquarium, Dana logged grades from her latest spelling test. Her wild bunch of second graders were released at noon and if Oswaldo didn't get long-winded during the training, she could get off work an hour early and get mentally prepared for her afternoon appointment. She had finally put her fears behind her. Today was her big day to visit a real estate agent.

The adjoining classroom door opened and Matthew Kerry, the new third grade teacher, entered her room. It was casual Friday. Some employees, like Matthew, took it literally. Dana dressed halfway professional by wearing a lightweight corduroy blazer with her jeans and wedge-heeled sandals. Matthew wore dungarees, a Benjamin Franklin T-shirt that read, *"Go Fly a Kite,"* and dilapidated running shoes. To Dana he looked like a fish out of water at 31st Street Elementary School.

"Hey there," Matthew said. "How's it going?"

"Slow."

"If you're headed over, I'll walk with you."

"Give me one minute." Dana found a pad and pencil, the most she needed for a short seminar. She and Matthew walked along the corridor, shaded from the sun.

"I didn't fully read the memo. What's the subject matter again?"

"Strengthening writing programs, again," Dana told him.

"A new strategy the district's come up with to fix our illiteracy problems, eh?"

"This program is supposedly better," Dana said, air quoting her words with two fingers. "Did you hear? We didn't meet the state standards last year. Our performance scores came in lowest in the district."

"You heard the saying 'Of whom much is given, much is expected'? The problem with kids of this type is the opposite. For whom much is deprived, much shouldn't be anticipated. Take the administration, for example. They expect us to work with insufficient tools and churn out *Einsteins.* I should write the U.S. Department of Education!"

Dana was laughing. "What brought on this fit of passion for the underprivileged?"

"The grim reality that I'm working off work sheets. How long does it take to get a textbook around here?"

"You'll get used to it," Dana said, then leaned over and whispered, "A word of advice... don't say 'kids of this type.' They're not of a particular type, Matthew. They're just kids."

"Right. Good looking out."

"Speaking of, what's an Ivy League grad doing in the ghetto anyway? Reclaiming your heritage or working off student loans?"

"*Danaaaa....*" Matthew sang, then tisked. "You have me pegged in a square hole. Maybe if you got to know me, you might discover that I'm not very square, but a pretty well-rounded guy."

"I think I know you, Matthew."

"I'm speaking of a less formal know," he whispered in her ear. Dana turned her cringe in the opposite direction. She saw this coming weeks ago and planned to tell Matthew, in a nice way, that he wasn't her type. She did not find him remotely interesting. He was simply too elitist for her taste, a true black conservative, and, in her opinion, only working in the community to connect to his lost roots. Matthew's overall wavy hair, fair skin, and conformist look was a turn off to her. Take Omar, for instance. He wore a natty Afro and a light goatee, which gave him a bad boy look amid his otherwise humble appearance. Now *that* was Dana's idea of a black man with sex appeal. Maybe the best way to turn Matthew down was to tell him she was in a committed relationship—a lie, but still a nice way to put it. What she and Omar had by no means met her standard of a relationship anymore.

Dana turned her head back to Matthew, ready to be brutally honest. "Matthew…" Her words stuck to her tongue.

"Not in front of our co-workers," he whispered before she could say anything. "I understand. Let me know. I'm right next door." He winked.

Approximately twenty teachers were sitting behind the banquet tables that faced the podium, waiting for the training to begin. Oswaldo was late, which meant Dana would lose the leisure time she had hoped for before her appointment. She and Matthew signed in and grabbed handouts from the display table. A vacant seat between Lauren Hendricks and Martha Mendes caught Dana's eye. She headed for it. She wasn't sure where Matthew sat and didn't look back to find out.

In walked Oswaldo, twenty minutes behind schedule. "This'll be quick. If you blink, you'll miss it," he said briskly, removing the pen wedged between his ear and stark white hair. Dana blinked more times than she could count to stay awake and Oswaldo was still explaining the new writing program that seemed indistinguishable from the old one. At three-ten, the training finally ended. Dana headed toward the parking lot at her usual time.

THE CONTEMPORARY AMERICAN REALTY office was on the fourteenth floor of First Interstate Bank. Dana sat stiff-necked, avoiding the credit report on the desk in front of her. She focused on Louise Brown's deep red lipstick instead as Louise broke down her credit score.

The woman didn't come across as eager to take on a credit-less client. She sat in her swivel chair with her hands clasped over her frilly white lapel and said, "Your FICO scores aren't great and you don't have a long history of employment, but I can work with you," as if doing Dana a favor. Dana shrank back, prepared to go through the same rigmarole the car dealership had put her through to drive off the lot.

"I've worked for the school district for three years, and what about my substitute teaching experience, and my paid internship back in college? Doesn't that count in my favor?"

"It's more of your DTI that flags a lender."

Dana was clueless. She hated to ask something that Louise assumed she understood, but she asked anyway, with hoarseness in her voice. "DT...what?"

"Your debt-to-income ratio compares the amount of money that you earn to the amount of money that you owe to your creditors to determine mortgage affordability." Louise was talking in tongues to Dana. While she droned on, Dana looked down at her credit report on the desk. Her shoulders slumped. Why did she buy a new car before she bought her house? Not wise. She had increased her debt unnecessarily. Her old car hadn't given her that many problems before she traded it in. On top of that, she let Tempest talk her into applying for a Nordstrom's charge card. She couldn't remember what she bought to run it up to a thousand dollars that was taking her a lifetime to payoff. And given the amount of her student loans, she would be dead and buried before she paid those off.

"...Most lenders will want your DTI to be lower," Dana heard Louise say, coming out of her reverie.

"I'm sorry, but can you explain DTI again?"

"Debt-to-income," Louise repeated as though tired of repeating herself. As Louise talked, Dana jotted down as much information as she could to research on her own.

"Don't look so discouraged," Louise said. "Interest rates are low enough and predicted to come down. And we can always look into different finance options: HUD, FHA loans...no downs. There are many options for young, single women. And I guarantee if there's something for you out there, I'll be the one to find it."

She must be a miracle worker, Dana thought.

When Dana left the real estate office, she made a stop at *Yogurtland* for a large New York Cheesecake sprinkled with Oreo cookie crumbs, her consolation prize for what proved to be a discouraging and wholly depressing experience. As soon as she finished off her yogurt and turned on the engine, Tempest called.

"Come by and see the gift Diamond tried to give Sterling that I intercepted," Tempest said.

"Who's Diamond?"

"The chick they flashed during the pre-game special."

"You met her, Temp?"

"Are you at home?"

"Close."

"Be at my house in ten minutes. Hurry up! I have to get back to work."

Dana shook her head. The entire ordeal with Sterling was confusing her. She found out Tempest had flown to Minneapolis to surprise Sterling only after Tempest returned. Now, a week later, Tempest tells her about a gift from a chick named Diamond.

Dana couldn't wait to see what this woman was trying to give Sterling, probably her panties. Gold diggers will stop at nothing to nab a ball player.

Tempest flung open the door the second Dana knocked. "What took you so long?"

"Traffic. What else? So, where's the gift and when did you meet this chick?" Dana followed Tempest toward the kitchen.

"She came by Sterling's house the night I got there."

"Is that so? How did she know where he lived, Temp?"

"Mark told her. He and Sterling *are* teammates and Diamond *is* Mark's sister." The way Tempest spoke meant she never considered the question. It would have been the first question Dana thought to ask Sterling. Dana sat on a bar stool, eager for details.

"Don't sit, girl. I have to get out of here." Tempest tossed a half-eaten sub sandwich in the kitchen trash bin, then moved fast past Dana; her silky black hair swishing across her shoulder blades as she walked. She was wearing a tan sweater with a faux-fur collar, a tan suede mini-skirt that showed off her long bare legs, and calf-length stiletto boots. A Nordstrom mannequin couldn't have been better put together. Dana hopped up from the bar stool and followed Tempest to her bedroom. Entering Tempest's room was like entering an Egyptian temple. A spool of sheer red fabric draped the four posts of Tempest's canopy bed, creating an exotic sanctuary. A glass computer desk took up a corner of the room, and over it hung a large knockoff painting of a goddess that Tempest claimed stood for "Truth, Balance, and Order."

Dana and Tempest stood in the walk-in closet as Tempest removed a shoebox from the stack on the top shelf.

"What is it?" Dana said, anxious to see *the gift*.

"I'll show you." Tempest opened the box excruciatingly slow, like the contents were the grand prize on a game show. Inside the shoebox was a rectangular gold jewelry box. Tempest removed the jewelry box and put the shoebox on the closet floor. She then opened the jewelry box so slow Dana thought she would snatch it out of Tempest's hand and open it herself.

"You're killing me, Temp," Dana said. A platinum chain with a charm clustered in diamonds appeared and hung from Tempest's French manicured acrylics. "What is it?"

"Sterling's jersey number, girl."

"I thought it was fifty-five?"

"It's fifty-three. Can you believe Diamond tried to give my baby *this*? She called it a small token of her appreciation. Quality is my middle name, girl. I deal in nothing but. This chain is worth dollars." Tempest tossed the necklace back into the box. They headed back to the living room.

"Did Sterling see it?"

"Freakin' no! I'm not crazy. By the time Sterling came home, I wasn't thinking about Diamond or her gift."

"I don't know, Temp. Watch her. White girls can be conniving when it comes to ballers."

Tempest smacked her lips and rolled her eyes. "Diamond is black, Dana, which proves that most women are conniving, white, black or purple."

"You have a point. But still, Sterling is there and you're here. You don't have to be a rocket scientist to know distance can affect a relationship, even one as rock solid as yours and Sterling's." Tempest had locked up in silence. They were halfway down the double flight of stairs when she commented.

"Maybe if Diamond could compete, I'd be worried. I shouldn't talk about people, but I'm sorry, she's not prom queen material. Take it from a prom queen." They neared their cars, where Dana had parked illegally in the assigned stall next to Tempest's car.

"That's what I love about you, Temp. You always find a rose in a field of weeds."

"Because there always is one," Tempest replied, with a genuinely optimistic smile.

"I sure hope you're right," Dana said.

EARLY SATURDAY MORNING DANA ANSWERED her cell phone with a growl.

"Hey there. I'll be by at ten. Culver City on Braddock Street, right?" With one eye open Dana glanced at the circular clock on the office desk. Eight-thirty on a Saturday morning was too early for Matthew to sound so jocular. They agreed on twelve, not the crack of dawn. Already Dana regretted agreeing to this date, for no other reason than to not hurt Matthew's feelings. That was the only explanation she could think of for her poor judgment.

"Why so early?" she said.

"You don't mind a little spontaneity, do ya?"

"Depends…"

"There's somewhere I'd like to take you before lunch, if that's okay by you?"

"Somewhere like where, Matthew?"

"Danaaa…," Matthew said, singing her name in that irritating way. "It's a surprise."

"Give me until ten-thirty, okay? It's *Saturday*."

"Cool."

Dana grunted and hung up. Why did men insist on surprising her? She really hated surprises, which never lived up to her expectations.

Matthew arrived fifteen minutes early. Dana saw his white Jeep Wrangler from her bedroom window as she slipped on her wedge-heeled sandals. Watching him walk toward the house, she waited to see if anything about Matthew excited her. He wore cargo shorts, a screened T-shirt and his bare feet in flip-flops. Not an ounce of excitement stirred within Dana at the sight of Matthew.

Just as her mother opened the front door for him, Dana entered the living room in an eclectic print skirt, and a tank top covered by a jean jacket to keep warm on an overcast day. She caught Corrine staring at Matthew with a curious smile.

"Matthew says he's here to take you to lunch." Her mother's statement was more of a question followed by an exclamation. Any man, other than Omar, coming to take her out on a date would raise a brow on her mother's face.

"Mom, this is Matthew Kerry. He teaches third grade in the classroom next door to mine. Matthew, this is my mom, Corrine."

"Matthew, did you say?" Corrine tilted her head up, squinting behind her reading glasses more than usual. Her mother had started a new project—painting the kitchen a pastel color. She wore a painter's hat that concealed her salt and pepper short afro and coveralls splashed with mint frappe colored paint.

"Nice to make your acquaintance," Matthew said, sounding ever like the elitist that he was.

"You two have fun." Corrine slowly closed the door behind them, leaving Dana with the feeling she was being watched.

During the drive, Matthew's obvious nervousness had him fiddling with the radio, indecisively switching from conservative talk radio, to rap, to rock, before settling on eclectic contemporary. Dana noted this as another problem with Matthew. Not only did they have different tastes in music, what else did they possibly have to talk about after covering the normal work-related subjects they covered in the first twenty minutes of the ride? Dana rolled down the window for boredom sake. A gust of wind blew in. The weather jump-started another conversation.

"Is it cool enough for you today?" Matthew asked.

"Cooler than I thought it would be."

"That's California weather for you, unpredictable or notoriously perfect." He flashed his tight smile, ending that topic. When they entered the 710 freeway, heading toward Long Beach, Dana became increasingly curious. Matthew and she were co-workers, nothing friendlier at this point. Giving it more thought, she didn't know much about Matthew to let him take her blindly to an unspecified location. The minute Dana opened her mouth to demand Matthew tell her where they were going, Matthew turned into the parking lot of the Long Beach *Aquarium of the Pacific,* a surprise that exceeded Dana's expectation.

"How did you know I love sea life?" she said.

"Let's see, there's the life-sized fish tank in your classroom to start with, but our field trip here was a dead giveaway. You bulldozed the kids to get inside."

"I did not," Dana said in the middle of her laughter. He laughed along.

"That might have been a bit of an exaggeration, but your excitement was obvious."

Throughout the entire one-hour private tour Matthew arranged, Dana followed the tour guide as her second graders had, gawking at sea lions, seals, sea turtles, sea horses, sea dragons, and diving birds. In the touch lab, she encountered bat rats and sea cucumbers. The three-story enclosure of killer sharks and giant sea bass awed her, as if discovering a world of hidden sea creatures for the first time. Dana couldn't get enough of sea life.

At *A Taste of Greek,* where they had lunch, Dana got to know Matthew over gyros, Greek salad and Spanakopita. She already knew, through campus gossip, that he was somewhere around twenty-seven years old, though his clean-shaven baby face led her to believe he was much younger. Today, Dana learned that Matthew lived somewhere off the beach in Palas Verdes, a community known for being swanky. How Matthew could afford to live there on a teacher's salary made Dana wonder about this guy. He also insisted he didn't have a girlfriend "necessarily" or any kids "that he knew of," and he was quick to add that he upset the applecart when he chose to be a teacher and not go into the family business.

"What kind of family business?" Dana asked for asking sake.

He smiled. "I wouldn't want to prejudice you against me. I know how you are."

"And how is that?"

"Hypercritical, you could say," he said and smiled tightly.

Dana didn't press the issue. If Matthew wanted to keep his personal life a mystery, so be it. She was more interested in his love for the outdoors than anything else about him. Finding out he spent his weekends sailing, hiking, surfing, dirt biking, and jet skiing, activities she could use to spice up her life after being cooped up with Omar, was worth her ear.

"How long have you been sailing?"

"When I was in diapers I set my first sail, believe it or not, and fell in love with it. If I had to choose between cruising, sailing and jet skiing, I'd choose sailing, hands down."

"I've never sailed in my life, other than a seven-day cruise to the islands, if that counts."

"You'll have to sail with me one day. It's an awesome ride. You'll love it." They talked for two hours, their conversation taking them from the restaurant to a leisure walk around the harbor.

Now standing at Corrine's front door, Dana and Matthew couldn't find the words to close their date, which Dana realized their outing had become—a real date.

"I like your spontaneity, Matthew," she said.

"You bet." Matthew extended his hand politely. Dana pushed his hand aside and rolled her eyes.

"Bye, Matthew."

"Are you suggesting I kiss you, Dana?" It was a joke that turned out not to be. Dana opened her eyes to find her hand pressed into Matthew's chest, holding his lips at bay. "Am I being too forward?" he said.

"This is our first date. You know how it is."

"Completely." He shook her hand professionally. "See you Monday?"

"See you Monday," Dana said with a smile.

A Sin Like No Other

"The holiday season is around the corner. If you haven't requested time off, sorry guys, it's too late. We're short staffed until the seasonal help is hired," Tempest told her staff, Hannah, Kelly, Roxy, and Tamika, who sat in the pink leather chairs of the chic ladies' lounge between her department, *Via C*, and *Savvy*. She relayed to her staff, verbatim, Linda's announcement from the weekly manager's rally, trying to sound upbeat without showing her true emotions—a manager's rule of thumb. In truth, she was as unenthusiastic as her associates looked to learn that overtime might be necessary and her weekends were shot. Visiting Sterling would be difficult the rest of the season without putting her job and promotional opportunities at risk.

"I'll be revising the shift schedule next week," Tempest said and dismissed her staff.

Before the doors unlocked for the early birds, the floors sparkled and the shelves and racks were organized and neat. It was Tempest's favorite time of day. She took extra care that her department was in impeccable order before starting her day. Today she only glanced around and headed straight for her office. With Diamond on her mind, she wasn't in the mood.

At the close of the day, Tempest took advantage of Nordstrom's handbag sale, purchasing a Dooney and Bourke that would go beautifully with the textured twill suit she bought her mother not long ago. She loved giving *just because* gifts. Her employee discount afforded her the luxury, along with her Nordstrom's credit card. She drove directly to Lynwood to surprise her mother.

Driving through her old neighborhood brought back fond memories for Tempest. She grew up in Lynwood and could remember when Nadine, Charlene and she ducked in and out of stores on Lynwood Blvd., mostly window shopping. They roamed the boulevard until dark before walking home. Tempest wouldn't be caught walking the streets at night in Lynwood anymore. According to her mother, there was a drive-by shooting every other weekend. According to Charlene, Lynwood hadn't changed that much; it was Tempest who changed after moving to Fox Hills, and now thought she was too good for Lynwood. There was never any truth to Charlene's lies. She simply worried about her parents' safety. They owned the only two-story house on their block, which outshined their neighbor's standard homes in renovations. Why reconstruct an entire house, add a story, install a pool and Jacuzzi, and surround the house with surveillance cameras? If you have the money, *move,* was Tempest's belief. It wasn't as if her parents were poor. Her Daddy may not have been traditionally educated, but he was a self-educated businessman who had acquired lucrative real estate over the years, and her mother worked as a lab technician for a hospital. Between their two incomes and the four pieces of income property they owned, they made enough money to move to a safer neighborhood.

Tempest pulled her sporty car in front of the two-car garage and parked in front of her parents' stucco two-story house. Now that it was dusk, she could see the light on in Salia's bedroom upstairs, which meant Salia was home from school to wash her clothes and eat a home-cooked meal. Tempest rolled her eyes when she saw Charlene's SUV parked in the driveway. She thought to drive off before reconsidering. She couldn't pick and choose family, she reminded herself. She had to accept Charlene for who her sister was. Anyway, whatever Charlene said or did, Tempest decided to take with a grain of salt.

Tempest used her old key to enter the house, walked through the black and white living room and headed to the family room, which was large enough to hold a pool table and a full bar.

"Where's Mama?" Tempest asked Charlene as she entered the family room where reality TV was showing live, loud and in color on the sixty-five-inch screen. Once Tempest surprised her mom with the Dooney, she was leaving.

"You know my baby sister, Yvette?" Charlene said to her client. Charlene sat on a barstool, fastening individual French braids to her client's hair.

"I think we met before." When Yvette tried to look up from where Charlene had her neck crammed forward, Charlene went crazy.

"Keep your head down, Yvette, or I'ma have to redo this braid! First, you walk in here an hour late, now you want me to be on your head all night! I got another client coming, girl. Keep still, okay?" Charlene may have sweetened her voice at the end of her tirade, but Yvette's face couldn't have been redder from embarrassment. Tempest shook her head, thinking she wouldn't pay Charlene two hundred dollars to be disrespected, even if Charlene was one of the best braiders in L.A.

"Hi, Yvette," Tempest said, giving Yvette a smile that said she understood her humiliation.

"What brought you to the hood?" Charlene said.

"Is Mama home?" Tempest asked, ignoring Charlene's comment. She placed the shopping bag on the bar counter, and took off her pumps, deciding to stay for as long as she could tolerate Charlene. Coming home comforted Tempest. She loved to relax on the blue leather sectional beneath the row of pane windows and look out into the lushly landscaped backyard lit up with garden lights. In a way, she was glad her parents refused to move. She hadn't lived at home in two years, but it still felt like home.

"What's in the bag?" Charlene said.

"A Dooney for Mama."

"Did you buy me one?"

"Why would I, Charlene? You won't use it. All the expensive handbags I've bought you, and you wear that no-brand black one every day."

"You bought Nadine one. She told me."

Tempest sighed. "I'll buy you one, but not a Dooney, okay. Is mama upstairs?"

"She and Daddy are in Palm Springs. I'm house sitting for 'em."

"Mama didn't tell me she was going to Palm Springs."

"Well, she told me. They're on one of those bus turnarounds with the church." Charlene stopped braiding and pulled the Dooney out of the bag.

"Charlene! You'll ruin the leather, putting your greasy hands on it."

"I'm just looking at it. See how my baby sister is, Yvette?"

Tempest politely removed the purse from Charlene's hands and carried it back to the couch with her for safekeeping. There was a time when she could spend the day at her parents' house, enjoying home-cooked meals and peace and quiet. Lately, when she visited, she ran into Charlene. If Charlene were at home half the time, where she should be, she could manage her parents' apartment complex properly, and the tenants wouldn't be thrashing the place. She should know. She managed it for a year before Charlene took over. In contrast to Charlene, she took the job seriously and wasn't doing it for the free rent.

Avoiding an unnecessary conflict, Tempest kept her opinion about Charlene's freeloading to herself. Mostly, she didn't want to get cursed out in front of Yvette. All day she guided the success of a multi-million dollar department, led and motivated her sales team, and was viewed as an expert in her field. But it didn't matter how her resume read, she would always be treated like a baby sister in her family.

"I'm going home," Tempest said decisively. "Can you put this on Mama's bed for me?"

"You must've found out something when you snuck out there to see Sterling. You haven't said nothing since you got back."

"There's nothing to say, Charlene." Tempest searched between the sofa cushions for her car keys.

"Before you leave, let me ask you something."

"Ask me what?"

"You and Sterling get down yet?"

While reaching for her purse on the floor, Tempest iced over. She couldn't believe Charlene asked her something so private in front of a total stranger. Charlene might share the vulgar details of her sex life with anybody willing to listen, but that didn't give Charlene the right to blab hers. In a hurry to leave, Tempest turned her purse upside down in search of her keys. Items scattered across the floor. Now she was on her knees, chasing down her lip gloss tube before it rolled under the sectional.

"Don't act like you didn't hear me?" Charlene said and laughed. "Everybody in the family knows you're the oldest virgin alive." Tempest put her purse back together and walked to the bar counter, appearing unfazed by Charlene's stupid question. She found her keys hiding behind Charlene's tub of hair grease.

"Too much information, Charlene."

"See how my family is Yvette? Don't nobody in this family think I'm smart enough to know shit, girl. I'm trying to help her, but she don't want to listen. If I was Nadine, she'd think I had something important to say, but that's okay."

That was Charlene's way of making Tempest feel guilty for confiding in Nadine more than her. Well, maybe if she knew which personality of Charlene's she would be confronted with, she would confide in Charlene. There were days when Charlene was sweet as pie, and days, like today, when Charlene acted as if the world had done her wrong. It wasn't anyone's fault but Charlene's that she chose not to go to college. She had the same opportunity as the rest of them. If Charlene didn't feel smart, why didn't she go back to school or get the cosmetology license she had been after for years. Nevertheless, pitying Charlene, Tempest stopped in the doorway.

"Okay, Charlene, tell me."

"The only reason Sterling's messing with that ho is to get a head job. If you haven't, that white girl will beat you to it. That's all I was trying to tell you, Tempest."

Tempest thought to walk out and let Charlene think whatever she wanted to think, before deciding to have her say. "If that's your theory, Charlene; I *know* Sterling's not cheating. So there!" Charlene stopped braiding and looked up. Yvette had permission to look up too.

"Oooo, Tempest! I'm telling Daddy." Charlene had herself a good laugh.

Tempest's heart started with small palpitations. By the time she got in her car, her heart was thumping out of control. She didn't know why she listened to Charlene. She wasn't going against her moral principles, doing something she vowed she wouldn't do until her wedding night because another chick might beat her to it.

But what if Charlene was right? And what if Sterling's rush to get married had more to do with sex than anything else?

Lately, his patience for holding off until their wedding night was thinning. Tempest's patience was thinning too. Her vow not to have sex with Sterling—again—was no longer as significant as it was six months ago. She had given into the flesh and her love for Sterling early into their relationship, before repenting and reestablishing her commitment to celibacy after their engagement. Sterling wasn't happy with her decision, but he loved her enough to go along with it.

Then there was her mother, who may not say it, but who had a strong opinion about pre-marital fornication. Why was she the only one in the family upholding her mother's Christian dogma? Nadine and Will had sex before they married and Charlene "got down" with Derrick regularly, practically lived with Derrick and their mother never batted an eye. Tempest wasn't sure about her baby sister, but with all the boys chasing after Salia, she wouldn't be surprised if Salia was more of a woman than she was by this point.

Tempest turned on the car radio to drown out her thoughts as she drove down the highway, headed for home. Not even music kept her negative thoughts from resurfacing, making her stomach burn like she had drank a cup of acid.

It was eleven o'clock Eastern Time. As soon as Tempest walked into her condo, she called Sterling. He didn't answer. She called his cell. No answer there either. Plus she hadn't received one call or text from Sterling for twenty-four hours. Two tablespoons of Pepto-Bismol was the only remedy that got Tempest through the night.

AS SOON AS THE CLOCK struck seven a.m., Tempest picked up the phone. "Hi Linda, it's me, Tempest. I don't know what's wrong with me, but I'm not feeling well...*again*. I made a doctor's appointment this morning, which means I won't be in today. You don't have to tell me. This is a bad time to take off. I'll be in tomorrow, if I'm feeling better, promise. I can be reached on my cell phone if you need me."

Lies. Lies. All lies. God forgive me.

After leaving Linda a voice message, Tempest packed a small carry-on bag, took a shower, and dressed in her travel gear—a body-shaping pair of black designer jeans, warm socks and tall-heeled boots. She layered her upper body in a long sleeve thermal to wear under a sweater, and grabbed the warmest coat she had to fight the Minneapolis climate.

TEMPEST'S VISIT DIDN'T SURPRISE STERLING this time. When he came home from practice, he expected to see her and couldn't have been happier. They ate dinner at "The Tin Fish," not far from his condo, one of their favorite eateries, a casual southwestern style pavilion off Lake Calhoun. They were eating when a woman walked up.

"My son would love to have your autograph." The woman pulled her freckled face son forward, who couldn't have been older than ten, and presented him to Sterling. Tempest admired how cordial Sterling was about the constant interruptions. A line formed. Not once did Sterling get agitated and turn down a fan's request. If they wanted to take a picture with him, he smiled for the cameras. Autographs, he signed, no problem. Tempest did what she could to support him while being mobbed. His fish tacos were growing cold. She flagged down the waitress, put in a new order, and had Sterling's food packed to go. The manager of the restaurant, a fan too, didn't charge them a dime for their meals and threw in dessert to top it off.

As they left the restaurant, Sterling wrapped his arm around her waist, pulled her close and kissed her cheek. "Thanks for taking care of me, baby. This is every day. See why I want you down here with me. I need a manager to handle my business. "

"I'll be handling everything for you soon, as your wife."

"That's what's up. I can't *wait.*" Sterling kissed her cheek again. They hadn't left the restaurant when up sprang a 36E cup-wearing fluffy blonde hair. Those were the only two physical attributes Tempest noticed of the chick who walked boldly up to Sterling, holding her breasts high and mighty in a deeply low-cut top. The woman didn't even freakin' say, "Excuse me. Do you mind me taking a picture with your man?" She shoved the camera at her and posed like a cheerleader, with one arm wrapped around Sterling's waist and one hand on her hip. Tempest took the picture politely, behind eyes of fire.

"See what I mean?" Sterling said when the chick walked off. It was as if the chick's pretty face was one out of a million he encountered daily and was no big deal. Tempest never let on, not for a second, how furiously jealous and paranoid she felt inside.

"You've reached stardom out here," Tempest said.

"You mean *we* have," Sterling said. "This don't mean nothing to me without you."

Tempest plastered on a sweet smile. A skilled manager could hide his or her emotions in the face of any offensive situation.

BACK HOME STERLING WANTED A MASSAGE. Tempest wondered if he wanted to pick up where he left off during her last visit. He sat on the floor, slouched between her legs, while she sat on the couch. She worked her way from the crown of his skull to his temples, making small deliberate circles with her fingertips. She moved to the rim of his ears then kneaded his neck and shoulders. Within five minutes, Sterling leaned his head back and looked into Tempest's eyes, begging her for more than a neck rub. Without hesitation, her lips met his. She loved Sterling's lips, their thickness, how they dominated hers. Tempest didn't let her devout thoughts stop her as she sucked them gently. She started with Sterling's top lip, then the bottom, drawing half moon circles with her tongue around his open mouth.

"You know what that does to me," Sterling said and stood on his knees between her legs. The feel of Sterling's bare chest pressed against her breasts made Tempest lose self-discipline.

"I want you so bad, Tee, I can't take it no more." Down came her tube dress. She and Sterling kissed and caressed each other as if they couldn't believe they were in the same room, in the same city, at the same time.

"Eight more months and you can have me for the rest of your life."

"What difference will eight months make?"

If Tempest weren't absorbed in ecstasy, with Sterling's tongue rediscovering her body, she would have told him it made every bit of difference to her, and if he loved her, he wouldn't be making her feel the way she was feeling—sinful.

"Sterling, we shouldn't…" Tempest said in such a whisper Sterling must not have heard her. He was too busy kissing down her abdomen, making her wet and squirmy. Tempest's mind fought for him to stop, but soon gave in to her perspiring flesh as her body slid willingly down the leather sofa. To hold her in place, Sterling gripped her legs firmly and wouldn't let go. It was too late to stop him now. She came, went, came, and went until she couldn't go any further.

"Don't laugh, Sterling. You were wrong for that." She threw her clothes back on, feeling naked in the eyes of God.

"I wasn't wrong a minute ago. You were begging me not to stop." He stretched out on the plush carpet and pulled her atop him. With her head rested on his chest of steel, Tempest closed her eyes against her burning tears.

"You mad at me?" he said.

"How do you think I feel, Sterling? Six months with eight months to go before our wedding day, down the drain."

"Tee…" Sterling forced her to look at him. "You're taking this celibacy thing to a whole new level. It wouldn't have come down to this if we got married back when I signed like I wanted us to. God already knows how much I love you, baby. Everything I do is for us. You want a mansion, don't you? With a design studio, an indoor pool, waterfall Jacuzzi, and what else?"

"A home theater, tennis court, and don't forget a playground for our only son."

"Is that your wish list?"

"You know it is."

"Then it's yours, baby. You still mad at me?"

"No," Tempest said, smiling.

Sterling pecked her on the lips. "I respect your morals. I do. But I miss you so much, Tee, I'm hurtin'. I can't take this long distance situation much longer. I want you out here with me, like *now*."

Tempest sat up and straddled Sterling. "I will be here soon, as soon as I get promoted to buyer."

Sterling smacked his lips. "That's always your excuse, Tee."

"It's not an excuse. Do you know how long it took me to earn my reputation for being a platinum seller with all-star customer service status *and* to promote to department manager?"

"Yeah, yeah. Five years. You told me."

"Yes, and for five years I've been working triple time to get promoted, brown nosing Linda every chance I get for the associate buyer position that's opening up. That's what you have to do to be successful in this business, plus have a strong knowledge of merchandising to back it up."

"What do you have to do to be my wife? That's what I want to hear," Sterling said.

"Try to understand, Sterling," Tempest explained passionately. "Nordy's is like the Super Bowl of the fashion industry, the best place for me to gain a sense of the business behind the scene. The more I learn, the closer I get to launch my own line."

"I've heard that story, Tee, too many times. There's a Nordstrom's in Bloomington. You can work there."

"A Nordstrom's *Rack*, Sterling."

"That's just as good."

"Put yourself in my shoes. I would never ask you to give up playing ball. It's what you dreamed of your whole life. I've been dreaming of having my own apparel line since I got my first Barbie."

"In a minute, I can buy you an apparel line. That's just another excuse." Sterling propped himself up on both elbows. "You know how I feel, Tee. Any given season I may have to pack up and move. I want my girl by my side wherever I go, holding it down for me. Admit it. You don't want to leave your family. Say it."

It was more than Sterling's hurt tone and his big brown eyes filled with disappointment that forced Tempest to rethink what she would say next. Nevertheless, she had to say it, even if it would anger Sterling more than hurt him. They both couldn't go on pretending it couldn't happen.

"What if you get cut?" Tempest said carefully.

"Why you gotta jinx me? I'm not getting cut!" Sterling barked. "Forget it, Tee. It's cool. Don't move. Stay home." Sterling shoved her aside, a gentle shove, but a shove nonetheless. This wasn't how Tempest wanted to end their one night together. She remounted Sterling like the black stallion that he was in her eyes and kissed him softly on the lips.

"I'm sorry. I was wrong. I trust your judgment, boo. I do. If you want me here, I'll move. I'll follow you to the end of the earth if I have to."

"You mean that?"

Tempest kissed him again, swallowing back the sob that rose in her throat. "I love you so much, my life depends on it."

Sterling pulled her face to his, inhaling her lips as if they were his breath of life.

"I'm feeling you so deep right now, Tee. I gotta have you, baby. I *got* to. We don't have to do nothing, just take care of me, *please.*"

Knowing exactly what Sterling meant by *take care of me,* Tempest froze up. Then Charlene's stupid theory popped in her head, then Diamond, and the image of that 36E chick. If she ignored Sterling's needs, it could make or break their future together. Torn between her love for the Lord and her love for Sterling, Tempest rationalized that oral sex wasn't necessarily classified as *sex.* Some women thought of it as foreplay. Her girlfriend Yasmine swore there was a difference. "God wants us to get some pleasure before we get married, girl, or he wouldn't have made us horny," Yasmine would say. Knowing God better, Tempest only laughed.

But what did God expect her to do with the well of love pinned up inside her for Sterling? Simply pretend it didn't exist, that her love for Him would satisfy her every need? Some days it did and some days, like today, the devil got the best of her. She loved Sterling so deeply her well ran over and spilled in tears down her cheeks.

"I'm sorry...I can't," Tempest said, holding strongly to her beliefs.

Sterling kissed her face tenderly. "Don't be sorry. It'll make feeling your pretty lips on our wedding night that much more special. Come here..." Sterling held her tight, freeing the breath Tempest had been holding. She felt as if she had shot up for air, out of twenty foot deep water, just before drowning.

She laid her head on Sterling's chest and closed her eyes, eager for the day when she could give herself, whole and completely, to her man with God's seal of approval.

A Step Somewhere

As luck would have it, Omar called disturbing her peaceful Friday night. Following their last date Dana refused to see him. Tonight, with nothing better to do, she fell for his *"Give me a chance to make it up to you,"* line. How could he make up for years of lost hopes and dreams? Omar promised that he would. This was her *real* surprise he said, that would make up for everything. Their last date, she supposed, was his sorry warm-up.

"Give me an hour. I'm in the middle of something," Dana said, not to act desperate. She hung up, topped off her nail polish with quick dry, and enjoyed the rest of HGTV at her leisure. After showering, Dana stepped onto the velvety maroon rug to dry off. Water dripped from her shoulder-length sister locks. Using a hand towel, she rang them dry until they flopped wild and loose, then walked back to her room wearing a bath towel. Blue jeans and a tank top should be appropriate to lounge around Omar's parents' house, Dana decided, predicting that to be Omar's last, if not first stop of the night.

"I KNOW WHAT YOU'RE THINKING," Omar said, reading Dana's thoughts as they pulled out of the driveway in his weathered Mazda.

"It's fine, Omar. But can we eat first? I haven't eaten a thing today." Omar drove on, heading in the usual direction.

"You don't have faith in me, do you, Dana?"

"I have faith that we're going to your parents' house. I'm just hungry."

He laughed. "I'll take care of you. Don't I always?"

"That's debatable."

When they passed 120th Street, Dana expected Omar to make a right turn. He made a sudden left down one street, then a right down another street. They were now heading in the opposite direction, away from his parents' house. Dana hoped they were going back to her favorite barbeque spot. No such luck. Omar stopped in front of a grubby melon-colored apartment complex between a sleazy motel and a liquor store, where two hard-faced Hispanic guys guarded the entrance. Omar opened Dana's door, a courtesy he offered when he was after sex.

"Where are we?" Dana asked. She wouldn't feel safe entering this place in broad daylight, let alone at night.

"One of my boys lives here. I want you to meet him."

"Which boy?"

"If I tell you, it won't be a surprise."

"If it won't be a surprise, I must know him. Why do I need to meet one of your boys I've already met?" Omar laughed. He laughed too much at the wrong times. Here was a man with a degree in accounting, an associate degree in restaurant management, and she swore he never graduated from high school.

"Come on, Dana. Let me surprise you this one time. It'll be the last time I try since you *hate* surprises." Dana sat firmly in her seat, waiting for Omar to close her door and either take her out to eat or take her back home. She listened to the cars zip up and down the busy street and watched the suspect Hispanic guys who watched her with equal suspicion.

Omar squatted by her open door. "If you really want to know, I'll tell you," he said.

"I'm listening."

"You're always saying our dates need more variety, right? I thought you'd like to do something different tonight. My boy is throwing a little social. He has a spread upstairs, all you can eat."

"Don't play, Omar."

"Do I look like I'm playing?"

Dana permitted a slight smile. "You should've told me."

"You should trust me."

"You need a TV, Homes?" One of the Hispanic guys said as they entered the complex.

"I'm straight," Omar said. He hiked the first stairwell they came to, with Dana under his arm. The motel lights brightened the courtyard, revealing a slum of a place. Dana sensed he was up to his usual games when he stopped in front of apartment twenty-one and used a key instead of knocking. It wouldn't surprise her if Omar had borrowed his boy's apartment for the night. Why didn't he take her to the sleazy motel next door? It would have been less insulting and more clear-cut.

When they entered the apartment it was empty of people and food. "Take me home, Omar!" she demanded.

"Dana, will you trust me?" Omar sat on the denim blue sofa, stretched his arms across its back, and sat his feet on the flimsy oak coffee table. "Have a seat. My homeboy is in the back. He'll be out in a minute. Where you at, homey!" Omar called out, as if in a stadium. He was acting entirely too stupid for Dana. She opened the front door to leave. In a flash, Omar leaped over the coffee table and stopped her.

"It's my place, Dana. I moved in last week. *Man,* you're a hard female to surprise." Omar's glower told her he was serious, for once. Dana surveyed the room. It actually wasn't as atrocious inside the apartment as out. The living room, connected to the dining room, made it rather spacious. And the kitchen, with decent wood cabinets, gave the place a nice facelift.

"You know how I get when I'm hungry," Dana said with a sheepish smile.

"I had the night laid out for you, if you would have faith in me." Omar walked to the kitchen, and pulled a large bag of Chinese food from the oven. He unloaded one carton after another of her favorite items. "I thought we could eat, play cards, watch a movie…and whatever else arises without Moms in the mix," he said and winked his brow.

Their love for good Chinese food, card playing and watching a good movie was a few of her and Omar's many compatibilities. Another, Dana remembered fondly, was their infatuation with black history. Early in their relationship, they would spend hours dueling over important historical facts. Omar out challenged her time and time again, in spite of the fact she minored in black history and his knowledge came from his unadulterated love for history in general. Tonight, Dana was as impressed with Omar as she was on their first date.

"When did all this come about?" Dana said, her face overtaken with affection.

"It's been in the making. Come on, I'll give you the grand tour, show you how I'm livin'." Dana followed Omar into the short hallway and peeked into the small white bathroom, clad with a green towel in place of a bath rug. There was nothing else present except for a wood magazine rack overflowing with the business magazines Omar read for pleasure like she did a good fiction novel, not for the purpose of making good use of his knowledge.

Across the hallway was the bedroom furnished with Omar's old bedroom suite. Right away Dana noticed the framed portrait of Omar's parents on his chest of drawers—the personification of a happy couple. Mr. Penn, a graying, twinkly-eyed man with a meek smile and Mrs. Penn, the matriarch of the Penn family. Her smile, donned in wine colored lipstick, dressed up her headstrong eyes that resembled Omar's in every other way. There wasn't anything Dana didn't love about Omar's parents. When Dana thought about it, she was nearly a member of the Penn family as far as Omar's father and older brother, Todd, were concerned. Omar's mother was another story. Dana didn't question if Mrs. Penn liked her, possibly thought of her as a future daughter-in-law, but Mrs. Penn didn't push Omar toward the altar either. As Dana saw it, she impeded Omar's manhood, making it impossible for another women to take her place.

Dana raised a brow when she saw her own photo displayed. It was the photo she had taken with her second graders last school year. It warmed her heart, but she couldn't help but feel as though she was being skillfully manipulated again.

They returned to the living room.

"I have another surprise for you," Omar announced, his smile reticent and childlike.

"You and your surprises. What is it this time?" Dana said.

"Sit down first," Omar instructed. Dana sat. This surprise she had to see.

At Omar's insistence, Dana closed her eyes and kept them shut. She heard a door open, next rumbling and what sounded akin to a snap of some sort. In the briefest of seconds, Dana speculated Omar had gone into the closet and snapped open a jewelry box containing her overdue engagement ring. Great misgiving interlaced her fantasy, but within those briefest of seconds, Dana's heart stood still. The next sound, however, eliminated her guesswork but was music to her ears. Dana couldn't stop the smile that spread across her face, and now she didn't want to open her eyes. Instinctively, she swayed to the seductive melody of Omar's B-flat tenor saxophone, each key playing the strings of her heart.

When Dana could pry open her eyes, she found Omar standing before her, his body bowed, his cheeks as tight as a blow fish, his eyes closed in rapture, as if he was making the sweetest love to every note his fingers stroked. Yet another reason she fell in love with Omar, Dana now remembered. He knew how to put her in the mood and one was coming on strong. If this scene had taken place a few years ago, in the days when simply serenading her with his smooth talking saxophone put her in a romantic frame of mind, Dana wouldn't be controlling her itch to make love to him tonight. She gave Omar a once-over—his nicely fitted jeans, his white undershirt layered with a plaid open-faced button-up, his heavy-lidded sexy eyes, and lean, sturdy physique. She really loved Omar, despite everything.

"That was beautiful, Omar," she said when he concluded his sultry jazzed up rendition of Alicia Keyes *"If I Ain't Got You."*

"Are you happy now?" Omar said, hitting a sour note. The way he said it rubbed Dana the wrong way. He said it as though he had fulfilled his obligation to make her happy for a lifetime, take it or leave it. Dana kept her agitation to herself, though whatever appetite she had for making love with Omar tonight was lost.

Sipping wine coolers purchased at the liquor store next door, they ate Chinese food, and then played spades. During their competitive game, Dana shared with Omar what Devon had shared with her about Carmen. His response was both interesting and surprising to Dana.

"When we get married," he said, "and I find out you got a little something on the side, I won't be leaving. You will!"

"First off, that isn't something you have to worry about," Dana said, referring to the getting married part. "And second, you're putting words in my mouth. I never said Carmen had something on the side."

"You don't have to say," Omar said. "I *know.* "

"Does that mean you had something on the side when you hung out with your friends half the night?" Dana lifted her brow.

"How did this conversation turn on me?"

"Uh-huh. Defensiveness is a sign of guilt." Dana slapped down a card. Omar threw out his winning card and laughed. "Whatever, Omar, and I saw you cheat!"

"You're a sore loser," he said, making Dana more sore. Omar had won three games, only because he threw out his spades early, took all of hers, and won with a three of diamonds or something ridiculous.

"I'm not a sore loser. You're a cheater!" Dana griped. They bickered like an old married couple, which would have been nice if by chance it came to pass. Knowing the unlikelihood, Dana grew tired of debating.

The lights were out now, except for the TV and neon motel sign streaming into the room. Dana and Omar lay on opposite ends of the sofa before Omar grabbed hold of her hand and pulled her into his arms.

"Can I have a kiss?" He didn't have to ask. Dana was hungry for one. "Can I have another one?" Omar's tongue was back inside her mouth before he finished the question. His kiss roughened; his hands wandered underneath her top and fiddled with her bra hook.

Dana pulled back.

"What's wrong?" he said.

"If that's the only reason you brought me over here, take me home."

"That's an insult. It's not the only reason, but since you're here…"

"Really, Omar."

"Next time then?"

"We'll see."

They lay spooned on the couch, her back to his chest, their feet playing footsies, while enjoying a movie. At least he made a move, Dana thought to herself happily. Even if it was a move down the street from his parents' house, it was a step in the right direction.

What Oprah & Dr. Phil Don't Know

*F*or Dana, visiting Carmen was more for selfish reasons and not simply to find out if Omar's accusation about Carmen was true. She rationalized that she had a right to make up for her time apart from her nephew. Not many weeks used to go by without Carmen coming by the house, if not to drop off DJ, to spend time with her and Corrine. These days Carmen called occasionally, and kept her conversations brief and pointed, as though she had something pressing to do. This time Dana didn't give Carmen a chance to come up with an excuse.

The house Devon and Carmen lived in was a page out of *Better Homes and Gardens*, the neighborhood as well. Dana parked on the street and loaded her hands up with shopping bags. She was looking forward to girl talk with her sister-in-law—about men, about sex, about whatever was on her mind, which so happened to be Omar tonight. Dana was counting on Carmen being her very own Dr. Phil and Oprah rolled into one. When she found the nerve, she would slip in a question or two about her brother and find out what was really going on in her brother's household.

As soon as she knocked on the door, Carmen answered and DJ's inquisitive face appeared next to hers. His little legs were clasped tightly around Carmen's waist, his arms clinging to her neck like a baby panda bear clinging to its mother. Carmen gave

Dana a hug, giving DJ the chance to leap from his mother's hip into Dana's arms.

"This boy thinks he's a little monkey, swinging on everybody," Carmen said, making Dana laugh. "Come on in, Dana."

"He can swing on his auntie anytime." Dana gave DJ's cheek a million kisses. Knowing she never showed up empty handed, DJ wasted no time tearing into the shopping bags.

"I thought you were bringing dinner," Carmen said.

"I only have two hands."

"You need help?"

"I can get it." Dana returned to the house with DJ's Kids Meal, and two Meal Deals for her and Carmen. To Dana's surprise, nothing appeared out of the ordinary in the house. The way Devon described Carmen's state of mind, she expected the house to be upside down and Carmen to look as crazed as she was allegedly acting. Carmen was as pretty and together as always, giving jeans and a basic Tee sex appeal without ever having exercised a day in her life. She should be so lucky.

"Get comfortable, Dana," Carmen said and poured two goblets of wine. Dana took off her shoes and prepared to relax, taking time to admire Carmen's eye for interior design. The warm pinks, sea foam green, crème colors and splashes of turquoise, gave the house a beach front feel and made Dana long for the ocean.

"When I get my new house, you have to help me decorate, " Dana said.

"I didn't know you were buying a house, Dana. What part of town?"

"I said *when*. I haven't bought anything yet, but I'm buying something soon, if it's the last thing that I do."

"You've been buying a house for a long time."

"You can say that again."

They finished their meals and relaxed in the family room, having girl talk while DJ played with his new toys. That didn't last long. DJ wanted their full attention, his tantrums entertaining Dana more than Carmen.

"Come on, boy. It's your bedtime," Carmen said.

"Let me put him to bed, Carmen. Do you mind?"

"Be my guest."

Dana scooped DJ up in her arms and carted him off. After bathing DJ, she read him his favorite bedtime story, "The Bear and the Big Red Strawberry." She read it five times more, putting DJ into a deep slumber. Dana could have read to him all night. It gave her that mothering feeling she longed for so badly she wanted to take every baby she came across home with her.

Life can sure throw you a curve ball, Dana thought. Getting married and having children came with age, she once assumed. She would be married by age twenty-five, have established her career, and have her first child by age twenty-six. By age thirty-five, she would have six kids running around her house with a picket fence and be a devoted member of the PTA. *Ha!* She turned twenty-six four months ago. The morning of her birthday, she awakened to a hollowness in her womb that wouldn't let go.

Dana returned to the family room to find Carmen on the pillow backed sofa, close to asleep. "If you're tired, Carmen, I can leave."

"I'm up." Carmen darted to an upright position and fluffed out her short hair. "What were we talking about again?"

"Do you have to ask?"

"Right..." Carmen picked up her glass of wine and nursed it. Dana didn't know how to broach the subject of Carmen's supposed bizarre behavior, so she stuck to talking about Omar.

"Do you think he's serious this time?"

"Because he moved to his own place?"

"It's about time, isn't it?"

"That's hard to say, Dana. Why would it make a difference?"

"You're right."

"Instead of reading into it, go with it, see where it leads," Carmen advised.

"If there was somewhere to *go*, I would. You made a good point a minute ago. So what if Omar moved to his own place? That could mean anything. What I need to do is to be done with him."

"Why don't you be?" That advice from Carmen made Dana draw back in surprise.

"You're saying I *should* be?"

"How will you know if you should be if you don't?" Now Carmen's advice was confusing Dana more than helping her. She thought to leave and let Carmen, who could barely keep her eyes open, get some sleep.

"Okay, skipping over that," Dana went on. "What do you think about him bringing up the *M* word? Did he forget we haven't been together in months?

"Men get stuck in a time-warp. I've heard from boyfriends I hadn't seen since the beginning of time, talking like I never got over them."

"Wouldn't it be nice if I had an old boyfriend I wanted to hear from? Can't name one."

"It's time for you to go fishing."

Dana laughed, thinking Carmen *must* be sleepy. "What does fishing have to do with anything?"

"There's plenty of fish in the sea, as they say."

Dana pursed her lips. "Where and in what sea?"

"The big ass blue one. Hell, what sea do you think?" They both had a good laugh, probably from the wine more than Carmen's joke. After three sips, Dana had had enough. Carmen gulped hers back like water.

"If I were single like you, Dana, I'd keep my pole and bait out. Fish are always biting."

Here was her opportunity to throw in a question or two about Devon. Dana leaped at the chance. "Is that what's going on with you and my brother, you both want to be single again?"

Carmen appeared flustered by Dana's question. "That was a figure of speech, Dana. I'm not trying to be single." She shrugged her shoulders. "But if it comes to that…" Carmen grew solemn, meditating on her glass of wine.

Dana tried to read into Carmen's expression. But Carmen could be as serious as she was playful, while holding an air of mysticism. Dana knew this the first time Devon flew Carmen home to meet his family. Right off Carmen said, "If you give me a hard time, you and I are going to have to fight over your brother." If Carmen was joking, she never let on, and being the overprotective sister that Dana was, she buried her inclination to scrutinize the prettiest girlfriend Devon had brought home, with almond-shaped dark eyes, flawless skin, and the bone structure of a model. If someone looked at Carmen once, they would look twice and get caught in a rude stare. After years of knowing Carmen, Dana still caught herself staring rudely at Carmen's beauty. Besides her beauty, Carmen was a self-assured, easy to befriend, family-oriented woman that Dana admired. Honestly, she couldn't have picked a more perfect match for her brother if she had picked Carmen herself.

Since Carmen and the conversation had livened up, Dana tucked her feet under a warm throw, ready to stay awhile. They gabbed for the next hour, about everything except Devon.

"Is your favorite position still missionary style?" Carmen said.

Caught off guard by the question, Dana stuttered for an answer. "I- like-it other *ways,* thank you very much."

"There's a whole lot of other ways to have sex, Dana. But based on my experience, how you are in bed is how you *are*." Carmen roughed her hair again, seemingly lost in thought. "Maybe that was a bad example," she added.

"The moral of this story is what? You think my problem with men is sex?"

"Did I say you have a problem with men?"

"You might as well have said it."

"You know what I think your problem is?" Carmen said, putting Dana on guard. "You're too cautious. Be more, I don't know, daring. Live a little. You're too young to be so serious."

"I can be daring," Dana said like a child eager to learn. Carmen laughed skeptically, propping her bare feet up on the coffee table and revealing the tattoo Devon made such a big deal over. It looked harmless in Dana's opinion, a feminine rose bud that gave no indication that Carmen was coming unglued.

"You have a tattoo?" Dana asked, jumping at another chance to pry. "What made you get one?"

"Nothing made me. You like it?"

"If I were more *daring*, I'd get one just like it," Dana said sarcastically.

Carmen laughed and finished off her wine. "I talked to your brother, by the way," she said in her cool manner. "He's coming home for dinner, for us to talk." A string of questions came to Dana's mind to ask Carmen. The ringing doorbell stopped her.

"Who the hell could that be?" Carmen jumped to her feet. "Stay here, Dana. I'll be right back." Carmen rushed off. Dana heard the front door open and close. While Carmen was away, Dana spent the time thinking about the one thing Carmen said that clung to her mind. "Be done with Omar." That was the simplest solution to a long drawn out problem. Had anything changed since she broke up with him months ago? No! Omar was the same old Omar. Dana had to admit that his move to his own apartment had given her a speck of hope. But she needed the sky to open up and the sea to part before she recommitted her life to a dead end relationship.

Twenty minutes had flown by and Carmen hadn't returned from answering the door. Dana made her way toward the living room, worried something was wrong. Before she could open the front door, Carmen flew inside the house, her eyes wildly annoyed.

"Who was that, a ghost?" Dana said and chuckled at the look on Carmen's face.

"What?"

"You look like you saw one."

"Oh. That was my neighbor…collecting the money I owed her for the Girl Scout peanuts I bought. It's that time of year. You know how people get."

"Collecting money this late at night? It's ten o'clock," Dana said, her expression puzzled. The revving of a motorcycle caught Dana's ear, along with its single flashing light shining through the living room shutters.

"Who is that?" Dana asked.

Carmen walked away, never answering the question. Dana's first mind was to question Carmen again. Her second mind dismissed it. She followed Carmen back into the family room.

"My neighbors don't care what time of night it is, girl." Carmen sat on the edge of the sofa and took a sip of the wine Dana thought was hers.

"Well, back to Omar," Dana said, reclaiming her comfortable spot on the sofa. "You never told me what you thought of him bringing up the M word?"

Carmen twisted her mouth and shook her head, saying nothing. Another sip of wine followed, one after the other. It didn't take long for Dana to see that Carmen's mind wasn't in the room let alone in their conversation. Whatever question Dana asked was met with the same vague answer and far off look.

"I need to get to bed, Dana," Carmen said, nicely kicking her out.

Taking Chances

$\mathcal{D}$evon was coming home for dinner tonight, which gave Carmen roughly two and a half hours after work to cook dinner and dress so irresistible Devon wouldn't want to leave. Thirty minutes before the close of her workday, she called her usual "close of the day" staff meeting to discuss the upcoming events on the books. Staff meetings, with Kendall present, were excruciatingly rough for Carmen lately, mainly because he would do or say things that made her go stark stiff. Hell-bent on not letting Kendall affect her job as he had her personal life, Carmen called the meeting anyway, armed in her toughest skin.

"Lillian, you're in charge of the Horton Family Christmas Reunion. How many rooms have they blocked off?" Carmen asked. Lillian sat next to Kendall around the small conference table in the glassed off room. Next to Lillian sat Brian, a quiet thirty-something guy who Carmen sometimes felt disliked being bossed around by a woman, least of all a black one. Lastly, there was Marissa, the oldest of her sales associates with the most seniority and in line to take Carmen's job should she leave. Kendall sat directly across from Carmen and he was looking directly into her eyes when she looked up from her planner. She was the only person in the room who saw straight through his professional exterior and into his eyes that said he couldn't wait to get her alone again.

Carmen's eyes jumped back to Lillian. "How many rooms, Lillian?" she repeated.

"Oh, uh.. the Horton family cancelled this morning. I forgot to tell you," Lillian stammered, knowing Carmen's rule on communicating the availability of prime dates immediately. Carmen was in too good a mood to lecture Lillian today and dismissed her slip-up with a tolerable nod.

"What about your events, Kendall?" Carmen said, looking Kendall's way but not.

"Yeah, Ken, what about *your* events?" Lillian teased. The way Lillian and Kendall looked at each other, Carmen would've thought Lillian had her hand between Kendall's legs, stroking his balls under the table. The idea sent a surprising stab to Carmen's stomach. Why the hell should she care? Lillian and Kendall could run off and get married for all she cared. Devon was coming home tonight.

Carmen clasped her hands on the table to control her emotions. "Whoever needs to see me about future events, stop by my office in the morning. I have to get home. I have a dinner date tonight." Why she felt a need to make that announcement baffled Carmen and rattled Kendall. His face twitched.

"Is your dinner date with your husband?" Lillian said in a way that sounded condescending.

"It is," Carmen said and couldn't keep from smiling.

"Dinner dates with your spouse are important. It keeps the marriage new and exciting," Marissa said.

Carmen straightened papers to do something with her hands and not look at Kendall. "We haven't found time for a date night in months. I'm looking forward to it," Carmen said.

"Can I have a word with you before you go on your *date*?" Kendall butt in. It wasn't the question Kendall asked but the way he asked the question, sounding more ticked off than anything else.

Carmen kept her composure. "Sure, Kendall."

"Not here. In private. It's personal."

Carmen froze. "In that case, it'll have to wait. I'm in a hurry."

"Wasn't it you that said if I have a problem to let you know? I have a problem, a very big one."

Carmen stood and leaned on the mahogany wood, pressing her hands flat against the surface, trying not to faint from dizziness.

"Okay, Kendall. We can meet, briefly, but it'll have to be on my way out. " Carmen hurriedly left the conference room. She was sure her face looked three shades of gray to her staff. In her office, with the door closed, she threw her face into her hands, hyperventilating. She was so sick of this shit. She had to get control of her panic attacks before they took control of her. At that, Carmen closed her eyes determinately, took in long, deep breaths and talked her anxiety down. When she opened her eyes, she felt strong enough to put Kendall's ass in his place.

His showing up at her house the night Dana came over was the absolute last straw. Was he that much of a fool to think she was going to invite him in and have round two of their sex session with her son in the next room? Carmen would regret, for as long as she lived, allowing Kendall into her house. Next, he would show up at her door with a suitcase, trying to move in. Their hushed spat on the side of the house went on for far too long. She was an emotional wreck when she returned to her conversation with Dana.

There was a hard, impatient knock on her office door. "Come in," Carmen said, ready to walk out when Kendall walked in. The furtive look she gave Kendall made him smile. It was their secret code that meant "Meet me down the street." On Sepulveda Blvd, blocks from the hotel, Carmen checked her rearview mirror to see if Kendall had followed her. She then turned onto a narrow street that led to a park. Kendall followed close behind on his motorcycle. They convened where they had in the past, in the darkest corner, hidden from the streetlights. The sexual aerobatics they pulled off behind a full-grown eucalyptus tree wouldn't be happening tonight. Carmen was determined.

"This meeting isn't what you think it's going to be, Kendall, so wipe that smile off your face."

"If you were trying to make me jealous about your... how did you put it, *dinner date,* I am very jealous. Cancel with your husband. You're having me for dinner tonight." He tried to wrap his arms around her. Carmen's arms flew up to deflect him.

"Can you understand basic English, Kendall, or do I have to spell it out for you? It's over! And tonight when my husband comes home he won't be leaving if I can help it. If that hurts you, I'm sorry. But I'm sorrier that I ever let you put your hands on me!" Carmen was breathing so hard she could see her chest rising and falling with each word she spoke. Obviously, Kendall wasn't taking her seriously. The smirk never left his face. He curled up his lips, his cat eyes twinkling with amusement.

"I don't believe you."

"Do or don't, I don't care what you believe anymore."

"You say you're sorry today. Tomorrow your mind will change."

"You're the one who's going to be sorry if you keep this shit up. From now on, unless it's company business, act like you don't know me."

He pulled her close to him. "Do you know how many women wait up for me at night? Do you, Carmen? It is you that I want, no other woman." Kendall kissed her convincingly, the sweet taste of his mouth brought about mini convulsions in the innermost region of Carmen's thighs. A forest fire between her legs couldn't have caught faster. How could it be? She loved Devon! She loved Devon!

"Show me how much you want me, Carmen." In the past this maneuver of Kendall's would have had Carmen tearing off his pants.

"I hate you!" she managed to say.

"You love me." Kendall suckled her neck, trailing his tongue to the valley of her breasts while hiking up her dress. To cool herself off, Carmen yanked herself back and slapped the shit out of him. To Kendall, a little smack or two was an aphrodisiac. He grinned, swiped off the sting, and held her so tightly she was bound like a fish thrashing to be set free.

"Let-go-of-me!" Kendall forced another kiss on her. This time Carmen controlled her sexual impulses. When Kendall finished his lone kiss, she slapped him again. "The next time you put your hands on me, it'll be your last time." Carmen straightened out her clothes and hurried back to her car.

"Carmen!" Kendall called after her. She jumped in her car and sped off, praying he didn't follow her home.

AT HOME, CARMEN SET THE dining table for two, doing her best to block out flashbacks of she and Kendall making use of the table in ways not fit for dining. "Honesty and transparency," Carmen repeated several times aloud. She wondered if being honest with Devon was the best advice Dr. Jessup could have given her. She swore the woman lived in a glass tower, seeing everything from one side of the ornate wooden desk she sat behind with folded hands and pitying eyes. Try sitting on the couch with her for once, and Dr. Jessup's own advice would sound like the bullshit that it was sometimes. Did the good doctor think this was a *Lifetime* movie of the week, where the doting husband forgave his wife for being a slut? Dr. Jessup, a white woman, had no idea who she was dealing with. Hell has no fury like a black man scorned. Once she confessed to having an affair, Devon would never forgive her.

After setting the table, Carmen poured herself another glass of red wine. The doorbell rang at eight o'clock sharp. Hastily, Carmen inspected her appearance in the gold-trimmed dining room mirror, raking her fingernails through her hair. The tight, cleavage-enhancing dress she wore with deep slits up both sides of her thighs was a look Devon loved on her. To enhance her sex appeal, Carmen wore platform sandals, showing off a fresh pedicure and the rose bud ankle tattoo that fool, Kendall, talked her into getting, along with a painful belly ring.

Before Carmen opened the door, Devon used his key to enter. Carmen didn't object. In fact, she was happy Devon hadn't disowned her and the house all together. It felt awkward from the time Devon walked in and their eyes met, as if they both stumbled upon a burglar and didn't know how to react, other than to freeze. After a moment of staring, Devon removed his blazer, yet held steady his face of stone.

"Where's my son?" he said. *No hello kiss, no it feels good to be home, you look sexy, or now I know why I married you.* Devon said none of his usual flattering remarks when he walked into the house from work. Feeling less than worthy, Carmen simply pointed toward DJ's bedroom and gulped back more wine.

Dressed for bed, DJ scooted around his bedroom floor with a toy car, making motor sounds. When he noticed his dad walk into the room, his little face turned as bright as the sun. "Daddy! Daddy! Daddy!" DJ sang, flopping on the floor. *At least DJ could get a smile and a laugh out of Devon*, Carmen thought. She stood in the doorway, watching father and son display a bond she would never understand. It wasn't envy she was feeling, but sheer remorse. DJ worshipped his father and vice versa. How could she have let anything come between the two of them? Plus, DJ was his father's miniature twin, so she would never be free of the man she loved, should tonight not work out.

Carmen fooled around in the kitchen while Devon inspected the house as thoroughly as a real estate appraiser might. She wasn't sure what he was looking for, but whatever it was, he wouldn't find it. She had combed through every square inch of the house. If she found a hair from Kendall's head, she flushed it down the toilet. Still, her heart wouldn't stop jumping each time she heard Devon take a step upstairs.

"I see you're keeping up the house," Devon said, entering the kitchen. He paused when he noticed the spider veined glass cabinet. "What happened here?" he said. She should have told him the truth—that she broke it out of anger at him for leaving.

"It cracked somehow," Carmen said, without further explanation.

"We better get it fixed before DJ gets hurt, don't you think?" Carmen liked the sound of "we." She hoped it meant Devon would be home soon to fix it himself.

They sat at the table. Between them sat barbecued ribs, baked beans and string beans from "The Smoke Pit," where Carmen stopped off to buy dinner. If Carmen wanted to cook, her nerves wouldn't let her. Her run-in with Kendall had her so frazzled she didn't know if she was coming or going. She picked up DJ, drove straight home, and took a hot shower to clear that fool out of her head. Even now, she was holding her breath, terrified Kendall would ring her doorbell and introduce himself to Devon as the man in love with Carmen.

Devon piled the black and white Asian style plate with food, plates they used only for special occasions. Carmen guessed tonight would qualify as special. She and her husband were having dinner together for the first time in months. The reality brought Carmen close to tears. When Devon moved out, her anger filled the hole in her heart that grew every day he was away. The real possibility of Devon coming home dissolved her anger, but left behind a gaping wound in her chest, making it hard for her to breathe with him sitting across from her. He was so close she could touch him, yet so far from where they used to be.

For nerve, Carmen sipped more wine. It was time she came out with the truth. If Devon found out any other way, he wouldn't give her a chance to apologize. In all the years she had been with Devon, he was honest to a fault and unrealistically expected her to be as well. Unfortunately, she lied like a cheap rug lately.

"You wanted to talk about something? What is it?" Devon said, after eating half his plate of food in silence.

"Your son sure was happy to see you," Carmen said, having lost her nerve to be honest and transparent, just yet.

"You know what he told me? He wants to be a fireman when he grows up. What does a three-year-old know about having a career?"

"DJ is smart. Every morning he tells me to *buck* up and drive safe, mommy, like he's a grown man."

"Does he really?" Devon said, as tickled as Carmen. "What're we going to do with him?"

"I don't know." Carmen delighted in the moment, loving the beam in Devon's eyes when he laughed, and wishing it were directed toward her. Laughing and talking about DJ was a safe subject to keep her from being honest. She and Devon laughed and talked through dinner, and wound up talking about work through dessert, a subject Devon readily latched onto. For five years Devon had been in insurance sales. Coming out of college, he sold whatever generated a paycheck—newspaper ads, vacuum cleaners, chiropractic services and lastly cars. Whatever the job, sales was Devon's love. It took a special man, Carmen thought for the first time, to get doors slammed in his face and wake up the next day as though the previous day's rejections and disappointments never happened. Now a manager at Tri-west

Insurance, Devon earned over six figures. Her salary was more than half his. They had finally achieved what they both worked so hard for—successful careers, a beautiful home, and a perfect family. Then she went and fucked it up. Tonight Carmen hoped to repair the damage.

If Carmen was bored listening to the tedious details of the insurance industry, she listened attentively anyway, holding back a yawn and dragging out the conversation with questions she never cared to ask Devon before.

"What's this about, Carmen?" Devon suddenly asked.

"What's what about?"

"You didn't invite me over to talk about my job, I know."

"I enjoy the stories. They're interesting."

He twisted his mouth. "I could say something about that, but I won't."

"Say what about what?" Carmen put on a sexy smile and ran her bare foot up the leg of Devon's pant. Sensing Devon's growing impatience, she had to do something to elude his question, and get past his stubborn attitude that wouldn't budge no matter how seductively she stared into his eyes. Sex was her most effective weapon.

"You've had too much to drink," Devon said, never altering his business expression. Carmen, more dizzy from love than the wine, feeling hot and sexy and wanting Devon, even if he didn't want her, decided to risk rejection. She swayed around the table and spread her legs over Devon's lap. What his stone face tried to hide, his erection couldn't. He wanted her as much as she wanted him. Defying her eagerness to make love to Devon where she sat, Carmen placed her hands on his face, feeling about like a blind person meeting a stranger for the first time. She ran her hands over his lustrous bald head, then used her thumbs to brush across his brows, the lids of his receded brown eyes, and down the robust bridge of his nose. Devon's lips she felt with her own, kissing them with gentle, fleshy pecks.

"I miss you," she whispered, brushing her lips across his.

"I miss *you,*" Devon said. His eyes spoke what she hoped was in his heart—forgiveness.

An insatiable desire came over Carmen, transforming her into a nymphomaniac. She begged for Devon to make love to her and not in those proper terms. They came close to making love on the dining room table before Carmen had flashbacks. To free her mind of Kendall, she said, "Let's go to our bed."

No matter where Kendall and she had sex in the house, the bed she and Devon shared was Devon's domain, to do with her body what he pleased. Characteristic of Devon's patient and caring ways, he gave her body uncompromised indulgence, his mouth only leaving hers to find other ways to give her pleasure. With Kendall, sex was an assortment of positions and locations. Carmen never knew where or how she would wind up, or what Kendall would do to enhance her orgasms. Lovemaking with Devon was a masterpiece, years of passion and love wrapped into one night. If Carmen didn't appreciate Devon's career choice before, she did tonight. It took a damn good salesman to have Devon's endurance. His persistence shot her straight to her sexual peak. When she thought she couldn't go a level higher, Devon shifted gears, setting off a series of orgasms that seemed never ending. The more Carmen cried and begged, the harder Devon drove, so rambunctiously Carmen thought she would die of pleasure.

In unison, they both collapsed into a heap.

"I shouldn't have to tell you I'm ready to come home," Devon said in a breath of satisfaction and exhaustion. Hearing those words topped another series of orgasms Carmen could go for, if her legs weren't limp as shoestrings. She left things as they ended, a night filled with love and passion, finding peace in Devon's arms as they slept.

In the middle of the night Carmen was jolted out of her peaceful sleep at the sound of a motorcycle tearing up the street. With Devon lying next to her, she was too terrified to look out of the window to investigate. She lay stiffly on her back, listening to the faded sound of a motor; which grew to an intolerable roar the closer it got to her house, then hovered near her driveway before skidding off again. How long she lay there tormented by the noise was a mystery to Carmen, but a bike race, starting in five-minute intervals, couldn't have been more disturbing to the quiet neighborhood. Who else could it be but that fool Kendall!

Lucky for her, Devon didn't stir and the roaring ultimately vanished before the sun came up. Carmen let some time pass, crept out of bed, threw on her heavy housecoat, and treaded softly downstairs. It was too dark and foggy outside to see down the street. Yet, she could rest knowing Kendall wasn't camped out in front of her house waiting to confront her husband. He must have watched her house all night and waited to see when or if Devon would leave. Well, he got his answer. She and her husband had reconciled. Now, hopefully that fool would stay the hell away from her.

Closing her eyes again was impossible for Carmen. Her mind was on full alert. While Devon slept, Carmen's heartbeat kept her awake. It was seven in the morning when Devon opened his eyes and found her face an inch from his, greeting him with a kiss. Devon mustered a tired, satisfied grin, mumbled he loved her and closed his eyes again. Carmen watched him sleep for another thirty minutes. When he finally opened his eyes again, they reenacted a shortened version of last night's masterpiece, long enough to satisfy Carmen's overactive sexual appetite for the day.

"What was it you wanted to talk to me about last night?" Devon said before she caught her breath. Carmen's face overheated until she could feel the edges of her hair curling from perspiration all the more. She smoothed them out with the tips of her fingers.

"You're going to be late for work. Go!" Playfully, Carmen attempted to nudge Devon out of bed with her foot.

"I know, but I sure don't want to move from this spot." He pulled her into his arms and squeezed.

To keep the conversation sidetracked, Carmen said, "Let's lay in bed all day."

"And do what?" Devon said, grinning.

"Make love for breakfast, lunch and dinner," she whispered in his ear.

"If this meeting today wasn't so important, you wouldn't get an objection from me."

"Do you have to go work?"

"Have to."

Carmen found the spot between Devon's legs that would change any man's mind. "Reschedule," she said. "Tell them something came up."

Devon laughed. "You're playing dirty."

"It's Saturday, Devon."

"I can't, babe." Devon turned her over, putting her eyes in direct line with his. "Now, what did you want to talk about last night?" His business face had returned, gone were his loving eyes from a minute ago.

Carmen sat up and leaned against the headboard. She had to tell Devon some form of the truth if nothing else. Besides, the unfiltered truth would only hurt Devon and destroy her marriage in the process. As Dr. Jessup said, she had to put the past in the past. That was the handiest advice Dr. Jessup had given her. Kendall was the past that would never repeat itself.

"Let me say this before you say anything," Devon said, delaying Carmen's almost confession. "We were friends before we were anything else, weren't we?"

"How could I forget?" Carmen quickly pulled away from Devon and sat up.

"Come on, babe, we've been together too long. You can tell me anything and I'll try to understand. But I have to tell you, a lot has to change for this marriage to work. I can't be married by myself, Carmen."

"I know. I promise I'll do better. Just come home."

"I *am* home." Devon assured her. "Now, tell me." He propped himself up on one elbow and stared at her. If eyes disclosed the soul, guilt was written across hers. Carmen looked down, wishing she had a glass of wine in her hand to sip.

"I wanted to tell you...that...I've been having attacks," she stammered.

Devon scratched his head. "Attacks? What kind of attacks."

"Panic attacks."

"Have you?" He said this as if his concern with her condition cancelled out any suspicions he may have had otherwise. His concern gave Carmen a reason to shed the tears pressing against her eyes. Sincere tears rolled down her face as she described the horror of her experience, how at any time of day an attack could strike her without warning.

"Is that why you're seeing a psychologist?"

"Partly."

"So, how long has this been going on?"

"My attacks?"

"Yeah."

"They started back in high school, when -"

"Your best friend was murdered...?" Devon finished her sentence as cool mannered as an anchorman on the nightly news.

That was how Carmen remembered hearing it. *"Sixteen year-old abducted and murdered; news at 11."* The story of how her best friend Nicole was murdered went deeper than Devon would ever know and ran like an ice-cold river through Carmen's veins. She wrapped her arms around her knees to warm herself. It could have easily been her naked body dumped in the woods like last week's garbage. She and Nicole had both jumped into the brown car, being cute and thinking they were too smart not to know the difference between a man who looked like someone's nice father and a cold-hearted killer. A short ride to school, what could it hurt Carmen said to Nicole. His smile would have fooled anyone. *Anyone.*

Carmen massaged her temples to stop the pain of the memory. She hated going back there, and she wasn't going back there this morning, whether it kept the conversation diverted from the truth or not.

"Babe, you okay?" Devon asked.

"I forgot I ever had them," Carmen said, her voice trailing off. "They just suddenly came back."

"Why didn't you tell me?"

"I expected them to go away. I didn't think they would get worse, attacking me two or three times a week, sometimes twice in one day. You don't know what it feels like...like I'm losing my mind!" Carmen wasn't putting on an act. Simply recalling her attacks brought down a sincere sheet of tears. "I feel so weak," she said. Physically, her body suddenly felt ten times heavier.

Devon sat up and cradled Carmen in his arms. "You'll be fine."

"You think so?"

"You got through it before, didn't you?" Carmen nodded, sniffing up the moisture in her nose. Devon cupped her chin and looked into her eyes "Then you'll get through it again. But promise me you won't keep something as serious as this from me again, or go off the deep end and not tell me, babe." Devon wiped away the last of her tears with the edge of the sheet. Not to make any promises she couldn't keep at this time, Carmen kissed Devon sensually; her way of saying she would do her best to be honest from here on.

"Promise me something?" Carmen said, pulling back from their kiss.

"What's that?"

"You'll never leave me again. Not for a day, Devon."

"I can't live another day without it. That's been my problem."

"I love you," Carmen said.

"I love you too, babe," Devon said, kissing her again.

"You want breakfast?"

"Sure do."

Not long later, Carmen served Devon and DJ, who was now awake and had joined their breakfast-in-bed reunion. "Breakfast for my two favorite men," Carmen said and presented them with a serving tray of toast, scrambled eggs, sausage, and an assortment of fruit. There was coffee for Devon, for Carmen a glass of orange juice and for DJ a glass of milk. The three of them sat up in bed, enjoying breakfast and watching DJ's favorite morning cartoons.

If Carmen had one wish left in life, this would be it, having her broken family whole again—if wishes came true.

Coming to Light

Tempest had a laundry list of wedding preparations to attend to today. The design of her wedding gown was her first priority. She drove across town to pick up Yasmine. Honking the horn was impolite, but she didn't have time to fellowship. On the second honk, Yasmine strutted out of her parents' quintessential View Heights home, set in a neighborhood full of prominent black professionals. That wasn't what stood out about Yasmine's parents' house for Tempest, however. Seeing the two-story black and white plantation home, with climbing Hydra decorating the black shutters, brought back warm memories of Yasmine's pool party, where she and Sterling first fell in love. Today the memory was above all uplifting for Tempest and helped clear up her quivering stomach. Now she could get on with the business of planning her wedding day.

"Where to first?" Yasmine said, looking in the mirrored sun visor to finger through her lavish weave. Yasmine could work a weave as if she was born with wet and wavy hair; colored contact lenses too. Blue eyes never looked so natural on a black woman. For years now, Yasmine had been working diligently to become a high fashion model. So far, she had only landed catalog work and low-budget runway jobs, but it wouldn't be long before Yasmine became an overnight success; Yasmine was definitely one of the "beautiful people" of the world.

When Tempest told Yasmine their first stop was Don Lou's, Yasmine's lemon-shaped eyes morphed into oranges.

"You got in to see Don Lou, girl! I read about him in a bridal magazine! You know he's a seamstress for the stars?"

Tempest laughed. Only Yasmine would know of Don Lou without her having to give a rundown. Since high school, she and Yasmine had been two peas in a pod. They were both on the cheer squad, both tall and fashion conscious, and now both in love with professional athletes (Yasmine was dating a rookie Lakers player.) Tempest couldn't have asked for a more compatible companion to take along for the ride.

Tempest searched for the address written in the bridal gown section of her wedding journal, a book well documented with her hopes for a memorable wedding day. When she located the address, she parked northbound on a side street adjacent Wilshire Blvd., five blocks east of Beverly Hills. Don Lou wasn't Hollywood's top-rated seamstress, but based on the bridal guide, Don Lou was as close to Hollywood as a bride could get, affordably speaking. Plus, the design she had in mind required a seamstress of Don Lou's caliber. Not many tailors had the stitching expertise to work with exquisite silk fabric, and Tempest wouldn't think of turning her life-long project over to an amateur, not with her wedding day being the best opportunity to show off her design sense.

As soon as Tempest and Yasmine walked into the upscale accommodations, keeping up their Hollywood appearances in oversized designer shades and classy/chic attire, they both opened their mouths to scream, but knew better not to. The large portraits hanging on the stark white walls framed the elegant images of Naomi Campbell, Heidi Klum, and Beyonce' draped in what had to be Don Lou's most popular gowns. It took Tempest two months to book this appointment and now she was actually here!

Excitedly, they sat at the table of Lou's assistant, a very Romanian and very fashionable woman. Tempest barely got out her swatch of silk when the woman, named Camellia, asked her to repeat her wedding date.

"The first day of summer," Tempest replied. It wasn't her ideal choice for a wedding day, but the best date before the official NFL season kicked off.

Camellia thumbed through her personal planner. "Who did you speak with here when making your appointment?" Tempest looked at Yasmine and back at the Camellia, whose remorseful smile sent hot liquid through her blood stream. She racked her brain for a name, scrabbling through her wedding planner. She always wrote down a contact person. *Always*!

"It's in here somewhere, " Tempest mumbled.

"Is that important?" Yasmine said, taking the words out of Tempest's dry mouth.

"*Very*. Mr. Lou never schedules his gowns less than a year out from the ceremony." Camellia then whispered, "Never," as if forbidden to consider the possibility.

"A year out?" Tempest said. "But I scheduled my appointment two months ago. Does that count toward my months as a whole?" The woman was shaking her head before Tempest asked the question.

"Whoever misled you here, I am so very, very sorry. We are to be clear with our brides. I can inquire about the date, but I am almost positive Mr. Lou cannot work you in. Think about the stitching that must go into a beautiful gown, the details he is so famous for." She whispered again. "You don't want to…how do you say… *skimp* on your wedding gown. It's the day of a bride's dream."

Tempest's eyes were full of tears, while Yasmine argued the lady down over the date. "It's okay, Yas. Let's just go," Tempest finally said.

"Don Lou ain't all of that, girl!" Yasmine said during the ride home. "Buy your gown, Tempest. I can think of five or six top designers you'll love!"

"Nobody understands. I've dreamed of designing my own gown my whole life," Tempest said, feeling her dreams slipping away.

THE WEEK ENDED MISERABLY FOR Tempest and the week following was heading in the same direction. If she didn't get fired, she was about to get a harsh reminder that she was a department manager and had to lead by example. Linda didn't have to remind Tempest. She had already reminded herself. There was absolutely no way she could visit Sterling again during the holiday season.

Standing in Linda's office, Tempest felt every single beat of her heart. With the phone to her ear and her sky blue eyes glued to the computer screen, Linda gestured for Tempest to take a seat in one of the cushioned chairs in front of her desk.

Linda had replaced her former boss, Bill, a year ago. It took some adjusting for Tempest. She had grown used to Bill's meek, personable management style. Linda was a petite blonde in her mid-forties, who had a kick-butt-take-names-later personality that Tempest admired. Tempest also admired the tangerine textured St. John suit Linda wore and wondered if Linda purchased it on clearance, or when it was tagged for a mere $1,195.00 dollars. If Tempest was going to get far in this industry, she had to dress like Linda and develop Linda's leather skin. Nothing seemed to ruffle the woman's feathers.

"Is everything okay with you, Tempest?" Linda said after wrapping up her telephone conversation.

"Everything is great." *Peachy freakin' king*!

"You've been sick more than usual—"

"I know," Tempest interjected before Linda could finish. "I'm sorry. But I'm feeling better!"

"Good. Have you hired your seasonal help?"

"I have five qualified applicants lined up for interviews, two of them this morning. I should be sufficiently staffed by the end of next week."

"Excellent. Update me at next week's rally," was Linda's final directive before she asked Tempest if she was interested in the associate buyer position that was opening up.

"I'm super interested!" Tempest said.

"Good. I think you'll make a great buyer, Tempest. I'm not making any promises—"

"No…I mean, yes. I understand. Thank you, anyway, Linda. Thank you!"

Tempest walked briskly out of Linda's office and down the hall to her own, which consisted of cubicles shared with other department supervisors and staff. Her first interview started in twenty minutes. Tempest sipped a cup of coffee and contemplated her meeting with Linda. *"I'm super interested?"* What a lame answer. "I'm very interested in the opportunity," would've been more professional. Linda probably changed her mind about putting in a good word for her as soon as she walked out of the office. And she couldn't blame the woman.

When Sterling called, the diffusing light inside of Tempest blew completely out.

"Tee, when you were here, did somebody leave something for me?" Sterling said, without a hello. Tempest initially had no idea what Sterling was talking about, then her brain dinged louder than a cash register.

"Hold on, Sterling, okay?" Tempest rushed down the hallway and found privacy in the staff bathroom. "Leave something for you?" she whispered.

"Yeah! Did somebody give you something to give to me?" Tempest couldn't answer Sterling's question with her turtleneck sweater suddenly strangling her neck.

"I have an interview in a few minutes, boo," she lied. "Can I call you right back?"

"Call me *right* back," Sterling ordered.

Tempest ended the call and stared at her reflection in the mirror. Heat permeated through her mahogany skin, turning her cheeks plum red. "You're in big trouble," she said to herself. She stayed locked inside the bathroom for a few minutes, thinking up one lie after another to tell Sterling. She hated to lie, knowing Sterling may never trust her again, but she had to. She completely forgot about Diamond's gift, which she put out of her sight and mind weeks ago.

With less than ten minutes remaining before her interviewee arrived, Tempest dialed up Nadine. Two heads were always better than one. And with Nadine being married for thirteen years, Tempest was sure her sister had concocted some pretty good lies of her own. After all, she was married to Will, the cheapest man alive. Tempest couldn't count the number of times she covered for Nadine when Will questioned her about the new clothes and shoes that magically appeared in Nadine's closet.

Calling Nadine was a mistake. "Clothes and shoes are one thing, Tempest," Nadine said. "But I would never lie to Will about something that serious. Stealing from him? What was going through your head when you took the gift? What's in the dark *always* comes to light, Tempest. Lying will only make it worse and mistrust in a relationship is difficult to overcome."

"Thanks for the advice, Nadine." Tempest hung up and called Dana for a less sanctimonious point of view. After Dana laughed for a full minute, she suggested Tempest tell Sterling that Diamond never gave her the gift, which would make it her word against Diamond's, and who was Sterling going to believe, his fiancé or a gold-digger?

"When did you get so good at lying, Dana?"

"You make me sound like a sociopath. You asked me to come up with a good lie. I gave you one. "

"A blatant one."

"A lie is a lie, Temp. If you can't tell Sterling a blatant lie, tell him the truth." Dana went on to pose a question Tempest hadn't thought of. "You can always ask Sterling why he cares about a gift from a total stranger."

"That's right! Why does he care and why is he mad at me over *her.* I'm calling him back now, girl! " Tempest hung up and lost her enthusiasm and her courage. If Sterling was angry with her, he had every right to be. She knew what she had to do, call Sterling back and apologize, right after her interview. By then Sterling wouldn't be as mad.

Tempest's eleven o'clock interview was waiting in the lounge area when she returned to the floor. Her name was Lydia, a spunky Asian girl with retail experience and an obvious eye for fashion based on the pink Juicy Couture outfit she wore. Tempest also loved Lydia's positive attitude. She would fit into the Nordstrom family perfectly.

"You're hired!" Tempest announced ten minutes into the interview, mainly to get rid of Lydia. She needed to call Sterling back.

"I am?" Lydia squawked.

"Welcome to Nordstrom." Tempest stood and shook Lydia's hand. Lydia practically bowed before Tempest's feet, thanking her profusely. "You'll be contacted soon about training."

Tempest had a forty-five minute window before her next interview. She informed one of her assistants she was taking a short break and hurried to the parking structure. Once inside her car, she lowered the windows to let the lemon scent out and fresh air in. She then dug into her handbag, found a stick of cinnamon gum and chewed, moistening her cotton mouth before calling Sterling. His cell phone rang and rang. Tempest sat in her car listening to the ringing much too long for a short break. Sterling never picked up.

THAT NIGHT TEMPEST SLEPT WITH the aid of Pepto-Bismol, partly dreaming of what she could say to Sterling, and partly waiting for her telephone to ring at 5:00 AM, Pacific Time, before Sterling went to practice. When the phone did ring, she was sitting at the bar counter in her gray chemise, drinking a cup of calming tea.

"Why didn't you call me back?" Sterling said, elevating his voice above a rap song vibrating in her eardrum so loudly she pulled back from the receiver.

"I did call you! Where were you!" she shouted.

Sterling lowered the music and got right to the point "What happened to it?" he said. If Tempest didn't know better, she would have sworn he dodged her question.

"What happened to what?" she said, playing the same dodge game.

"Don't try to game me, Tee. Whatever it is somebody gave you to give to me."

"Oh, *that*? I brought it home by accident." Her lie manifested on its own.

"Why would you take something of mine and not tell me?" Sterling wasn't yelling. He sounded more surprised, as though he found out in a nick of time that his fiancé was a kleptomaniac.

"I didn't open it, Sterling."

"So, where is it?"

Tempest's anxiety had her walking in circles. "I don't know off the top of my head."

"You're clowning, Tee. I already know you took it. Diamond told me she gave it to you almost two months ago. You never mentioned it to me."

There was something in the way Sterling said Diamond's name that made the hair on the back of Tempest's neck rise. Her name rolled off his tongue too intimately, as if he talked to Diamond not once but on more than one occasion, maybe as recent as last night. Tempest stopped her nervous circling and stood pond water still.

"When did she tell you, Sterling?" Her tone was not so sweet this time.

"When did she tell me what?"

"About the gift?"

"Does it matter?"

"It matters if you don't know her, Sterling."

"I never said I didn't know her. I've seen her around. I told you, she's Mark's sister."

"You didn't answer my question."

"Forget about it, Tee, all right. I have a big game this week. I don't need this right now. I'm already stressing."

Whatever womanly intuition Tempest had was lost in her sympathy. "I'm sorry. I know how you get before a game."

"You know me, baby."

"I know. But I just don't get why a total stranger would leave you a platinum chain valued at over three thousand dollars. I had it appraised, Sterling, so I know." Tempest wasn't sure if the phone went dead, but the silence coming from Sterling was deafening. "Sterling…did I lose you?"

"I thought you said you didn't open it." His voice was coming through loud and clear now. Tempest was back to circling the room, the carpet feeling as if it were quicksand ready to cave in under her feet. The God's honest truth was her only chance of recovery.

"I opened it, okay, Sterling? I'm sorry for lying to you. But how would you feel if a man came to my door and handed you a gift to give to me worth that much money?"

"Tee, I can't control what people give me. People are always giving me stuff. That's the nature of the business I'm in. But in the future, if somebody comes to the door and leaves me a piece of *bubble gum*, I expect you to give it to me."

Tempest opened her mouth and gagged on her own tears.

"I still love you, though." Sterling assured her. "I gotta go, baby. I'll call you later, all right?" By the time Tempest got a word out, Sterling was gone. Tempest hung up and called Nadine.

"Will and I have been through worse," Nadine said, half asleep. "It'll pass in a few days." Tempest didn't have a few days. She snatched her Visa Gold from her wallet and sat down at the computer. This trip was going to run her a thousand dollars and up. She couldn't worry about that right now, her job either.

Falling

Tempest's flight leaving LAX was delayed. By the time she arrived in Arizona, she missed her connecting flight to Minneapolis and had to wait another hour to depart. She couldn't sleep and she couldn't read. Not even music relaxed her. To kill time, Tempest talked to Dana until she was down to one cell bar, a conversation she could've done without. "Be careful, Temp," Dana had said. "You might find what you're looking for." She loved Dana, but sometimes Dana could be as negative as Charlene.

"At this time, we will begin the pre-boarding of flight 1667 to Minneapolis/St. Paul," she heard over the intercom. The flight was sparse. Half the seats in the waiting area were empty. No one rushed to line up behind the pre-boarding passengers, nor did Tempest. There was no sense in rushing to get nowhere fast.

In the pre-dawn hour, the airplane taxied toward the terminal at MSP International Airport. The queasiness in Tempest's stomach was in her throat, and the snacks she ate on the plane only heightened her urge to vomit. With only a carry-on, she didn't need to make a stop at baggage claim. She wheeled her small suitcase as fast as she could in stiletto boots toward the nearest bathroom before picking up her rental car. The Minneapolis/St. Paul airport was one of the busiest airports in the world. Usually, when she arrived, it looked as busy as an indoor mall on a Saturday afternoon. Other than the few people she arrived with, the airport was lifeless, even going to the bathroom alone made Tempest edgy. It was vacant and cold and could stand cleaning. She hurried into a stall to take care of her business quickly and leave.

Wiggling back into her jeans, she heard the door open. She zipped up and rushed out of the stall. The janitor didn't say anything when their eyes met. With small brown teeth, he sneered at her as though he trapped the mouse he was after. Everything about this man was sinister looking, hard and heartless eyes, cratered face with sunken cheeks, oily hair combed forward and to the side. He had the look of a parolee who begged his way into a job. And tonight, of all nights, he decided to forgo rehabilitation.

If Tempest wanted to run out, she couldn't. His cart blocked the entrance. Tempest thought only of Sterling and how devastated he would be when he found out she flew up to surprise him and never made it out of the terminal alive. Her only defense was to bluff her way past this man. If she let him see the sweat staining her cashmere jersey tee, he would know he had trapped the right mouse. Tempest straightened her shoulders and looked ten feet tall compared to his scrawny stature.

"Excuse me, sir. This bathroom is for ladies only." She stepped toward him fearlessly, her voice sounding powerful and professional, as if she knew his boss and could have him fired at the drop of a dime. The man held up his hands like she was going to beat him over the head with her Louis V bag. She would if she had to.

"This bathroom is closed, misses. Din't cha' see the sign?"

"Sign?"

"Outside," he said.

"No, I'm so sorry. No, I didn't see it," Tempest said, embarrassed for making assumptions about the little old harmless-looking man. To compensate for her guilt, she took her time washing her hands and left him a five-dollar tip on the sink, then hustled to pick up her rental car.

Her day started off bad enough and was quickly becoming nightmarish. Somehow, the rental company lost her reservations, leaving her without a car. Tempest talked herself out of crying and maintained a positive outlook.

"It's okay. I can take a cab," she said to the woman behind the counter. A cab was waiting in the taxi zone when she got there. It would be quicker anyway and save her money she didn't have after charging her credit card to the max. She would drive Sterling to practice in the morning and keep his truck for the day if she had to. *See? Keeping a positive outlook helps.*

"To where?" the Haitian driver asked with a French accent. He wore a black beanie and black gloves with the tips of the fingers cut out.

"Uptown. Ewing Street, please," Tempest said, giving him Sterling's address. During the ride, Tempest relaxed for the first time all night, enjoying the soft R&B music playing on KMOJ 89.9. When she opened her eyes, the taxi was turning onto Sterling's street. The closer the taxi came to Sterling's complex the faster her heart raced. It dropped to her knees when a white X5, parked in front of Sterling's condo came into view. Tempest sat erect in her seat, having the sickest feeling in the pit of her stomach.

"Right here," she told the driver. The taxi stopped behind the X5.

"Twenty-eight dollars," the driver announced. He must have noticed she didn't know what time or space she was in because he repeated the fare.

"My fiancé plays for the Spartans," she began to explain in a stammer. "I'm not sure if he's home. Can you wait for me?"

Tears stood in her eyes, gearing up to fall. The driver's somber look didn't change, but he nodded.

Tempest stepped out of the car, her boots wobbling to stand on solid ground. When she could stand firmly, she took a step forward, then another. Sterling's SUV sat in the driveway like it hadn't moved for the day. As she approached the door, it seemed to recess into the darkness. It took a million steps to reach the porch on legs too weak to carry her.

When she reached the door, she didn't knock or ring the bell. Her arms were too feeble to move. She felt dazed, only aware of her existence by the chatter of crickets in the nearby bushes. She found the muscles in her arms to remove her keys from her handbag, then glanced back to be sure her ride hadn't left her stranded. The driver was leaning against the passenger door, smoking a cigarette, as though waiting for a show to start.

On the strength of your blood, Jesus, please don't let that X5 belong to Diamond.

Tempest had difficulty unlocking the door, her hand trembling more from nerves than the blistering cold. She forced the key into the lock and made the first turn, the clanging of her keys bringing the crickets to a hush. Once inside, Tempest stepped into the darkness. As she did, a light flipped on in the hallway. In the next second, Sterling bolted around the corner.

"Tee...shit!" Sterling said and turned away. He then turned back as if he didn't know which way to turn next. Other than his white boxers, Tempest saw only the blackness of his skin. Everything else was a blur before her eyes took in Diamond, who stood in the background as naked as Sterling.

"I told you to stay in the back!" Sterling yelled over his shoulder at her. In a flash, Diamond vanished and Tempest, for a split second, wondered if she had seen a ghost. Sterling turned back to her. "Tee!" he said. "What're you doing here?"

He sounded more upset with her for putting him in this predicament than sorry for what he had done. "Baby, it's not what you think." Sterling stepped toward her. Tempest took as many steps back, gasping for oxygen as tears gushed from her eyes.

"How could you? How could…how?" Tempest garbled. Her hand lay on her chest to keep her heart in place as she descended to her knees, floating down, down, down, as though falling from a hundred-story building at the velocity of a feather. Sterling fell to his knees with her, his weight bearing down on her with the might of a defensive back tackling his opponent. Somehow, Tempest wound up on her side with Sterling cradled behind her, the two of them stuck together like welded spoons.

"Let me leave, Sterling," Tempest heard herself whisper from a million miles away.

"I can't let you, Tee. I love you too much. I love you, baby. I love you. Let's pray about this, all right? I swear to God this is the first time she's been here. I'll tell her she's gotta get the fuck out. All right, baby? Don't leave."

Tempest's voice rose to an animal's howl. "God, *pleeeease*! Let me leave!" If she had the strength to beat Sterling off of her, scratch out his eyeballs, kick him where it would hurt most, tear into his skin with her teeth, throw her engagement ring at him, she would have. Whatever strength she had must have come from God almighty. Tempest found herself back inside the taxi, and didn't recall how she got there. She could have crawled out of the house backwards, for all she knew.

Split Decision

$\mathcal{D}$ana took a quick shower, threw a pair of shorts and a tank top over a bikini, slipped on flip-flops and found a nice sized beach towel before hurrying to her car. She went from a life no woman would trade her for to two dates in one day, first with Matthew then with Omar. She was more excited about her date with Matthew; or rather thrilled about doing something new, different and fun for a change.

She zoomed out of the driveway and zipped across town. Matthew was waiting for her at the foot of the Manhattan Beach pier. He too wore shorts, though his were knee-length Op swim trunks.

Matthew leaned on her window seal with folded arms. "You showed. Wasn't sure if you would."

"Why not? It's a beautiful day for the beach."

"Always," Matthew said with a smile. Dana wore a smile as broad as his, and once again questioned her excitement. There were no two ways about it. She wasn't interested in Matthew, in a romantic sense.

She parked across the street in a free zone, as directed by Matthew and joined him by the water. For a Saturday afternoon and a week before Thanksgiving, the pier swarmed with beachgoers. Matthew had carved out a vacant spot in the sand not far from the pier and set up a mesh tent. Before stepping in, Dana came out of her flip-flops, loving the feel of the warm sand creeping between her toes. Her last trip to the beach was so long ago she forgot she loved it so. The simple joy of watching water and land unite was one to behold. The whooshing sound of waves was music to her ears. She stood immobilized, appreciating nature's awesomeness and realizing how much she had missed out on in three years.

Inside the tent was a quilted blanket. Dana sat atop it, in front of one of the two serving trays Matthew had set up.

Laughing, she said, "Why do I have a sneaky suspicion I'm not the first woman to get the royal treatment in this tent?"

"No, not the first, but would you believe the first black one?" Matthew said.

"You're not serious?"

"Does that surprise you?"

Dana shook her head. "Not much. You look like you're open to dating any race, put it that way."

"Variety is the spice of life, they say. What about you?"

"Am I open to dating other races?" Dana shrugged. "I do what comes natural for me, but don't change the subject. Why don't you date black women, Matthew Kerry?" Dana narrowed her eyes.

"I'm not black enough for black women," he said and flashed his tight smile.

"You'll have to come up with a better excuse. I'm not buying that one."

He laughed. "You shouldn't take me so serious, Dana. I'm a funny guy when I try to be. To be kosher with you, you're not the first black girl I've been out with, only the most beautiful black one."

"Good save," Dana said with a smile. "Should I take you serious this time?"

"You bet." He went on to unpack the cutest wicker picnic basket, with cute little salt and pepper shakers, utensils and checkered cloth napkins. "I hope you don't mind store-bought chicken salad."

Glad to switch subjects, Dana said, "What else do you have stuffed in your little basket?" She bent forward to see. Inside was a bag of crisp red grapes, a miniature box of Ritz crackers, a Tupperware bowl of salad, potato chips, and bottled water. Dana picked up a bottle, unscrewed the cap, and sipped.

"You know what I like, I see," she teased.

"I eat lunch with you most days, remember? You're quite the food critic."

"Because I know what I like and what I hate doesn't make me a food critic."

"You hate most everything."

Dana laughed. "So, what is it that I like, since you think you *know* me so well?"

"That's a no-brainer. Frozen yogurt is your favorite dessert, smoothies for breakfast and peanut butter power bars after a good workout. Close enough?"

"You're scaring me."

"Never heard that before. I'd better not tell you I know your favorite flavor frozen yogurt." He placed a plate of chicken salad, Ritz crackers, and grapes on her tray, and watched her with a wry grin.

"No. Tell me." Dana was eager to know.

"I don't want to scare you."

"Sure you don't. You almost had me. It's okay, Matthew. I didn't expect you to know."

"New York Cheesecake, if I took a wild guess."

Dana felt a tingle in the pit of her stomach. "How did you know?"

"What else scares you about me?" Matthew asked.

Dana wanted to say it scared her that he knew more about her than Omar, who couldn't remember her favorite flavor yogurt to save his life, though she had told him enough times. It further scared her that she was beginning to find Matthew subtly sexy.

"Next time lunch is on me," she said, letting his question go unanswered.

"Are you saying there'll be a next time?"

"Maybe…" Dana chomped on a crisp grape and smiled. Matthew pulled the last item from the basket.

"For you." He presented her with a single long-stemmed rose that she accepted with an open heart and mind. They ate, laughed and talked with ease.

"You play Frisbee?" Matthew asked after their walk on the beach, cooling their feet in the moist sand.

Dana grimaced. "You're not going to make me play, are you?"

"Come on. It's a blast!" He pulled Dana by the hand.

Dana found it hard to believe she was having fun chasing down a flying disk, a game she hadn't played since childhood. It felt awkward initially. Trying to navigate in rough sand was probably as daunting as walking on the moon. She laughed to tears at her clumsiness. She had to remind herself that if she could endure an hour of turbo-boxing, she could do this. It didn't take long before her athletic agility and competitiveness returned. Dana breezed across the sand like the wind, her well toned legs standing the test of a rigorous workout. Then Matthew introduced her to "Ultimate Frisbee," and she thought she would pass out.

That was the beginning of Dana's second date with Matthew. She ended their date with her arms wrapped tightly around Matthew's waist, jet skiing at high speed across the Pacific. Dana screamed from fear and delight, all the while awed by the beauty of the setting sun painting the horizon a fiery orange.

DANA ARRIVED HOME WELL AFTER the sun went down and was met at the door by Corrine. "Did you forget Omar was coming over?" Corrine whispered. "He's been here for an hour. I'm sure he's hungry. I would've fed him, but he said he's taking you out to dinner."

Dana wanted to laugh. Was that supposed to make her feel guilty? Knowing her mother's love for Omar, Dana was sure it was. Regardless of what Omar did, Corrine found a way to defend him. In her mother's opinion, Omar was not only "cute as a button," but a respectable young man that would make a good husband, if Dana would be patient with him. She was sure Omar didn't mention to her mother where he planned to take her for dinner tonight—straight to his apartment, and dinner would be the last thing on his mind.

"No. I didn't forget, mom. I told Omar seven o'clock. It's his problem for coming an hour early."

Corrine shook her head. "He probably got the time mixed up, Dana. He's waiting for you in the den."

Dana moseyed toward the den, not in any hurry. Her attitude toward her date with Omar had changed considerably after her date with Matthew. She wasn't looking forward to being cooped up in Omar's rundown apartment tonight. In all honesty, she wanted to cancel her date with Omar and go straight to bed. Her day with Matthew had caught up to her.

When Dana walked into the room, Omar sat up from where he was lounging in the recliner, watching TV. He wore his dressiest attire—black slacks, a collared button-up shirt untucked at the waist, and black soft bottom dress shoes.

"You look like you've been to the beach," he said.

"I have."

"When did you start going to the beach?"

Dana didn't know how to answer that question. Had he asked her when she stopped going to the beach, she could have easily answered. Anyway, what business was it of his where she had been and with whom? He hadn't put a ring on it.

"I'll be ready in a minute," Dana said and walked out.

"Wear something nice!" Omar called after her. Dana paused in the hallway and thought to ask "What for?" She didn't bother. After showering, she vacillated over what to wear and how "nice." Dana chose the jeans and dressy top number. Why get her hopes up? After dressing, she found Omar in the kitchen with her mother, impressing her with his charm and feigned choirboy ways.

"You see this, Omar? Can you help me clean it up?" Corrine said. Omar examined Corrine's hit and miss paint job.

"No problem. I can get this finished for you in half a day or less, Momma Corrine."

Corrine was charmed. "Thank you, son. It's the edges that I had the hardest time with, or I would've gotten it done on my own," Corrine, forever the independent, said.

"Dana can help me, won't you, Dana?" Omar winked at her, trying to be funny.

"Of course Dana will help you," Corrine said.

Humph, Dana thought. She doubted if Omar would be around long enough to finish the job.

DANA DIDN'T KNOW WHAT STUNT Omar was trying to pull tonight, but reserving seats at a romantic, fine dining restaurant on Melrose Avenue, with expensive cuisine meant Omar had a hidden agenda. He had opened her car door, pulled out her chair, and given her permission to order liberally. Maybe he sensed another man was making inroads into her life.

"This is a nice surprise." Dana spread the white napkin across her lap, taking in the serene atmosphere.

Omar looked pleased with himself "Tonight is your night," he said. Dana forced a smile, then buried her rolling eyes behind her menu. They ate and did their usual small talk. Dana put forth her best listening ear, taking little interest in the conversation with her mind back at the beach and her heart on the fence.

His mom and pop's fortieth wedding anniversary was coming up, and he asked if she could think of a nice gift "they" could buy. His older brother Todd had a business proposition he might take up, and a new basketball session at the Boys and Girls Club had started. His numbers were growing so big he might have to form two teams; one for the girls and one for the boys. "And by the way, when are you coming by to check out a game?" he went on.

"Let me know when and I'll come," Dana said, snapping back to their chat. The conversation fell silent. For the next ten minutes or so, there wasn't much left for the two of them to chat over—nothing fresh, no uncharted territory. In three years, she and Omar had covered the most they were going to cover. To the front of them was a dead end street, blocked by a full-scale brick wall. The only direction from here forward was in reverse, a course Dana wasn't taking.

If Omar hadn't asked her about the latest on Carmen and Devon's separation, he never would have engaged her in a conversation. Dana relayed the little she knew, that Devon moved back home and he and Carmen were going away for the weekend to spend time alone.

"He must not know about her side action," Omar said and snickered.

"You're way off base. As usual."

"If you say so."

"What about your brother?" Dana said in defense of her own.

Omar laughed. "Why're you dragging my brother into this?"

"No offense to Todd, but every time I see him, he's with a different chick. My brother has a wife and a family, which is more than your brother can say." Dana eyeballed him, hoping he got her hint.

"You should see the girl Todd's got now." Omar whistled low and long. "She's a dime piece. I'd marry her." He laughed heartily at the scowl on Dana's face. "I'm just playing with you. You're the only girl I want to marry."

"Give me a break."

"What?"

"Don't include me in your future plans, that's what."

"I got my own spot. Isn't that what you wanted?"

"Among many things."

"I need to do more to have a future with you?" he said, as if exhausted from putting forth his best effort. "What else? Get a new car, a better job, what?"

Dana finished off the last of her dinner salad before answering Omar's question. "I'm really glad you finally moved out on your own, I am, but don't you think it's past time you invest in something more than an apartment? This is the best time to buy, that's what my agent says. If I can do it, you can, Omar." What Dana wanted to say was why didn't he invest in a place with her? However, that would lead the conversation down another dead-end street.

"Trust me, Dana. I have a plan."

Dana strained her voice not to disturb the serene environment. "That's all I keep hearing from you, Omar! What plan?"

Omar sat back in his seat and smirked. "My approach is different than most cats. They're rolling on twenty-fours, living larger than their means and don't have money in the bank after working forty. You see what I roll in…a bucket. My apartment may be a roach trap, but at *seven -hun* a month, I keep my overhead under budget. I could wine and dine you like this once a week, take you on vacations, the whole nine, but that's not the best way to build a savings."

Dana never doubted Omar's intellect to accomplish his goal, whatever it was, only his motivation. He wasn't exactly behaving like Donald Trump at the moment. What's more, when had her love for him been based on how much money he had in the bank or the kind of car he drove? If so, she would have kicked his cheap butt to the curb three years ago.

"What ever happened to your plan to release a CD?" *And write a book, start your own business; open up a non-profit for the underprivileged?* Dana thought, but didn't say.

"That's my backup plan. This plan has been a goal of mine since high school."

"And I'm just hearing about it? Nice to know I mean so much to you."

"When my plan is in motion, you'll be the first to know. I promise. When you think about it, I'm a toddler in the scheme of things. Say I live until I'm a hundred years old. That's a quarter of my life expended, which means I have a good seventy-something years to accomplish my goals. See, you Dana, you're a typical female with the immediate gratification syndrome. You want to start a family, buy the house with a picket fence, the whole nine. Not that I don't want that too. That's my master plan. But if we rush things, what is there to look forward to?"

"What about having kids, growing old together, spoiling our grandkids? That's something to look forward to." Dana hated the sound of her own voice, which crackled worse than broken eggshells.

"And all of that takes money." Omar stopped talking to order dessert. "You want something?" he said.

"Save your money," Dana snapped. Omar laughed with the waiter, as if they had a private understanding of women that only men could understand.

"Make mine to go, man."

"Please do. We're leaving." Dana slammed down her napkin on the table.

"We haven't finished eating."

"I'm finished," Dana said. Omar and the waiter chuckled again before the waiter walked off. Dana put on the shrug that kept her shoulders warm in her sleeveless top, preparing to storm out of the restaurant.

"You're not coming over tonight?"

"Why should I, Omar?"

"Dana, whatever my plans are, you're a part of them. Doesn't that prove anything to you?"

"What it proves is that we're two different people with different values. Like you said, I have immediate gratification syndrome. And it's clear you have delayed gratification disorder." Dana's cynicism wouldn't quit these days, not after years of comprising herself from fear Omar would label her "a difficult black woman," giving him another excuse not to marry her.

Omar watched her curiously. "What'll make you happy, Dana? Seriously. I want to know." There was genuineness in Omar's tone, but Dana had heard it before. Omar's genuineness had kept her imprisoned in possibility opposed to reality.

"If you don't know what will make me happy by now, you never will, Omar."

"You want to get married? Is that what you want? Let's get married." A smile played around Omar's lips as if the entire night was a joke. Something in Dana's heart broke in two. She recognized the bitter taste in her mouth for Omar now. It was hate. She hated that Omar didn't live up to his promise, that he kept giving her hope only to disappoint her, that he expected her to wait around until he got his act together, or until he decided she wasn't right for him and found someone else to share his plans with. She hated him as much as she loved him.

"Don't do me any favors," she said.

"The favor would be mine if you say yes. I've never been more serious in my life, Dana. Let's do it. Let's get married." He was up to his old games again, playing with her heart like a clump of meaningless clay. Dana wasn't falling for it this time. She took a calming breath and let Omar have it.

"After the day I had, with someone who doesn't mind wining and dining me, or taking me on vacations, or sharing his *plans* with me, you think I'm going to jump at the chance to marry you now? Thanks, but no thanks!"

Omar looked as if she had thrown a glass of water in his face and woke his butt up. "You're seeing some other cat?"

"What did you expect me to do? Wait around for you for a hundred years?"

"Why wouldn't you?"

"Like I said, give me a break, Omar."

"If the shoe was on the other foot and I was the woman and you were the man, I'd wait for you."

Dana could have said much in response to Omar's absurd comment, but didn't. She took another bite of her Dungeness crab with cherry blossom vinaigrette and sweet peas, and thought she was eating cardboard. Her taste buds were completely lost, her appetite too.

"So, who is he?" Omar asked.

"A friend."

"You like this cat?" Omar clasped his hands at his chest and leaned back in his chair, waiting for her reply. In their three years together, Dana had never hinted of being with another man nor did she want to be. Had Omar been with another woman, he had done a good job hiding it from her. Faithfulness wasn't the problem with Omar; lack of commitment was, together with his arrogance to think she had nothing better to do with her life than wait around for him. For the heck of it, she should tell him she was in love with Matthew.

Dana leveled her gaze at him. "You don't really want me to answer that question, do you?"

"You must like something about him, you brought him up." Omar said this suggestively, as though she had invented a man to make him jealous.

"If you really want to know, I like that he surprised me with a trip to the aquarium because he appreciates that I'm a fish buff, that he took me on a picnic and jet skiing today and that he knows my favorite flavor yogurt. Do you know my favorite flavor yogurt, Omar?" Dana intended to damage Omar's ego. The fire in his eyes confirmed she had.

"Come on. I'll take you home," he said.

"I was ready to go ten minutes ago," Dana said with a leer.

That concluded Dana's date with Omar. He didn't have much to say to her on the ride home, and let her out of the car, saying, "If you want to know, your favorite flavor yogurt is New York Cheesecake."

Dana rolled her eyes and slammed the car door. It took him long enough to remember.

Later that night, Dana reminisced on her day. She had to admit she had a blast with Matthew. Yet, her surprise dinner date with Omar overrode a picnic on the beach and jet skiing into the sunset. What if that was Omar's idea of a romantic proposal, she mused. If so, she missed her one chance to say "I do."

Give Me Strength

Not much kept Tempest down. She could always control her moods by going on a shopping spree, sewing or sketching a new design, and afterwards she would be in an up mood again. Not this time. Darkness had become her days and nights. She hadn't eaten, showered, or brushed her teeth for two days. Or had it been three? Tempest didn't know anymore. Time was insignificant now that she had nowhere she wanted to be and nothing to look forward to.

What hurt most, so much that her heart felt stampeded, was Diamond couldn't enter a beauty contest let alone win one. If Diamond were prettier than her, it may not have hurt as much. Or maybe it would hurt more and she would still be lying in bed in the middle of the day, staring into space and wanting to die.

Charlene called while she was contemplating death. Tempest heard when people really don't want to die, they'll tell someone as a way of reaching out for help. Maybe that was her way of reaching out. Anyway, she told the right person.

"If you kill yourself over Sterling," Charlene told her, "I'll kick your ass, Tempest." Charlene then told Nadine, who set off the alarms. Her whole family put her on suicide watch, even though she promised them she wasn't seriously going to kill herself. It was only a passing thought to get back at Sterling.

Her family traipsed in and out of her condo day after day. Her mother held a one-woman prayer session in her room. Nadine cried every time she walked through the door, mainly because Nadine found out she was pregnant for the fifth time. And Charlene took it upon herself to set up shop in her condo, bringing along clients and all. Tempest was surprised to see Charlene's sweet side come out. Her big sister watered her plants, washed her clothes, and even kept her condo neat and clean. Tempest never recognized it before, but Charlene was stronger than all the Perry sisters put together. Spending a few days with Charlene gave Tempest strength enough to get out of bed, shower and brush her teeth.

Salia stopped by too, and laid next to Tempest, watching the soaps half the day.

Her Daddy stopped by once. Years ago, he would have threatened to kill any man who hurt one of his daughters. Now, being in his late sixties, he didn't have much fight left in him.

"Love is a gamble, Princess," he said to her. "You can roll a winning number more times than not and still crap out. If Sterling doesn't recognize a good woman when he's got her, he's not much of a man. That's how I see it. " He shook his head like his own son had disappointed him. "From now on, if you need anything, you come to me, you hear?" Tempest sure hoped he meant that literally. She would need him sooner than later now that Sterling, who talked her into renting this freakin' expensive condo in the first place, wouldn't be paying half the rent.

Tempest thanked her father with a long hug and laid her head on his shoulder, pacified by her Daddy's strong embrace. It reminded her of her childhood, sitting on her Daddy's lap and staring at him with stars in her eyes. His skin shined in the silkiest black satin around his deep-set stern eyes. "How's Daddy's beautiful princess?" he would ask her. She was too young to tell her Daddy how much she loved him, admired him, and wanted to marry a man exactly like him, so she would smile, lay her head on his chest and feel beautiful. She believed with all her heart a black prince like her Daddy would gallop into her life, seat her in her rightful place next to him on the throne, and love and cherish her forever. Her Daddy loved and cherished her mother for thirty-nine years. Why wouldn't her future hold the same fate? Yet, when Tempest looked into her Daddy's eyes that night, she noticed how much he had aged. His beautiful skin was now creased with deep smile lines, and permanent stress lines had settled into his forehead. It made Tempest more saddened.

Maybe it was time she gave up her childhood fantasy of finding a prince like her Daddy, one who loved his family more than his own life, who sacrificed and worked himself closer to the grave to make sure his girls had something to pass down to his grandchildren, and who would cut off an arm for her mother. Tempest thought she found a man like her Daddy in Sterling. She thought dead wrong.

Days passed without Tempest leaving the house. Her best friend Yasmine came over and brought flowers. "I'm not dead yet, girl," Tempest told her and found something to laugh about for the first time in days. Dana stopped by too, every day after work. Today Dana forced Tempest to dress and take a ride. They wound up at Santa Monica Pier, sitting in Dana's car with the top down and talking into the night. The tide, framed in foam, rumbled in and rolled out quietly. Tempest stared into the endless dark sea, where the sky seemed to swallow the ocean. When she and Dana were kids, and their families got together for a beach day, they would take turns covering each other in mounds of sand. Dana would lie stiff as a corpse, admiring the sky like there was something fascinating up there to see. As soon as the sand touched Tempest's knees, she wiggled herself free, afraid of being buried alive. Tonight Tempest wanted to submerge herself in the cold, damp sand to feel anything other than numb inside.

"Look alive, Temp," Dana said.

"I'm alive, just thinking."

"About what, should I ask?"

"About work. Linda's letting me get away with murder. I've called in sick for a week, knowing I have new hires starting. I need to get back before I get fired." Tempest said this not to admit what Dana suspected was on her mind. Not a minute passed when she wasn't reliving that awful night in her head, trying to convince herself that she imagined it all. The more she tried to alter the truth, the more apparent the truth became. All the signs were there—from the pre-game special, to Diamond's gift, to Sterling's sudden desperation to break their pre-marital vow, down to the bad feeling in the pit of her stomach.

Bits and pieces of what happened that night flashed in her mind, followed by a blur. The taxi driver had the heart not to charge her a dime for the fare from and back to the airport. Sterling claimed he came after her, even had her paged at the airport several times. He wouldn't have found her if he seriously tried. She hopped the first standby flight she could get on and was back in L.A by 9:00 AM the same day.

"Have you talked to Sterling again?" Dana asked.

"Yes and I'm tired of listening to his lame excuses."

"What excuse could he have after being caught with his pants down?"

"He said that was the first and only time he got with Diamond, like it makes a freakin' difference to me."

"And what did you say to that?"

Tempest looked Dana squarely in the eyes. "I know what you think, Dana, that I'm not strong enough to stand up to Sterling. Want to know what I told him? I told him I never want to see or hear from him again, and if he passed me on the street, give me fifty feet and keep his dog ass stepping!"

Dana hiked her brow. "You told him that, Tempest?"

"Sure did."

"I guess I thought wrong."

"You and everybody else. You would've been proud of me. And to make sure I never talk to him again, I'm having all my numbers changed. Remind me to give them to you."

"You think that's a good idea, Temp? Give it another week before going that drastic. If you want my advice, put closure to the relationship first or you'll be stuck wondering if you made the right decision."

Tempest couldn't hold back her tears that were bound to fall for years to come. "I have to do it this way, Dana, or I'll never get over Sterling. I already feel sorry for him. I know I shouldn't, but I do, girl. Daddy said it right. Sterling will never find a girl who loves him more than I do. I mean, *did*, whether he plays for the NFL or not. Let's see if *Diamond* has his back if he gets cut or breaks his freakin' neck. Let's just see!"

Dana laid a hand on Tempest's shoulder. "You did the right thing," she said. Whether Tempest felt she had done what was right or not didn't reduce the lump in her throat, heal the ache in her heart, or settle her stomach long enough to keep a meal down. That feeling, equal to being robbed of everything she owned and left with nothing to live on, clung to her like a bad dream.

"I am so sick of crying over Sterling!" Tempest swiped her face dry with one sweep of her hand. "You're sick of me crying too, aren't you, Dana?"

Dana laughed. "Sorry for laughing, but I'd think something was wrong if you didn't cry, Temp. You were always a big cry baby."

They both laughed.

"But honestly," Dana went on. "I know you love Sterling. That's not going to change overnight, even if you want it to."

"I wish you were wrong, but you are so right. I can't help loving Sterling and you can't help loving Omar. What's wrong with us, girl?"

Dana pursed her lips. "Speak for yourself. Omar and I are history."

"Again, Dana?"

"I sound like a broken record, don't I? But this time it's mutual. He hasn't called me and I'm not calling him, ever again. I'm fine with it."

Tempest didn't believe Dana, not for a minute. "You really like this new guy, Matthew, Dana?"

"He's growing on me, slowly," Dana said. She went on to say Matthew had taken her out twice this week, one night to a sushi bar and last night they caught a movie. This weekend they had plans to go parasailing. Tempest found herself absorbed by the twinkle in Dana's eyes. Nothing got Dana so excited.

"Let's face it," Dana continued. "Omar and I are finished. The string we were holding onto finally broke, that's all. Did I tell you he asked me to marry him?"

"You turned him down, didn't you?" Tempest shook her head. "I knew it."

"Well, you would've too if you heard the way he asked me. That wasn't a proposal. It was barter. Had I said yes, Omar would've set our wedding date for the year three thousand and expected me to wait."

Tempest felt an ache in her heart at the mention of a wedding date, flashing back to how perfect her life had once been.

When the bright lights of a utility truck making its way across the sand glowed through the foggy night, Tempest and Dana headed home.

A Fight For Her Life

"We needed this, didn't we, babe?" Devon said to Carmen, standing on the balcony of their beachfront villa overlooking the ocean. From where they stood, they were close enough to the water to jump in. The villa they rented, with walls and décor sheathed in inviting gold and white tones, had stimulated Carmen's sexual appetite the minute they arrived at the quaint hotel she got for a steal of a deal through her industry connections.

Carmen agreed. Time away was exactly what she and Devon needed. Mostly, she needed a break from Kendall. After Devon moved back home, Kendall lost his mind. First, he made biking up and down her street his second job. It took Carmen placing an anonymous call to the police, complaining of noise abatement, to quiet the disturbance. Then came the childish prank phone calls, calling her and hanging up or texting her all damn day and night. When Carmen cut off communication with Kendall completely, blocking his number from her cell, the fool started following her halfway home after work, likely hoping for a roadside *quickie*. One day Carmen did pull to the side of the road, waited for Kendall to walk up to her car window, then threatened to have him deported back to the Dominican Republic if he didn't quit stalking her. He looked furious, like he wished he had never confessed to Carmen that he was working in the United States illegally. He mumbled something in Spanish and walked away.

It was a threat Carmen had not planned to carry out, but hell, it worked. She hadn't seen that fool, outside of work, since.

Over the weekend, Carmen put that headache behind her. DJ stayed with Momma Corrine for two days, and she and Devon had nothing but time to seal their reunion. Their lovemaking was a ball of fire and energy, and noisy enough to get a visit from security telling them to "pipe down." If she and Devon got a ray of sun, it was from their balcony, where they ate breakfast each morning, watching the seagulls soar and the beach come alive. For the most part, they closed the weekend having never left the confines of their room. They made love and talked, and talked and made love. When they weren't talking and making love, they were ordering room service or a good "in theatres now" movie.

Driving home, there wasn't anything left for the two of them to talk out. Their faces were aglow with satisfaction and peace as they coasted down the highway. Their weekend away was perfect, and life was as right as right could get for Carmen.

WHEN CARMEN WALKED INTO WORK after her refreshing vacation, she felt like a new woman with a new lease on life. That was before she saw the look on the hotel manager's face, which cut short her merry strut. Normally Francisco, a good-looking fifty-year-old Hispanic man, was flashing his flirtatious smile at her or complimenting her on a job well done. Now his stern look indicated there was a problem.

"You have a minute, Carmen?" Francisco said.

"For you, always, Francisco," Carmen flirted. "What's wrong? Did somebody burn the place down while I was gone?" She chuckled. He didn't.

"It's nothing. I'm sure we can get this cleared up in no time." He placed his hand gently on her back and guided her toward his office. Not only did Carmen fear Francisco's unusually serious tone, she didn't like the feeling in her stomach. If she took a wild guess, Kendall had something to do with this *problem* she was about to face. Carmen was too terrified to speculate what Kendall had said or done, but it was something serious enough to invoke Francisco to make a special trip to her office and wait for her to arrive to work.

Francisco's office was the size of a suite, but felt two times smaller when Carmen sat on the leather loveseat near the conference area. Francisco didn't sit, but stood with his hands in the pocket of his suit pants, rocking on the heels of his dress shoes as though anxious to say what was on his mind. He couldn't be more anxious than Carmen. She caught herself involuntarily picking her teeth with her thumbnail.

"First, let me say that I respect you and your work, Carmen. If this was in my hands, I wouldn't be having this conversation with you."

"If what was in your hands?" Carmen kept a steady voice in the midst of a full-blown internal panic.

"It's the craziest thing I ever heard. Someone lodged a formal sexual harassment complaint against you. I can't give you any names." Francisco let his statement hang in the air, and that was where it stayed. Carmen had not a word to say to contest the charge. She knew the company's policy on sexual harassment. Hell, she was required to complete the training along with her staff. The charge was as serious as it could get for a supervisor and more serious for a married one. Carmen blinked back her furious tears while Francisco took her hand into his and patted the back of it.

"Once," he said, "an employee accused me of harassment years ago. Aye-yi!" Francisco swatted the air. "It was nothing, a little harmless flirting. We all do it. You are a good-looking girl,

Carmen. This person perhaps has an eye for you. Not to worry." He patted her hand again. "I'll do everything in my power to get this cleared up quickly."

Carmen released the breath she was holding, but the weight on her shoulders continuously pulled her down. She was sweating to the point of soiling her silk blouse. Her heart felt like it was in her throat, choking her to death. The biggest fear running through Carmen's mind was Francisco asking her about Kendall. If he did, the truth might pour out of her like toxic waste. She was exhausted of lying, cheating, and hiding.

Thankfully, Francisco didn't ask her one question. He made clear it wasn't his job to investigate these complaints, almost like he wanted to wash his hands of it.

Not once did Carmen hyperventilate, get the shakes, or feel like she would lose her mind. But it was by a thread that she got through the day. She moved about robotically, smiling when required, troubleshooting on command, and treating her staff extra pleasant, not to appear on the verge of a nervous breakdown. If Kendall was the "someone" who lodged this complaint against her, he pulled off the performance of the year, acting as if nothing was out of the ordinary; a game Carmen knew how to play just as well.

Throughout the day, Carmen's thoughts stayed on the last thing Francisco said to her. "A designated human services advisor given the authority to investigate and evaluate sexual harassment related charges will contact you." She was not to discuss the allegations with other employees or it might be viewed as "threatening."

Keeping this scandal bottled up and airtight was Carmen's main goal. When it came to Kendall's ass, on the other hand, it was going to take everything in her not to call him personally and chew his ass out! Sexual harassing *him*? From the start he harassed her!

Before today, the specifics of how her affair with Kendall began were vague in Carmen's mind. She always blamed herself, thinking she did something, in some way, to tempt Kendall—the laughing, the smiling, the flirting. Now, Carmen could recall, detail for detail, how the relationship came about. Kendall came onto her in the elevator, and it wasn't for the first time. "I had a dream I made love to you last night," he said. "When are you going to make my dream come true?"

Whenever they were alone, he seized the opportunity to brush up against her and whisper obscenities in her ear. Her fault lay in being turned on by Kendall's sexual attraction to her, for meeting him after work for drinks, for enjoying the excitement and thrill of it, and not putting a stop to the affair before it started, but mostly for forgetting how much she loved Devon.

Maybe the affair wouldn't have caught up to her had she ended it as a *fling*, a brief sexual relationship without emotional involvement. Her liaison with Kendall had gone on for over six months, and Kendall's emotional involvement was steadily moving toward obsession. Besides, it was too late to go back and start over, and she didn't have time to let guilt and fear grip her to the point of inaction. The most she could do now was fight to save her life.

Carmen had to talk to someone before she fell apart. A few blocks from home, she made a call to Maryland. Having to confess her affair to Tan wasn't the easiest conversation she ever had with her sister.

"This is too good," Tan said, after hooting and hollering like she was watching the season finale of *Sex and the City*. There was a brief pause on the line and a long exhale, which meant Tan had lit a cigarette for the occasion. "Was the little shit worth it?"

"Worth this kind of trouble? What do you think, Tan?"

"Well?"

"Well what?"

"Don't leave me hanging. I want to hear the good parts."

"There weren't any *good* parts."

"Was he packing a pistol? Was he fine? You don't have to tell me, honey. Those Dominican men are fine as - "

"Tan!" Carmen interrupted. "Did you hear me? This isn't one of your soap operas. This shit is real! I can lose my job!"

"Well, calm down, honey."

"I can't calm down!"

"You're not in love with him are you?" Tan said, going from jokey to serious.

"In love with Kendall? Nowhere close."

"Are you sure, Carmen? It's hard for women to separate their emotions when they have an affair, cause honey, my girlfriend went to pieces over a married man she had no business with, got pregnant, had the baby for the man and he never left his wife. Please don't tell me you're pregnant - "

"Tan, I need your help not the drama."

"I don't see how I can help from way out here."

"You can help by listening."

"Go on, honey. I'm listening."

"You worked for human services once?"

"So long ago I forgot when and where. Why?"

"I'm scared they'll come to my house and start asking questions. What if Devon is at home?"

"You think they will?"

"I can't count on what I think. I'll feel better if I know how this investigation is going to go."

"Did you forget your ex-brother-in-law is now the VP of Human Services?"

"Carl?"

"Yes, Carl. You think they charged him with sexual harassment for screwing his *secretary?* No, honey, they gave him a promotion and a fifty thousand dollar raise. Men get away with it; women take the fall. That's the way of the world."

"Will you call Carl for me?"

"He dropped off the twins yesterday after having my babies all week. I have to say this was the loneliest week of my life."

"I'll call you back, Tan, okay?"

When Carmen arrived at the house, she cleared her voicemail and unplugged it in the event the investigator called the wrong number. As a precaution, she told Francisco to have the investigator contact her by cell, which was the best way to reach her anyway. Thank goodness Devon called to say he was stuck in traffic and running late picking up DJ. Still wired and spacey, Carmen didn't know what to do but stress out. A hot bath didn't help. Neither did one glass of wine. Carmen had two glasses before she relaxed.

When Devon came home, he inquired about her workday. "Work was work, nothing out of the ordinary," Carmen said indifferently.

"Wish I could say the same for my day," Devon said. Over dinner, Devon bent her ear about his stressful day at work. Carmen half listened, contemplating her own. They went to bed and made love. For Carmen, their lovemaking was lukewarm at best.

In the morning, Devon saw her off with a kiss, never once aware of her frantic frame of mind.

As Carmen was arriving to work Tan called. "You didn't tell Carl it was me, did you, Tan?" Carmen said right off.

"I didn't mention any names, and he didn't ask. How are you feeling?"

"Biting my nails and pulling my hair out."

"Call your therapist, Carmen."

"Whatever good that'll do me. What did Carl say?"

"Honey, Carl was too happy to tell me the protocol, citing laws and case studies like I was going after his job. He's blessed I never did. I know better than to cut off my nose to spite my face. Every bill he pays around here helps - "

"Tan, I only have a few minutes."

"Wait. Let me get my notes." Tan disappeared and returned to the phone. "Let me see if I got this right. Carl was talking so fast, but I think he said…if I could read my own writing… it must be severe or pervasive enough to create a hostile work environment. Was it?"

"That all depends," Carmen said and chewed her thumbnail.

"Depends on what?"

"If slapping him counts."

"You didn't! What would make you slap the little shit?"

"It's hard to explain."

"Well, explain it to me, honey, because I don't understand. You are his boss, Carmen."

"You think I don't know that?"

"I have to know these things if I'm going to help you," Tan said.

"What are you getting at?"

"If I got this right, Carl said as long as nothing threatening or humiliating took place, or you didn't do anything to affect his psychological state - "

"Affect *his* psychological state?" Carmen shouted. "What about my psychological state? Kendall is driving me crazy!"

"Don't shoot the messenger. These are Carl's words."

"I could kill Kendall for this, I swear!"

"That's the last thing you want to do, honey."

"Did you ask Carl about the process?"

"I got it right here in my notes. Hold on for a minute."

Carmen was out of patience and time. "Tan, I'm at work. I'll call you later, okay?"

After hanging up, Carmen thought for a minute. Had she threatened or humiliated Kendall somehow? She slapped him, yes. What else could she have done to keep Kendall off her? And what about his offenses? Following her home, barging into her house, disturbing her peace of mind. None of that would matter in the end. The evidence Kendall had on her would put her out of a job and the hospitality industry.

THAT NIGHT CARMEN WENT TO bed early, emotionally exhausted to the point of sickness. She hoped whatever she was coming down with would give her an excuse to miss work for a few days, and time to get her story together before meeting with the investigator. She snuggled up, fighting against the fever overtaking her body.

While waiting for the flu medicine to take effect, Carmen closed her eyes and tried to sleep. If she was awake, it felt like a dream she was trapped in. Racing, racing…

…*Racing toward a brown car. Her best friend Nicole raced alongside her. The wind was on their backs, the sun kissing their faces. "I got the front seat!" Nicole said, sprinting ahead of Carmen. Something in Carmen's mind wanted to say, "Let's both sit in the back." She never had the chance.*

"You two girls on your way to school?" the man said, his eyes twinkling from his friendly smile. Nicole struck up a conversation with the man. Carmen didn't like the way he asked Nicole questions no stranger should ask a young girl. Don't get scared now, her mind echoed. It was your bright idea to bum a ride. Carmen counted the blocks to school.

Three more blocks…

Two more blocks…

One more…

"Thanks for the ride, Mister. We can walk from here." Carmen had her hand on the door handle, ready to leap to safety as soon as the car stopped. The brown car never stopped. It rolled on, taking them along.

Terror took over Nicole's eyes. "What should we do, Carmen?" Nicole's eyes screamed.

"I don't know!" Carmen eyes screamed back. Their implicit conversation went on for blocks. The brown car rolled on and on. Its operator looked straight ahead like a bus driver oblivious to his passenger's final destination.

"Nicole, jump!" Carmen screamed as she clubbed her fist against the man's head mightily. Nicole isn't jumping. Why won't she jump? "Jump, Nicole! Jump!" Carmen opened the back door, ejecting from the moving car. Her body slammed into a dirt field and rolled down a hill. The hill steepened, whirling her endlessly. The brown car sped on, taking Nicole with it. At the bottom of the hill was a long, barren road. Carmen ran for her life. Her legs wanted to give out as if chained down by bricks under water. Her lungs shorted out and her heart thumped in her eardrums.

"Somebody help! Help!" Carmen screamed, running against a windstorm it seemed.

No one came to Nicole's rescue. No one.

"Sometimes the adolescence in us is killed off too soon in more ways than one."

Carmen's eyes shot open at the sound of Dr. Jessup's voice in her head, uncertain if she was dreaming or awake. In the dark, images slowly became familiar to her eyes—the twin set pelican paintings, the white shuttered windows, the turquoise painted walls, even the feel of her silk duvet was a comforting reminder of home for Carmen. She pulled the duvet over her shoulders and curled under it. The effects of the medicine and the dream had her nerves crawling like an anxiety attack brewing. At the same time, she wanted to sleep. Her nerves wouldn't let her. Carmen lay on her side, pondering her predicament. She never remembered the ending of that reoccurring dream, but the reality of its conclusion always awaited her when she opened her eyes. Once again, she had gotten herself into a fatal situation, knowing better.

Carmen reached over, turned on the lamp light and picked up her cell phone. She had deleted Kendall's number from her cell but not from her memory. With a tentative hand, Carmen punched his number into the text box. When her text message was complete, her index finger hovered over the send button. "You are not to discuss the allegations with other employees." Francisco's warning had Carmen so petrified she felt like her fever had shot up to a deadly degree. She shouldn't be crazy enough to contact Kendall, but if she didn't, his bogus complaint would go too far. What Kendall wanted was her, however and whenever he could have her. *Fine!* She would agree to meet with him and that would be as far as their meeting would go this time. In the end, she hoped to convince that fool to drop the complaint and leave her alone for good. Carmen hit the send button.

"You must be feeling better," Devon said, bursting into the room and startling the hell out of Carmen.

"It feels like I'm dying," she said and curled under the covers with her cell phone, praying a text message from Kendall wouldn't beep right back and alert Devon.

Back in the Game

During the Thanksgiving holiday, Tempest's ordeal with Sterling was the center of her family's debate. It didn't surprise her, though, not when it came to her family. After emptying pots, pans, and casserole dishes full of delicious food, they usually became loud and boisterous. Nadine kept yelling for everyone to lower their voices before her Woodland Hills neighbors reported her for disturbing the peace.

The debate started over one question: "Why do men cheat?" The women in the family insisted on clarifying the reasons, while the men kept their opinions to themselves and their attention on a holiday bowl game.

"Men cheat because they are unhappy and sexually unsatisfied," per her cousin, Makayla.

"Insensitive, egocentric, and insatiable," per Nadine.

"Men will be men," per her mother and her Aunt Jackie.

"Because their plain dogs," per Charlene.

Tempest could have answered the question in one word before the shouting got started. It boiled down to heart. If Sterling had one, he wouldn't have done what he did. No other reason could justify his actions, in her opinion.

After dinner, they gathered in Nadine's blue and white country-style kitchen around the half-moon island. Tempest lounged in one of the bar chairs, dipping a dinner roll in cranberry sauce, her mood fluctuating between red hot and jet blue. She gave herself credit for keeping her feelings tucked inside and not shedding a single tear while Sterling's named floated around the room.

Charlene, who wouldn't give the subject a rest, said, "Next time you decide to get married, Tempest, I hope you pick a dress I can wear out somewhere. That dress you picked cost too much money to wear for a day."

"What a thing to say," Nadine said, bouncing and pacing with her eleven-month old son, Ali.

"Not everybody has money to throw away like you, Nadine. I got bills to pay."

"You never know what's going to happen. Tempest may forgive Sterling," Nadine said.

"I think she should," said Nadine's husband, Will, who was eating a slice of cake with his coffee after wolfing down two full plates of food. Will wore his hair in an old-fashioned fade-top, his mustache as thick as Steve Harvey's, and had the powerful voice of the successful criminal prosecutor he was. Though he was a big softy when it came to Nadine.

"I wouldn't take Sterling back if he signed a fifty-million-dollar contract," Charlene said.

"You're one to talk, Charlene, after what you've put up with from Derrick," said Nadine.

"I don't put up with shit from Derrick!"

"Paying his parking tickets to get him out of jail, letting him live in Daddy's place rent free, babysitting his illegitimate kids while he runs the street, should I go on?"

"Derrick will get cussed out too."

"And that's the sum of it, Charlene. You blow smoke and haven't gone anywhere in six years. If Tempest wants to forgive Sterling, that's her prerogative. At any rate, she'll be married for her trouble. That's more than you can say."

Tempest braced for a screaming match.

"Some men learn their lessons the first time around, don't they, Waverly?" Makayla interjected, sparing a family feud.

"How would I know?" Waverly said, eyes bucked.

The room filled with needed laughter. Even Tempest had to laugh at Waverly, who could pass for a man of the cloth when he wore a suit and had a Bible in his hand. He and Makayla had been married so long they looked more like brother and sister. Both were stout, top heavy and had eyes that protruded in their sockets.

"Nadine wants everybody to be like her, stuck in the house with a bunch of bad ass kids," Charlene blurted out of nowhere. That was Charlene, resorting to insults to win a debate. Between Will and Nadine, Attorneys at Law, she didn't stand a chance in this household. Will intervened in the nick of time, advising Nadine to take Ali upstairs with Mama and the other kids. By this time, Nadine was in tears. Pregnancy wasn't agreeing with her this go around.

Tempest had had enough. She raised her hand. "Excuse me," she said. "In case you forgot that I'm here, I can speak for myself. Charlene, you don't have to worry about paying for a dress you'll never have to wear. Nadine and Will, thanks for your optimism, but I'm never going to forgive Sterling—ever! I don't care if he learned his lesson the first time around or the tenth, *Makayla.* Lastly, if anyone in this family cares about how I feel, you won't mention Sterling's name around me ever again." Tempest left the room and her family speechless.

Scheduled to work on Black Friday, Tempest headed straight to Nordstrom's from Nadine and Will's house. While coasting down the highway before the moon fell, her cell rang, sending her into a cold sweat. Before answering, she remembered she had her numbers changed, so it couldn't possibly be Sterling calling.

It was Yasmine. Tempest's chest caved in, partly from disappointment and partly from relief. Yasmine said she was already standing in line, "freezing to death," while waiting for the store doors to open. She asked Tempest if she wanted to go to a Lakers party in Hollywood. Yasmine didn't have to ask Tempest twice.

"Count me in," Tempest said. She couldn't think of a better way to get her mind off Sterling.

NOT ONE THING IN HER closet was worth wearing to the party. Selecting the last dress she set her eyes on, Tempest slipped on a powder pink strapless sequin mini, looked at her reflection in a full-length mirror, and then kicked off her platform stilettos. Why should she freakin' have to worry about what to wear, when at one time all that mattered was how she looked to Sterling?

"I can't go," Tempest said when Yasmine called.

"You're going to miss Andrew Bynum, girl. He's hot and single." That was Yasmine's way of cheering her up.

"I don't have it in me, Yas. Sorry."

"If I didn't understand, I'd give you a hard time. But I understand. If you change your mind, call me. I plan to be fashionably late and turn heads walking in the door, girl."

Standing over the bathroom sink, Tempest cleared her face of makeup, going from glamorous back to sad and pathetic. Not to look at herself, she clicked off the bathroom light and got ready for bed. She was nowhere near sleepy at nine-thirty on a Saturday night.

The two dozen roses Sterling sent with a card that read, "Tee! I love you! Call me!" were smelling up her place. To date, that totaled ninety-six long stem red roses, two pounds of chocolate, and a life-sized stuffed bear with "I love you" stitched on its belly—all sent special delivery from Sterling.

Tempest half expected him to turn up on her doorstep after he went as far as sending his mother to deliver his message personally. "I don't know what Sterling did to you, and I don't want to know," Ms. Alexander said. "But whatever he did, please call my son, so he'll stop calling me crying over you, child."

Tempest loved Sterling's mother, but nothing Ms. Alexander said made a difference. She was grateful to God Sterling was stuck in Minneapolis until the season ended. Now she didn't have to worry about seeing him until she was strong enough not to care if he was dead or alive.

Tempest opened the refrigerator and stared at empty shelves. She hadn't grocery shopped in weeks. Even if she had, she didn't have an appetite. Tempest prepared a cup of tea, sat on the couch, and stared at the black TV screen. After a minute, she picked up the remote, turned on the TV, and turned it back off minutes later. She wasn't up to watching TV either. Had what happened not happened, she would have more than enough to do to take up her time and mind. If she wasn't looking through the many bridal magazines she bought, or orchestrating her wedding plans, she would be living in the future, romanticizing about her life as Sterling's wife. If not that, she would be on the phone, talking to Sterling half the night.

Determined to do anything but cry, Tempest forced herself off of the couch, stalked to the hallway, and rummaged through the dark, narrow closet, tossing aside empty shoeboxes, wrapping paper, recycled gift bags, and other junk until she came upon her box of leftover fabric. Sewing always cleared her mind. She would start on the quilt she planned to make for Nadine and Will's new baby. She could always buy one, but it was so much more special to Nadine when she made it with her own hands. It had become sort of a tradition. At the baby showers, people now expected to see one of her famous baby quilts, anticipating the pattern she had crafted, stitched with *T. Perry Designs* in the corner. For Nadine's first baby, she created a quilt in the shape of a yellow bus, with happy babies in the windows. For Nadine's second baby, she filled the quilt with cute purple, blue, yellow and green dinosaurs. For Nadine's third child, she went with a traditional quilt pattern and fabric, stitching colorful letters and numbers for the trim. Nadine's last baby received a quilt in the shape of a big bright sun. Her quilts always got "oohs and ahs," from the crowd and requests for a duplicate. If Tempest had the time, she would take orders, but she only quilted for fun and in her spare time. With plenty of time to spare these days, she might as well get started early.

Tempest hadn't decided on a pattern for Nadine's fifth baby. It would come to her naturally. She was going with unisex, since Nadine and Will wanted to be "surprised," this time. Inside the fabric box was the quarter yard of the ivory chiffon fabric she used for her drapery, two yards of sea green velvet fabric she never used for anything, and several yards of scarlet red cloth left over from her canopy draping. The rest were scraps. She doubted Nadine would want a Christmas-colored quilt for a spring baby.

"This is so muffed up, the whole freakin' situation!" Tempest screamed. She kicked past the junk on the closet floor and marched back to her bedroom to call Yasmine.

"You sound lit up," Yasmine said.

"I am! Come and pick me up. I have to get out of here."

"I'll have the limo driver cut back to Fox Hills. I'm on my way."

"Limo?"

"Trenton had it sent over, girl. I told you, I'm turning heads walking in the door. Those basketball bitches won't outdo me tonight."

Tempest decisively selected what to wear to the Lakers party, and it wasn't a conservative glam-girl dress. Attacking her closet, she searched high and low for the hottest, eye-catching dress she owned, then wiggled herself into the body-hugging, one-shoulder mini and slipped on sexy tall, high-heeled boots that made her legs look a mile longer. She reapplied her make-up, fastened on extra large hoop earrings, unwrapped her hair that fell over her shoulders like black silk, and was ready to walk out the door when the limousine arrived. If she was going to get over Sterling, she had to get started.

The black stretch limousine Trenton sent for Yasmine seated a total of ten to twelve people. Yasmine and Tempest were the sole occupants taking up the circular seat furthest to the back. Anyone peering in through the darkly tinted windows would have thought there was full-fledged partying going on inside. Yasmine had the strobe lights going and music videos blasting on the flat screen TV, doing her best to cheer Tempest up. Nothing Yasmine did could lift Tempest's mood tonight. The limo ride turned out to be a big fat downer, reminding Tempest of the last limousine ride she had with Sterling during the weekend he proposed under the Vegas lights.

The limo cruised down Sunset Blvd, and maneuvered its way around the circular driveway of a Hollywood nightclub. Out front, white Christmas lights draped the palm trees and crystal icicles hung from the arched rooftop. On a street packed with nightclubs for the stars, the building wasn't easy to miss. Yasmine stepped out first, wearing a face fiercer than a movie star's. She wore a pewter strapless mini dress and four-inch heeled sandals that only Yasmine could work better than a top model on a cat stroll. Next to Yasmine, Tempest felt like Yasmine's personal assistant, and now hated her outfit. She should have stuck with her glam-girl dress.

As it so happened, her outfit was perfect for the occasion. It kept the eligible men at the party away from her and gave her peace in the darkest corner of the crowded room. After trying hard to get her on the dance floor, Yasmine took off with Trenton, who turned out to be the guest of honor and the only Lakers player present as a lure. Three-fourths of the crowd was basically gold-digging groupies out to catch a glimpse of a baller. Tempest fumed inside each time one flounced by with fake breasts, fake hair, and fake attitudes.

"You look lonely over here in the corner by yourself," Tempest heard a man say. She looked up, up and up into the face of a seven feet tall man. He was either a basketball player or fronting to be one. "I'm lonely too. You want company?" He joined her at the belly bar covered with abandoned drinks.

"What's your name?" he asked her.

"Tempest," she said.

"I guess you know my name," he said, as if she should.

Tempest sighed. *I might as well get this over with.* "I'm not interested."

"Give me a chance. I might change your mind," he said, showing off his pretty smile.

Tempest considered this man for a moment. At least he had kind eyes and didn't act or smell like he had drowned himself in alcohol like the last man who approached her. She felt she could confide in this man, that maybe he would sympathize with her situation, make her feel better about professional athletes once again.

"Want to know why I'm lonely?" she began. The tall man listened tolerantly while she narrated her relationship with Sterling, how he played for the Spartans, how they were engaged to be married, how she loved and trusted him with all her heart, and how he fixed it so she would never trust another ball player in her life, even one with eyes as kind as his. After she finished her sad story, the man handed her a napkin.

"Maybe I can help things start looking up for you," he said. Tempest mustered up a smile, wiped her eyes with the napkin, and wrote down her new cell number on it before handing the napkin back to him.

Later, Tempest learned that the tall man played for the San Antonio Spurs, one of their veteran ballers.

"This is your big chance to get over Sterling," Yasmine said, overly enthusiastic."One rotten baller don't spoil the whole bowl game, girl."

Sailing Away

"Dana! I left the gate open!" Matthew yelled as Dana turned the corner toward an exclusive section of the club where luxury yachts lined the dock. She couldn't begin to count how many boats were anchored at the private Windjammers Yacht Club, of every conceivable size and shape. The extravagant ones put the dinky ones to shame. Dana tugged at the security gate that Matthew left ajar and stepped onto the dock.

Lady Maya, named in honor of Matthew's great grandmother, was a tri-level pearly white yacht, berthed last on the north end of the dock. Seated in one of the two swivel chairs anchored on the bridge, Matthew waved her over. He wasn't alone.

"How goes it?" Matthew said, helping Dana aboard.

"It goes," Dana replied. Fearing she might tumble backward into the water, Dana kept a secure grip on the stainless steel rail running along the length of the 58-foot Navigator. She followed Matthew toward the roomy sundeck.

"Dana, this is Niles, a friend of mine. Niles, meet Dana, more than a friend," Matthew said with a smile.

Dana and Niles shook hands. "Hi, Niles," Dana said.

"I heard a lot about ya. Matt never lies. You're a real beaut. Love the locks," Niles said.

"Thanks." Dana wasn't sure what to make of Niles with his shoulder-length blond hair simulating locks of his own, sun-kissed copper skin, and long-lashed emerald eyes. Dana had never seen a white guy she considered fine. Niles was the first. Mid-thought, she happened to catch the glance Niles and Matthew exchanged. It was a universal language apparently all men understood. Translation:

"*Are you hitting that?*" Niles had communicated to Matthew covertly.

"*Tonight,*" Matthew had communicated back before hiding his smiling eyes behind reflected sunglasses.

So, inviting her to stay the weekend on his family's yacht was evidently Matthew's way of making a booty call. The thought, honestly, hadn't crossed Dana's mind. And now that it had, she almost laughed out loud, nervously. In Dana's mind, this date was just another one of Matthew's innocent adventures. Did he really expect her to sleep with him when they hadn't kissed? That goes to show how seriously she had taken Matthew. Well, regardless of what Matthew was after, she wasn't backing out of this date. It was time she be more *daring*. The most daring move she had made in the last few years was growing sister locks and breaking up with Omar—decisions that took her too long to make. Tonight, wherever this adventure with Matthew led, she would dare to cross that bridge when she got there.

"Check you later, bro," Niles said while hopping off the deck and hitting the dock on bare feet. "We're cruising to the Mexican waters tonight! You game?"

"What time?" Matthew called after Niles.

"Sundown!" Niles yelled back. A few minutes later, Niles appeared a distance away on the deck of a red, white and blue sparkling torpedo-shaped vessel. Dana noticed three ambiguous women on the bridge. There were two other guys standing at the helm of the boat, holding drinks and talking. With the waterfront backdrop, a portrait of a great vacation get-away advertisement couldn't look more inviting.

"You game for a voyage?" Matthew turned and asked Dana.

"I don't see why not, if you're game? To let you know up front, though, I don't party, not the kind of partying your friend looks like he's into."

"Niles?" Matthew chuckled. "That's his persona to hook the babes. He's an architect, believe it or not, and a pretty successful one."

"And here I thought he was a beach bum."

"Just an average Cornell grad with an Einstein IQ. His family owns an empire."

"Did you say that to impress me?"

"Impress you, Dana? That's next to impossible."

"Only because I know why white boys got it like that."

"Danaaaa…you're speaking in general terms again."

"Generally, they do."

"You're not going to spare me a lesson in black history, are you?"

"If you spare me the average white guy routine." They smiled into each other's eyes and moved indoors.

The 'galley' as Matthew called it, flaunted maple-stained glossy cabinets and an L-shaped marble countertop. Dana leaned over the countertop, with a knee resting on the white leather seating behind it, while Matthew grabbed bottled juice from the refrigerator.

"Would you like one?"

"I'll take apple." He handed Dana a small bottle of apple juice from a refrigerator fully stocked, beer and wine coolers included.

"Gotta love your tenacity, Dana," he said after he chugged his juice.

"Does my tenacity bother you?" Dana gave him the "*If so, maybe we should end this dating charade while we're ahead*" look.

"Will it offend you if I'm Kosher?"

"I prefer *Kosher.*"

"It's what I love most about you—your *ferocity.*" He practically growled the word.

Dana laughed. "You call that a compliment?"

"You bet. A sincere one. I love your intensity, Dana. It turns me on." He leaned over the countertop, removed his shades, and stared at her with a quirky grin. As Matthew moved in closer, the butterflies in her stomach fluttered. Why was she so nervous, likely because so much was riding on this kiss.

Dana thought that the extent of her participation in their kiss was simply holding her mouth open while Matthew's tongue tickled and played with hers. But given Matthew was so into it, and her inner thighs were tingling, she must have been kissing him with as much fervor as he was kissing her.

"That didn't offend you, did it?" he said when their kiss ended. Speechless, Dana shook her head, pressing her fingers to her lips as if to confirm they had indeed kissed and she had indeed enjoyed it. As though he had misplaced something, Matthew looked around the lounge.

"You haven't changed your mind about staying the weekend, I hope. No luggage?"

"It's in the um, car…," Dana said, and cleared her scratchy throat. She had left her luggage in the car in case she changed her mind.

"I'll get it for you." Matthew held out his hand.

Dana reached into the pocket of her jean jacket and handed over her car keys.

THE THREE WOMEN ON BOARD the torpedo vessel stood around the spacious galley, nibbling cheese and crackers, drinking wine coolers, and gossiping. Dana learned the brunette's name was Whitney. She wasn't much taller than five feet and had the body of a teen who lived on popcorn and diet soda. The blonde was Amanda, tall and statuesque, and trying hard to be friendly. Ebony was the black one. Her complexion was truly ebony, her corkscrew afro parted down the middle and shooting out in all directions, an eccentric look that Ebony wore well.

"What do you do for a living?" was the first thing Whitney asked. Dana hated labeling as an introduction, but she answered nice enough that she taught grade school. The next question was, "Is that how you met Mattie Poo?" Ebony asked this in a lilted twang that burned Dana's ears, given her low tolerance for the elite. She never got around to answering Ebony's obvious question. Matthew had come up from below deck to introduce her to Kyle and Alan.

The seventy-two foot yacht with a hired captain at the helm hadn't left the dock, and Niles and his crew were already getting their party on. There were drinks in abundance and trays of hors d'oeuvres to enjoy. Dana didn't want to eat or a drink; she wanted to leave. She parked herself on one of several bench-style dinettes with glossy cherry wood tables, and nibbled on chilled shrimp and cocktail sauce.

Niles surfaced from below deck, his amazing emerald eyes noticeably bloodshot. "Dana! There's a shit load of grub over here. Help yourself!" he called out.

"Thanks. I will." she said. Niles hadn't heard Dana's reply, rapt in an intimate embrace with Ebony. It was becoming clear who was paired with who. Niles obviously had a thing for black women. Kyle and Amanda looked somewhat compatible; then there was Whitney and Alan, the perfect Calvin Klein looking couple. That left her and Matthew as the final and questionable pair. As daring as she wanted to be, if she backed out now, she wouldn't have to worry about what Matthew assumed their kiss would lead to over the weekend.

Dana stepped onto the deck. She was wearing jeans, warm socks, gloves, boots, and a hooded fleece lined jacket, but that didn't keep the chilly bay breeze from ripping through the fabric, making her shiver worse than cold water to her bare skin. Dana bore the discomfort, unable to tear her eyes away from the view. If she was enjoying anything about the night, it was the breathtaking skyline of the marina, the festive lights making it all the more magnificent to behold.

"There you are," Matthew said, walking up and putting his arm around her waist from behind. "It's beautiful out here, isn't it? Perfect cruising weather. You'll love the ride."

"I changed my mind," Dana said right off, reluctant to face him.

"Not about the weekend, I hope?"

Dana faced him. "About cruising to Mexico."

"Did something happen to make you change your mind?" Matthew massaged her shoulders, staring into her eyes for an explanation.

"No... nothing happened."

"If you're not game, neither am I."

"Don't disappoint your friends on my account," Dana said, hoping to encourage him to leave with his friends.

"They won't miss me."

That night, after they ate dinner at a seaside restaurant, she and Matthew strolled around the marina, where they enjoyed a free outdoor concert and Matthew bought her a silver dolphin anklet she admired. Saturday morning, in the early hours, they ate breakfast on the go and hit the water, canoeing around the marina until Dana thought her arms would fall off. It was nonstop from then forward: a bird watching guided tour, lunch on the boardwalk, an afternoon bike ride around the marina and cruising the marina on *Lady Maya* that evening, watching the sunset.

Inside, *Lady Maya* was as plush as a penthouse suite. It was becoming clear to Dana that Matthew wasn't the average teacher living on a meager teacher's salary. Yet, he continued to front as Joe Blow for some reason. They parted ways for the night, Dana going to the master stateroom and Matthew to the VIP guestroom.

If this is what it felt like to live on the water, Dana never wanted to leave. It was better than sleeping in a luxury hotel. The master stateroom's king-sized bed was the softest she had ever been in. She was under a velvet goose-down comforter, in a cozy room with dimmed recessed lights. All she needed now was her book to snuggle up with. As Dana reached into her overnight bag, there was a tap on the door.

"Thought you wouldn't mind company tonight," Matthew said, entering the room uninvited. He wore nautical pajama bottoms and a bare chest.

"I'm not that easy, Matthew," Dana made clear.

"Definitely wouldn't think that about you."

"As long as we're clear, I wouldn't mind company."

Matthew was quick to make his way to her bed and stretch out next to her. "Is it any good?" he said, looking over the jacket of her book.

"I'll have to let you know. I'm just getting into it."

"You're a reader, are you?"

Dana was forced to look into Matthew's dreamy light brown eyes. His head lay flat on the pillow. His hair, freshly washed, glistened with short loose curls. Dana never imagined she would be sexually aroused by Matthew, but something was stirring inside of her. She blamed it on the romantic setting. Any healthy women would be stimulated under the circumstances.

"Fiction mostly, inspirational sometimes," she said.

"Can I ask you another question?" he said.

"Depends on the question."

"Don't get intense on me."

"Do I look intense?"

"You look like you're going to bite my head off."

Dana had to laugh. She was doing her best to look indifferent, with her desire to kiss Matthew lying on the tip of her tongue. "Ask me," she said.

"What are you looking for in a guy?" Matthew said. Right off, Dana could have named a number of attributes she was looking for in a guy, if not a husband. She wasn't asking for much, basically a somewhat ambitious, non-attached, authentically heterosexual man; one who wasn't threatened by her independence, who was attentive, romantic, spontaneous and fun; who wasn't commitment phobic, and didn't call her a red bone or Creole as if giving her a compliment.

"I'm not looking for one," she replied curtly. Matthew flashed his million-dollar smile, and moved in close enough to make Dana's heart skip a beat. The novel in her hand kept him at a safe distance. *Here goes the booty call,* Dana thought. She geared up to be brutally frank with Matthew. He propped himself on one elbow directly in front of her and twirled her locks in and out of his fingers, soothing Dana in many ways.

"This is a great look on you. I've always wondered what your hair was like before you went Reggae."

"Long and unmanageable," she said without looking up from her book.

"Have I told you about the first time I noticed you on campus?"

She glanced up. "Not that I recall."

"In the Admin building going through your mailbox. I thought to myself, if she looks that fantastic from behind, she must be a knockout head on." Matthew stroked her face with the back of his hand. "You're more than beautiful..."

"Thank you," Dana said. To ignore the tingling in the pit of her stomach, Dana lowered her eyes back to her book.

"You're hard to read," he went on.

Dana looked up again. "Am I? What are you looking to find out?"

"A sign that you like me as I like you."

"I like you, Matthew," Dana said, sounding apologetic.

"Maybe *like* isn't what I had in mind," he said.

Love sure couldn't be. *Sex* was likely the word on his mind. Dana didn't care how entrancing Matthew's gaze was; she wasn't going to let him manipulate her as easy as Omar had.

"Would you be offended if I kiss you again?" He moved in for the kiss.

"Matt," was all that came out of Dana's mouth when his lips pressed against hers. Dana hadn't fallen for Matthew's "You're so beautiful" line, but his delicate kissing, massaging and gentleness, combined with the sensuality of the sea, worked its magic on her. Before the trance wore off, Matthew had shed her clothes and his, down to nothing more than his pale skin and a prophylactic.

"You're a fucking turn on," he said, moving inside of her like he hadn't been on this journey in awhile and didn't know how to navigate the waters. When he finally broke through his fog, they couldn't find a compatible rhythm. Gradually, the yacht swayed to their love making under the stars and the moon. Or rather, Dana wanted to imagine that to be her experience. She had to fake an orgasm to get through it. She couldn't blame Matthew for her lack of arousal. Her mind was at fault. It wouldn't stop thinking about Omar long enough for her to relax and go with it, regardless of how hard Matthew was working to please her.

When Matthew stopped trembling inside of her, he said, "Fucking awesome!"

The next morning, Dana woke up intending to sit on deck and watch the sunrise. Through the porthole she could see the sun hiding behind the clouds. She clasped her hands behind her head and closed her eyes, appreciating the sound of nearby geese ebbing and flowing with the tranquil swaying of *Lady Maya*. There was a sudden thumping on deck that brought her out of tranquility. She listened for another sound. Seconds passed before she heard footsteps.

She shook Matthew awake and whispered, "I think somebody is on board, feel that?"

"That's a current," he said.

"A current doesn't have footsteps."

"It's probably someone motoring by," was Matthew's next speculation. Dana wasn't crazy. It couldn't be someone motoring by and there was no telling who it could be. She shook Matthew again to wake him. When a dog started barking fiercely, Matthew raised his head with a panic-stricken look that told Dana he had some idea who might be walking around upstairs.

"Who is it?" Dana said, ready to jump out of bed behind Matthew.

"I'll be right back." He hopped into his PJ bottoms and left the room in a hurry. Dana *really* hoped the intruder wasn't some chick dropping by unannounced. She thought to put her clothes on. When reaching for her pajama set crumpled on the floor, she changed her mind. If anyone got caught with their pants down, Matthew would. Let him explain to this chick why a naked woman was in his bed. Dana picked up her book and waited with a tight face for whomever it was to walk in, probably a wholesome white girl Matthew had on the side, or should she say she was on the side, and his girlfriend was his main dish. She should've known Matthew was too good to be true, taking her on extravagant weekend getaways, fun adventures, and wining and dining her two and three times a week. No man was *that* perfect.

Matthew dashed back into the room. "Dana…."

"Who is it, Matthew?"

"I know this is going offend you."

"Forget offending me! Who's up there?" Matthew stammered for an answer. "Never mind. She can stay. I'll leave." Dana found her clothes.

"Dana, it's my parents," he confessed.

"So what's the problem? They don't know you're sexually active? I'm lost." She fastened the string of her sweatpants with a yank and threw on her hooded sweatshirt.

"They weren't expecting us to be here."

"If we have to leave, why didn't you say so?" Clearly, Matthew wasn't being *Kosher* with her. If so, his eyes wouldn't be roaming the room for more lies. "Enough with the lies, Matthew. What's going on?"

Matthew sighed. "I beg you not to take this the wrong way, Dana."

"Try me."

"The deal is my parents will shit bricks if they see you. I promise, it's not you, Dana. It's because…well, you're not the kind of girl they approve of for me."

A fly could have flown in Dana's open mouth.

"I'll explain it to you later? You mind hanging out in here for a sec?"

"I'm not hiding from your parents!"

He pressed his finger to his lips. "Shhhh…I'm begging you, Dana." Dana had never seen a grown man look so petrified. Sweat beaded around his upper lip and hairline, and his eyes were practically watering. "I'll get them off deck somehow. Then you can haul ass," he said.

An hour crept by before the yacht was quiet and motionless. Never in a million years would Dana believe she would hide from a man's parents like she was in high school. No, make that junior high.

THE MINUTE DANA PULLED INTO the school parking lot Monday morning Matthew's jeep drove in behind her. She heard his horn toot but pretended not to. She passed up one parking space after another. Once Matthew parked, Dana did as well, far away. She lingered in her car, waiting for Matthew to get lost before exiting. The rest of the workday, Dana avoided Matthew and with good reason.

"Line up, munchkins," Dana told her class at the end of the day. "When you're quiet as mice, I'll open the door." Dana pressed her hand to her lips. The ragged line of black and brown faces squirmed to stand like obedient soldiers until the bell rang. When the bell sounded, she opened the door. Her kids shot into the sun.

"Walk!" she called after them. "Follow me, Juan," she said to a long-faced student left behind. Dana closed her door and walked toward the administration building for a parent/teacher conference in the counselor's office.

They sat in a small circle: Juan's mother, Mrs. Ortiz, Shirley Wyatt, and Dana. "Ask her what's been going on in the home, Dana," Shirley requested. Shirley was the school site counselor assigned to the campus ten days out of the month, and on the verge of retirement. Shirley had worked for the district long before Spanish was a necessary language in California, and felt she was too close to retirement to bother with learning a second language. As a result, she couldn't communicate with many of the students' parents and needed Spanish-speaking teachers to translate. Dana was one of them.

Dana didn't know what was going on in Juan's home. She only knew that Juan was her sweetest student and now he had become a little hell-raiser. It was time she implement a behavior modification plan.

Following an emotional conference with Juan's mother, Shirley handed Dana a business card from her purse. "If you're still on the hunt for a real estate agent, I have a nephew," Shirley said. "He can help you find a good deal. His name is Reginald. I'll tell him to expect your call."

"Thanks, Shirley."

"Glad to help. Root canal. Gotta go." Shirley rushed out of the office for her dentist appointment.

Back at her classroom, Dana stopped mid-step near the door when she found Matthew sitting at her desk.

"Hey there," he said, standing to greet her. He wore his tight smile, loose-legged cargos that could stand ironing, and a short sleeve plaid shirt. "I bought something for you." A vibrant iridescent blue Betta fish with its long flowing tail swam in a fish bowl on her desk. It was the most striking Betta Dana had seen, pure beauty.

"I don't know what to say," she said.

"I thought he might complement your collection."

"I need to get in my desk." Dana tentatively approached Matthew.

"I screwed up, didn't I? Can I explain?"

"You've explained and I understand."

"Dana, it's more complex than you think."

"I'm not the kind of girl your parents approve of. That's pretty plain and simple. Would you have introduced me to your parents if I was a white girl?"

"Danaaa…it's not that either."

"Why don't you come back when you figure out what it is? Excuse me." Matthew blocked her from getting her purse and leaving.

"This weekend wasn't about a lay for me, if that's what you think."

"Really? What was it about, Matthew?"

"Would you believe much more?" He took hold of her hands. Dana wished he wouldn't, not in her classroom, not where anyone who walked by her open door could see them faced off intimately. The sound of balls bouncing and the laughter and chatter coming in from the playground couldn't block out the uneasy quiet. He reached up and caressed her face. Dana pulled away.

"I'm leaving." She found her purse in her desk drawer. "If you're staying, lock up."

"You want the truth?" Matthew said.

Dana decided to listen. "I think you owe me that much."

"It's my parents, Dana. They are fucking die-hard elitist extremist who expect me to uphold the family pedigree. Personally, I disagree with their conformist code of beliefs."

"If that were true, Matthew, why'd you ask me to hide? I introduced you to everybody important to me, and you didn't give a second thought about hiding me from your parents! Do you know how that made me feel?" Dana hated she raised her voice a note, giving Matthew the satisfaction of knowing she cared.

"I feel obliged to them for many reasons, Dana, but it's becoming a real pain in my ass, I tell ya." He held both her hands again. "You're coming to my parents' house."

"What for?" Dana said, her smirk making clear her lack of interest.

"Their annual Christmas party. I told them all about you. I don't care what they think. I know how I feel about you. Will you come?"

Against her better judgment, Dana gave Matthew a slow, reluctant nod. This relationship was headed for another dead end. She could see it coming head on.

Never Wonder

Tempest invented compelling, eye-catching scenery to draw clients to her department. Vivid, sexy colors attracted the eye. She kept that in mind when displaying new merchandise. This winter, shades of powder pink, dark olive, chocolate, and slate gray were vogue.

She usually wore whatever style was in and encouraged her staff to do the same. Today Tempest wore a powder pink button-up, a chocolate mini skirt and calf-high chocolate leather boots. Three customers stopped her and asked where they could buy her exact outfit. She directed them to her department. While she was helping Susan coordinate outfits, her cell phone vibrated at her hip. Tempest let it go straight to voicemail then peeked at the number. It was Robert. She rolled her eyes and ignored the call.

She knocked on the dressing room door. "Let me know if this works…with this?"

Susan opened the door without inhibition, her nakedness as normal to Tempest's eyes as the sun. She couldn't count how many naked bodies she had seen, from pale lean figures with swooping pear-shaped breasts and bright pink eyes, to chocolate ones with areolas as dark as hers. She handed Susan a pair of black herringbone gauchos and a Tarantola grape angora cardigan.

Susan was one of Tempest's oldest and most loyal customers, as far back as when she was new to Nordstrom and working to establish her reputation in retail. With the help of customers like Susan, who never left the store without a receipt tallying thousands of dollars, Tempest was able to develop a following. If she moved to another department, her loyal customers would track her down. It was her service they loved most. She followed the legendary Nordstrom service policy to the letter, making the customers feel special and pampered. Now that she was a department manager and had assistants to help with day-to-day sales, customers like Susan continuously requested her help.

"If you need anything else, Susan, I'm around the corner," Tempest said. She hadn't made it back to the service desk before her cell phone vibrated again. This time it was *Quinton*. She had gone overboard giving out her number. She met Quinton at another Hollywood club she had gone to with Yasmine. He's a fireman, bald, black and beautiful as the night. *Robert,* she met in Westwood while on her lunch break. *Parker,* she met while at the gym with Dana. She was bored out of her mind, walking in place on the treadmill. Parker was running next to her, making her laugh. He asked if he could call her sometime. *Why not,* Tempest thought. She didn't know what Parker did for a living. "*I'm a businessman,"* he told her. Dana summed him up as a drug dealer. He was rolling like one in a candy red, convertible Jaguar XK. Tempest went out with him once. Otherwise, she wasn't interested in Parker, Robert, Quinton nor the tall baller with the kind eyes, and was ready to have her number changed again.

Her plan to get over Sterling backfired. The more guys she met, the more she thought about Sterling. She knew what happened between Diamond and Sterling really happened, but she could no longer conjure up the hurt and pain linked to the experience. It didn't help that the season for the Spartans was close to over. Their losing streak would take them out of the playoff lineup, which meant Sterling would be home sooner than later.

"I'm positively in love with it all," Susan said, and dumped a pile of clothes on the sales counter. "I need shoes. Shoes, shoes, shoes."

"Jennifer is waiting for you downstairs. I had her pull several of your favorite brands to go with your outfits."

"That's why I love you, Tempest." Susan kissed the air on both sides of her face. Tempest's cell phone vibrated again. This time it was a guy named Latrell. He went straight to voice mail.

After work, Tempest had things to do, thanks be to God. Her favorite fabric store on La Brea was her first stop. She was searching for the right fabric for the quilt she had yet to sew for Nadine and Will's new baby. She took slow leisurely steps down the aisles, feeling like she always did in a fabric store – tingly inside as she examined the striking fabrics she came across. There were linens, chenille, velvets from Italy, paisley, Indian prints, and whatever fabric fanatics like her fancied. Everybody had their muse. Fabric was Tempest's inspiration. She loved to walk the floors of top-rated fabric stores for hours, buying fabrics she sometimes never used, dreaming of her designs and forgetting the time. When Tempest finally came across the fabric she wanted for her quilt, she was running late for praise team rehearsal.

She and Yasmine arrived in the church parking lot at the same time, ten minutes late. Yasmine was mad about spending the next two hours rehearsing, and possibly missing *Dancing With the Stars,* her favorite show, now that an extra day of rehearsal was added in preparation for the Christmas program. Tempest talked Yasmine into joining the team, mainly because the program could use Yasmine's songstress voice, as well as give Tempest something to do other than think about Sterling all night. In addition, Tempest recommitted herself to helping out in Children's Church on Sundays, and was contemplating the usher board, just to keep busy.

Yasmine marched up in her winter white designer jogger with the face of Evileen. Stewardship wasn't Yasmine's thing. She paid her tithes, attended church on Sundays, and Bible study on Wednesdays. Anything more with church folk went beyond Yasmine's patience, especially the gossip. Word did spread like wild fire at New Jerusalem, Tempest must say. The entire congregation heard she had cancelled her wedding plans, practically overnight. They were worse than the Paparazzi with the questions. But even gossip couldn't keep Tempest out of the one place that lifted her spirits and gave her hope.

"Don't ever say I wasn't a best friend to you," Yasmine said, with one hand on her hip and her Bible in the other hand.

"You need Jesus," Tempest said and laughed.

"Throw the Bible at me all you want. I'm missing my show!"

Following rehearsal, Tempest begged Yasmine to go to dinner with her. With thirty minutes left of her program remaining, Yasmine couldn't be convinced. As a back-up plan, Tempest called Dana, who was having dinner with Matthew.

Tempest's awaiting loneliness met her at her front door when she arrived home. Before she entered her condo, her next-door neighbor, Emit, stopped her. Emit, who was about her father's age, was nice enough to listen for her to come in safely on late nights.

"I have something that belongs to you, young lady," Emit said, appearing at his door. "I've been meaning to give these to you. Every other day I get something in my box of yours. I don't think that postman can tell the difference between two fifty-six and two fifty-seven."

"Thank you, Mr. Emit," Tempest said, taking the stack of mail from his outstretched hand.

"Haven't seen any fresh flowers on your doorstep lately. Your boyfriend run out of money?" he teased, his coffee-stained smile half hidden behind his graying mustache. Emit must have detected her mood switch and noticed the tears in her eyes. He reacted by withdrawing indoors.

"Well, you have a good night," he said and closed the door in her face.

Tempest closed herself inside her condo, fell back against the door, and sighed. "Get over it already," she told herself.

The letter from Sterling was the first envelope she noticed in the pile, making her heart descend at record speed and her hands forget their purpose. "Jesus," Tempest whispered and dropped down onto her sofa. She picked it out of the pile of junk mail, holding it like it contained a lethal dose of anthrax. She had survived Thanksgiving, was close to surviving Christmas, and by the grace of God hadn't lost her job from those stupid spur-of-the-moment trips she took. Hearing from Sterling, after weeks of not, might throw her headlong into another depression.

She sat the letter aside and threw the rest of the junk mail in the trash. She then walked to her room to change out of her work clothes and into a night chemise. The letter followed her. The television, she hoped, would take her mind off it. She turned to *E! True Hollywood Story,* a rerun of Vanessa Williams. Visions of the letter dominated the television screen. She got up and walked to the bathroom to brush her teeth. The letter was there too, in the vanity mirror.

Tempest tried to sleep, laying face up in bed, watching the canopy fabric flutter from the night air blowing through her bedroom window. She curled up on her side, staring through the chiffon drapes, watching the shadows of the trees rustling in the wind. On a clear, smog-free day in L.A, she could sometimes see the marina from her bed, one of the benefits of living in Fox Hills she loved so much. Everything was nearby. The Westfield Mall was in walking distance, Marina del Rey a hop, skip and jump away, and she had easy access to major freeways, she thought to keep her mind distracted.

Her name and address written in Sterling's cryptic penmanship inserted itself back into her mind. She closed her eyes, pressing her widespread hands to the bed like Jesus on the cross, fighting her impulse to rush into the living room, tear open the envelope and read what was inside. Just when she had gotten through the night without crying herself to sleep, without suffering through nausea and chest pains, this shows up. She should have thrown the letter in the garbage with the rest of her junk mail.

Throughout the night, the letter stayed in the living room like a visitor that didn't belong, keeping Tempest from closing her eyes. She lay for as long as she could, staring at the television, seeing images and hearing no sound.

"Forget it!" She had to find out what Sterling had to say. It would kill her if she didn't.

Tee,

I know you don't want to talk to me, but I hope you'll read this letter. You are the air that I breathe, baby, my life. You're my everything, Tee. Nothing feels the same without you, no tackle, no interception, making the Pro Bowl. Nothing. You know how I do, celebrate on one knee, thanking God for every win. You taught me that, baby, to be grateful for everything God gives me and never to take my blessings for granted. When we took the Broncos Monday night, I didn't get on my knees to thank God. I got on my knees praying you'll come back to me. I pray every night, Tee, hoping somebody up there will hear me. I don't know what else I can do to get you back, to show you how sorry I am for hurting you. You know I don't believe in losing. I can't lose you, Tee. I love you more than my own life! Hit me back.

#53

Raindrops of tears funneled down Tempest's chin and splattered the white paper. She read the letter repeatedly, reading more between the lines than what was written. It wasn't like Sterling to pour out his heart. She pictured tears in his eyes as he wrote. She had seen Sterling cry only once, when he ran across his father in downtown Los Angeles, who was passed out drunk on a bus stop bench, almost unrecognizable to Sterling. Tempest cried with him, her heart feeling Sterling's pain like his dad were her own. Every tackle Sterling made was for his dad, hoping he was out there watching. Every dime Sterling earned was, in part, for his father, to help his dad get off the streets and clean up his life. Otherwise, Sterling rarely showed the softest side of himself. Tempest knew that side of Sterling better than anyone. With the letter in her hand, she dozed off wondering when Sterling was coming home.

WHY DID SHE LET HERSELF wonder? The next day after work she wandered near Sterling's mother's house, like a police cruiser casing the neighborhood. By the second go round, she wondered what she was doing, but couldn't get the steering wheel to turn westbound and head toward home. She had a deep craving, worse than Nadine's craving for sour pickles, to find out when Sterling was coming home.

By her third casing, Tempest drove slowly down the cross street of his mother's house. Ms. Alexander lived in a section of south central Los Angeles where the houses could use an extreme makeover. Rumor had it, many of the people in the neighborhood were on welfare, and because of gang violence, entering the neighborhood was like entering a war zone. But looks were misleading and rumors weren't always true. Tempest knew for a fact Sterling's mother had never been on welfare and was a hard-working woman who did her best raising three kids, for the most part alone, and keeping Sterling away from the drugs and crime of his neighborhood.

Tempest cruised past Sterling's mother's house too afraid to stop, but it was just her freakin' luck Victoria, Sterling's sister, stepped out of her boyfriend's car, catching her dead to rights. Tempest thought of sliding down in her seat and driving on. She stopped and rolled down her car window, lowering her sunglasses.

"Victoria...Hi!" Tempest said. Victoria's boyfriend drove off without speaking.

"You looking for Sterling?" Victoria asked dryly, like Tempest wasn't the only chick to cruise by the house looking for Sterling. Obviously, he had a fan club. She didn't take Victoria's crabby attitude personally. Victoria was that way with everyone, much like Charlene.

"Is Ms. Alexander home?" Tempest asked, not to tell a lie.

"I wouldn't know. I haven't been here." Victoria walked off carrying two-year-old Roland on her hip, and rubbing her expectant belly. For twenty, Victoria walked and acted like a tired forty-year-old woman. Having babies so young, Tempest guessed, aged a person.

"You coming in or not?" Victoria said, looking back.

Ms. Alexander lived on a narrow street. Tempest made a three-point turn and parked out front. The duplex Ms. Alexander lived in was a one story Victorian style house that the owner of the property had visibly split down the middle, converting a four-bedroom house to maximize profits. Ms. Alexander had occupied the right side of the duplex long before Tempest knew Sterling. The occupancy on the left side of the duplex was like an expressway, residents moving in and out month after month. The "For Rent" sign on the lawn meant currently no one was living there.

Walking toward the duplex, Tempest tugged at her skirt, which suddenly felt unprofessionally short. When she stepped onto the porch, she had to rub her stomach to settle it.

"Ma! Somebody's here to see you!" Victoria called out from inside.

"Who?" Ms. Alexander called back.

"Come and see!"

"Who is it, Vicky?" Ms. Alexander insisted.

"Come and see!"

"Child!" Ms. Alexander said, as if not in the mood to play guessing games with Victoria. Tempest remembered that way back when, during the time Sterling lived at home, Ms. Alexander ate dinner early and went to bed early after working the graveyard shift as a nurse's aide. Tempest wasn't sure where Ms. Alexander worked these days, but she felt bad for disturbing her. She recalled how Ms. Alexander fussed at everybody in the house for waking her up.

"Why're you standing outside? Come in," Victoria said.

Through the screen door, Tempest watched Victoria leave the room. She took a deep breath and entered the house. Alone in the small living room, Tempest sank into the soft cushions of the sofa. On top of the colossal oak entertainment center across from her were Sterling's trophies, dating back to flag football. Framed pictures of Sterling and his two sisters were everywhere, and Ms. Alexander's collection of crystal filled what space remained on the shelves.

Tempest wouldn't say anything in Ms. Alexander's two-bedroom apartment was high quality, except for the champagne-colored sofa she was sitting on, the six-chair dining table and large flat screen TV purchased by Sterling with his signing bonus money. Otherwise, most of the furniture was outdated. The white walls were yellowed and the wood floors needed refinishing. Everything had its place, though, and Ms. Alexander did her best to keep a neat and clean home. If for no other reason, Tempest prayed Sterling would sign a new contract so he could buy his mother the house of her dreams and move her to a better neighborhood.

"Tempest?" Ms. Alexander said, speaking her name as though she had forgotten her. "Child, I didn't know it was you out here. Vicky, why didn't you say it was Tempest?" Ms. Alexander sucked air through her teeth and shook her head. "I'm sorry, Tempest." Tempest came close to crying when Ms. Alexander welcomed her with a big hug. "It's so good to see you," she said, kissing Tempest cheek to cheek, her smooth skin, close to the color of black licorice, feeling as soft as lambskin. If Sterling didn't get his height from his father, he certainly inherited the gene from Ms. Alexander. Tempest wore heeled boots, Ms. Alexander house slippers, and they stood eye to eye.

"Hi, Ms. Alexander," Tempest said softly.

"What'd I tell you about calling me *Ms.* anything? I ain't but forty-nine and you making me sound *old*. You must be coming from work. You're always dressed so nice. Look at me." Ms. Alexander tightened the belt to her robe and smoothed back her hair that hung stiffly at her neck. "Bree!" Ms. Alexander called over her shoulder.

"What, Momma?" Bree called back from another room.

"Don't be whatin' me, girl! Come out here. Somebody came by to see you! And bring me my cigarettes!" Ms. Alexander sucked air through her teeth again. "Sit down, Tempest." They both sat on the couch.

"I caught her driving by like she wasn't fixing to stop," Victoria said as she walked back into the room and sat little Roland in his highchair.

"I was going to stop," Tempest lied.

Bree came running out of the room. "Tempest!" Bree nearly jumped into Tempest's lap and hugged her. "You came to take me shopping?" Bree asked.

"That's all this girl thinks about." Ms. Alexander flicked the lighter and took a long drag of her cigarette, her colorful acrylic nails fanning her face. "Can you say hi first?"

"Hi!" Bree flashed an exaggerated smile. "Now, can we go shopping? Please, please, please! I need new clothes, *bad*." She laid her head on Tempest's shoulder and pouted her bottom lip. Tempest absolutely loved Sterling's little sister. At twelve, Bree was too funny and cute. After divorcing Sterling's father, Ms. Alexander had two kids by the Puerto Rican man she once lived with, Victoria and Bree's father. Both Victoria and Bree inherited his bedroom black eyes and bronzy skin. And with lips like Sterling's, the kind that steal attention away from their eyes, Bree was already supermodel material in Tempest's book.

"You need, you need," Ms. Alexander parroted. "What you need, Bree? Sterling sent you money for school clothes, child." Tempest's heart skipped a beat hearing Sterling's name. She wanted to ask about him so badly her mouth salivated.

"Sterling's a cheapskate," Bree declared, making Tempest laugh inside.

"You hungry, Tempest?" Ms. Alexander asked her.

Tempest wasn't hungry and hadn't intended to stay. It was only right for her to stay, however, and at least act as though she came by to visit Sterling's mother. She sat at the dining table with Bree, admiring Bree's new school pictures, while Ms. Alexander fixed her a bowl of chili beans and Victoria fed little Roland.

Tempest didn't need to ask about Sterling. Victoria and Bree volunteered everything she needed to know, but didn't care to. It wasn't easy for her to hear Sterling's name repeatedly and breathe at the same time. The more Tempest heard, the angrier she became. She listened, blank faced, never letting her true feelings show past the tears burning behind her eyes.

"Sterling's not coming home. He got picked for the Pro Bowl," Victoria said.

"Don't tell half the story, Victoria," Sterling's mother chimed in. "He's staying back to work out some more, Tempest."

"It's not fair! Why can't we go to Hawaii?" Bree whined.

"Who's gone pay for us to go?" said Sterling's mother.

"Your son can pay, that's who? He got enough money," Victoria said.

"I don't want him wasting all his money on *me*."

"When he signs his new contract, he'll be rich, and I can go shopping anytime I want to. Ha-ha," Bree said.

Whatever, Tempest thought, concluding Sterling stayed in Minneapolis to hang out with Diamond. If Tempest had it in her heart to forgive Sterling, she didn't any more.

Ms. Alexander handed her one of Sterling's latest game cards, featuring an action shot of Sterling making a tackle. Then came his recent article in *Sports Illustrated*. Tempest gave both a quick once-over and kindly placed them on the table. Besides, she had read the article, compliments of Will. Basically, the Spartans will likely re-up Sterling's contract. If not, Sterling will have his pick of teams as a free agent, as if she freakin' cared.

"I'd better go," Tempest said, after eating a spoonful of chili beans and taking one bite of her cornbread.

"Don't leave," Bree hung onto Tempest's arm.

"I'll be back. I promise," Tempest said.

"When?" Bree wanted to know.

"Soon," Tempest said vaguely. She hugged Victoria, promised Bree she would take her shopping one day, and walked quickly to the door with Ms. Alexander following her.

"When I talk to that son of mines, I'll tell him you stopped by."

"Don't, please, Ms. Alexander, " Tempest begged.

"You and Sterling are too much for me," Ms. Alexander said, shaking her head and chuckling. "You ain't fooling me none. I know why you came by. I wish Sterling was here. He'd be too happy to see you!"

Right, Tempest thought.

"He finally fessed up to what he did and I don't blame you for telling him where to go. Start having babies with a man, you put up with more than you oughtta'." Ms. Alexander glanced over her shoulder at Victoria and turned her annoyed eyes back on Tempest. "You wanna know what I told Sterling? Nobody made you eat the cake, boy, so live with the bellyache."

That, Tempest found worth a laugh. Had things worked out between her and Sterling, it would have been nice to have a mother-in-law like Ms. Alexander who never let her son get away with making excuses. There wasn't an excuse for what Sterling did to her.

"Thanks again for dinner," Tempest said sincerely.

"You didn't eat but a bite."

"I'm sorry." She gave Ms. Alexander a hug. Sterling's mother returned her hug so tightly she squeezed the hurt and disappointment out of Tempest—temporarily anyway.

"If you want to know, Sterling will be home in January for that Super Bowl game out there in San Diego. Stop back by then."

Tempest couldn't think with a clear head when she drove off. Anticipation jetted through her bloodstream, filling her head with crazy ideas.

For the Sake of Brotherly Love

Dana's new realtor was Reginald Moore. He had called Dana about a property he thought might interest her.

"What do you think so far?" Reginald asked Dana. He wore trendy black frame glasses that made him look more shady than businesslike. His dark complexion was blotched with a lighter shade, and he looked like he could stand some exercise.

"Did termites live here? What's with the floor?" Dana's boots crunched down on the wood scarred with cigarette burns and other atrocities when she took another step inside the house.

"Before you run out, check it out. You may like it."

Dana's mouth contorted. "Maybe...I don't know," she said tiredly.

This was the fifth dump Reginald had shown her. The house was a fixer-upper that had been on the market for six months. Dana guessed that meant her chances to buy it were better, if she wanted to buy it. She wasn't bubbling with excitement given the location and the looks of the place. The grass hadn't been mowed for God knows how long; the wood was splintered; the windows were barred, and the architecture was from some prehistoric time.

Finished with his burger, Reginald was now slurping down coffee. "You mind?" he asked and lit a cigarette, not caring if she minded or not. "You asked me to show you houses in your price range," Reginald continued with smoke coming out his wide nostrils. "You're looking at it. I can make an offer on this dump, but let's talk turkey. I know you think you need a *house*. But I know of a two-bedroom condo priced below market value—"

"No condos, please, Reginald," Dana interjected. "I want a house. Having a backyard is important to me."

Reginald found that funny. "With a tire swing too? You must have kids."

Dana cleared her throat. "No…but I will..one day. And even if I don't, I read somewhere that I'll gain more equity buying a house versus a condo."

"Worry about tomorrow when tomorrow comes. If you let me be your guide, Dana, show you what I know, you'll love me for it in five years. This listing I'm talking about just came on the market, and won't last past tonight. We can ride over right now."

"Where is it?"

"Paramount, part of a new development."

"Paramount?" Dana shook her head. "Sounds like too much of a commute and too far from my job. I hate traffic." Reginald delayed his response while he opened the security screen to flick out his cigarette butt. He returned to the fireplace mantel to slurp more coffee.

"Nine times out of ten you'll change jobs before you change residences," he said.

Dana let out a heavy sigh. "I don't know…" She sighed again, now wishing she had accepted Matthew's offer to tag along. She needed someone with real estate sense to consult.

With evening traffic backing up the highway, it took Dana forty-five minutes to get to Paramount. What a waste of time. She couldn't get inside. The key to the condo wasn't in the lock box as Reginald thought. Dana wouldn't have been so disappointed if her hopes weren't raised when she entered the complex. Despite the deteriorating community nearby, with laundry airing in public and rowdy kids taking over the street, the condo looked ideal for her first piece of real estate. The stucco complex had forty units total, a gated entrance, one-car garages, and a private patio on ground level units, perfect for relaxing on the white patio furniture she recently seen advertised.

The listing agent couldn't show the place until the next day, Reginald reported. Dana hoped and prayed it would be on the market when she returned.

On her way home, Dana traveled the back roads to avoid the 405 freeway. The drizzle coming down made traffic unbearable. If she had to sit in it for another minute, she would pull her locks out. She had come out of the airport tunnel and was driving up Sepulveda when Carmen's Acura caught her eye. The *"D.C. Is For Lovers"* bumper sticker on the back window made it instantly recognizable.

"Carmen!" Dana yelled, blowing her horn and waving her hand out of the window to flag Carmen down. Carmen drove on like she was in a hurry. Dana sped up to catch her and missed the green light and Carmen too. "Great!" Dana slumped over the steering wheel. Carmen was the perfect person to talk to about buying the condo she adored. She quickly thought to dial Carmen's cell phone. Carmen didn't answer.

Not far ahead, Dana saw Carmen's car slow and the brake lights flash before turning onto a side street. As soon as the light changed, Dana shot through the intersection and missed her turn because of oncoming traffic and impolite drivers. To catch up to Carmen, she took a back street, searching for Carmen's car in the night. How could Carmen have disappeared so quickly? To the left of her was an airport parking structure, to the right of her a strip of park. As soon as Dana saw Carmen's car parked on the side of the road, a crazy motorcyclist cut her off, forcing her to swerve to avoid a side swipe. The man parked and hopped off his bike like he owned the road. Curse words came to Dana's mind, ready to fly out her mouth. Dana lowered her window. Seeing the man without his helmet, however, stopped Dana from saying anything. She couldn't think of a bad word to say to a man that gorgeous.

A car horn blew and sent Dana on her way. She glanced in her rearview mirror to steal a final look at the man and swore she saw Carmen emerge into the light. The guy wrapped his arms around Carmen, or the woman Dana swore looked just like Carmen, that is. Dana found herself caught in the middle of the intersection, questioning if she should go home or turn back. She decided to turn back.

Dana crept her car up the street, increasing the tempo of her windshield wipers to combat the escalating rain. The woman and man had disappeared. But why hadn't Carmen's car moved, and how far could the guy have gone without his bike? Inkling told Dana to park on the opposite side of the street and wait. She had to be sure it wasn't Carmen, for her brother's sake. Although Omar was the last person Dana wanted to agree with, his certainty that Carmen had something on the side didn't escape her rational mind. And what about her gut feeling and what Devon had said about Carmen's bizarre behavior?

While watching for Carmen to return to her car, another clue came to Dana's mind that made her gasp. The motorcycle! That night at Carmen's house, she heard one outside. She also remembered the crazed look in Carmen's eyes and the lie Carmen told her about her neighbor selling peanuts at ten o'clock at night. *Give me a break!*

Dana needed only to sit a minute longer to confirm her suspicions. Carmen and the guy suddenly appeared out of nowhere. Instinctively, Dana slouched in her seat and rolled up her window a fraction, not to be seen or heard. She felt silly watching the two of them having what appeared to be an innocent conversation. That changed in the next minute, however. Their muffled interaction rose to shameless shouting. Dana sat up, clinging to the door handle, ready to run across the street to intervene, fearing for Carmen's life at one point before realizing Carmen was the aggressor in this lover's quarrel.

What happened next made Dana cover her mouth. "This cannot be real...," she mumbled. Carmen then jumped into her car and sped off. The guy took off after her, his bike leaving a trail of rubber behind. It all happened so fast Dana wouldn't have believed it if she hadn't been a spectator. Devon wouldn't believe it either, nor her mother. Good thing she had a camera phone.

DANA RUSHED INTO THE KITCHEN expecting to find Corrine. Instead, she found Omar and a room reeking of fresh paint.

"I didn't know you would be here," Dana said, caught off guard.

Omar looked down at her. "What's up?" he said. He was standing on a ladder, adding finishing touches to his paint job. Dana covered her eyes like a visor to adjust to the bright lime green room. She started to smile. Maybe if Omar had smiled, she would have. Omar went back to painting as if she wasn't there. *Be that way*, Dana thought and went about her business. She made her way around the clutter in the room to pour herself an ice-cold glass of water. Corrine's project was finally complete, and apparently, Omar had spent the day working on it. Dana threw back the glass of water, relieving her burning throat and cooling her temper. She rinsed out her glass in a hurry and left the kitchen.

Closed in her bedroom, Dana paced from one side of the room to the other. A minute ago she was boiling over inside to tell Devon, her mother, somebody about what had to be reality TV. Now she couldn't get Omar off of her mind. She removed her corduroy blazer to cool off. First Carmen, now this! Her mother's little ploy wasn't going to work.

After coming completely out of her work clothes, and changing into shorts and a tee, Dana sat on her bed to think before doing something she would regret. What should she do with the information she had on Carmen, information that would hurt her brother so deeply she wanted to hurt Carmen in return?

The door unexpectedly opened. Omar had the nerve to stick his head inside her room without knocking. "Let your mother know the leftover paint is in the garage," he said.

"Are you in a hurry?" Dana said.

"Yeah. Why?"

Dana thought for a minute, wondering if she should consult with Omar or not. "I need your advice on something," she said anyway.

"On what?"

"Something, Omar, okay?"

"I'll stay where I am, if you don't mind." He gestured toward his paint-stained old jeans and T-shirt like he didn't want to dirty up the place, then stood like a barricade in the doorway with crossed arms. Dana didn't want to be any nearer to Omar than he visibly didn't want to be near her. She didn't even know why she was telling Omar any of this, but she had to tell somebody before she picked up the phone and called Carmen herself. Aside from that, telling Omar was a safe place to deposit her secret until she could decide what to do with it.

"So, what advice do you need from me?" Omar said. Dana handed him her cell phone. "What's this?"

"Just watch, Omar."

Omar hit the video play button. Dana didn't have to watch with him to know what his eyes were taking in. She sat, as if on needles, waiting for his reaction. Scene by scene, Dana replayed in her mind Carmen yelling at the guy, telling him how much she hated him for whatever he had done to her; him shouting back how much he loved Carmen and would never do "that," whatever *that* meant. Next came the slap. Dana winced hearing it again, having a vivid account of how violently Carmen whacked the guy across the face. She recounted him grabbing Carmen by the shoulders, jerking her like he intended to return Carmen's slap with equal force, and Carmen coming close to beating him to death.

"This part you won't believe," Dana said, her face burning with anger and embarrassment over what Omar was about to see next—Carmen and her man kissing as if they would screw right on the park grounds. When Omar hit the stop button, Dana waited for classic Omar to show up.

"Okay," he merely said without a twitch or a laugh playing around his mouth.

Dana threw up her arms. "After what you saw, you say okay? You could at least say I told you so. You know you want to. Go ahead and say it, Omar."

"I don't have anything to say, other than I know how your brother must feel." Omar sounded so somber Dana wanted to shake a laugh out of him.

"The thing is, Devon doesn't know and I don't know how to tell him."

"Why would you?"

"Why?" Dana jumped from her seat. "Did you not see what I saw? That lying, cheating bitch was kissing another man in my face! It's my business to tell my brother. Carmen could be up to anything. What if she runs off with this man, leaves my brother in the cold and takes my nephew with her?" Dana waited for Omar to laugh and say she was being melodramatic. He shifted in his work boots, watching her from another angle, his expression still somber and unchanging.

"Not every man wants to know his girl has something on the side." Was that a poke at her for telling him about Matthew? If so, she felt it.

"The difference is, Carmen is not Devon's girl. She's his *wife*, Omar. "

"If it was the other way around, would you tell?"

"What does that mean?"

"If you caught your brother cheating, would you tell Carmen?"

"For one, Devon would never cheat on his wife. Don't you think I know my own brother?"

"Don't be so sure." Omar glanced at his cell phone. "You good? 'Cause I gotta go."

A crushing feeling in Dana's chest clogged her larynx. "Bye," she managed to say.

Omar hurried off, leaving Dana no surer of what to do than before she confided in him. All he did was prove they had lost whatever brought them together to begin with and had nothing in common anymore, not even the same viewpoint. Making sure Omar was out of her sight and mind, Dana peeked between the living room blinds, wondering where he was speeding off to so fast that he forgot to turn on his headlights. The thought of another woman crossed her mind.

For advice that she could use, Dana called Tempest.

"I was just thinking about you, girl," Tempest said before Dana could get a word in. "Guess where we're going?"

"Where?"

"To the Super Bowl!"

"Who's we?"

"You, me, and whoever else wants to roll. You know it's in San Diego this year?"

"Where are we staying, and even if I could afford to go to the game, it's sold out by now, isn't it?"

"We're not going to the game. We're getting our party on in the streets, girl!" Tempest said.

"Party in the streets with egotistical ball players and gold-digging scuzzies? Count me out."

"You're such a party pooper, Dana."

"I hate those scenes."

"Come on. It'll be fun!" Tempest begged.

"I really can't, Temp. It's not worth the money I don't have. I may be putting in an offer on a condo tomorrow, if I like it."

"That's good, girl. We can celebrate at the Super Bowl. If I cover the hotel and food and we do a turnaround, will you go with me? Please, Dana. I really need you there, for support."

"Support for what?" When Tempest grew quiet, Dana said, "Don't tell me sorry Sterling will be there! I should've known you were up to something. Ask Yasmine to go with you, Temp. That's more her scene than mine and she'll be better support than me when it comes to Sterling. You know how I feel."

"I was kinda hoping the three of us would go and split the cost. I'm broke too, girl."

"When did you talk to Sterling, anyway?"

"It's a long story. And I'm not trying to see Sterling. I want him to see me."

"Am I supposed to get it?" Dana said.

"Just think about it, Dana, okay? You have a whole month. You never know, maybe you'll have the money by then. Pray on it, girl."

"Yeah, maybe some money will fall out of the sky."

Tempest laughed. "Bye, girl." She hung up, not giving Dana time to ask for her advice, which was probably best. She needed to sleep on this Carmen situation before she acted. Like Omar said, what if Devon doesn't want to know the truth about Carmen?

As if her mother was waiting in the wings for Omar to leave and her underhanded plan to reunite the two of them to work, Corrine returned home not long after Omar left.

"How does the kitchen look?" Corrine said, walking into the house.

"Omar finished the job, Mom, if that's what you're asking."

"That wasn't what I meant, Dana, but I'm glad to hear it." Corrine placed her armload of textbooks on the formal dining table and made a beeline to the kitchen. "Beautiful! Beautiful! Beautiful!" Her mother squealed with clasped hands. Dana begged to differ. Omar left smudge marks on the ceiling, and she could see areas where the old color was bleeding through. But at least he took his time to clean up after himself. With room to roam, Dana prepared herself a salad.

"How's your house hunting coming along?" Corrine asked, biting into an orange slice.

"Better than I thought. I think I found something I like."

"Take your time, Dana, and don't rush."

"Rush? Do you know how long I've been looking for a place, Mom?"

"Well, try not to buy the first piece of property you come across. A home is one of the most important investments you'll make in a lifetime."

"Did you feel this way at my age?" Dana asked, while dicing fresh carrots and cucumbers from the garden.

"Eager to buy a house?"

"No, like you were stuck in a rut when you should be transitioning to the next phase of your life."

Corrine laughed. "Transitioning to what phase?"

"You know, making progress."

"A word of advice: your next phase won't get here any faster worrying about it, and when it does get here, you'll wonder why you were in such a rush to get to it. But to answer your question, when I was your age I was married and had your brother. Plus I had too much to do than worry about the next phase of my life. Why don't you do something to occupy yourself in the meantime? What about getting your master's degree in education? That ought to keep you busy." Her mother slipped that little suggestion in whenever the chance presented itself.

"Never mind," Dana said. "Speaking of marriage and kids, how's Devon and Carmen getting along?" Dana said this casually, although her mother probably picked up the sarcasm in her voice.

"Doing as well as any other married couple I suppose," Corrine said. Her mother's philosophy on marriage was to stay out of it and let married people work out their own problems. That position didn't seem to stop her mother from staying in her business. Being single must not count. Dana shook her head and kept her thoughts to herself. She handed her mother a bowl of her famous homemade chicken salad and sat across from Corrine to enjoy her own.

"You could have told me Omar was coming over, Mom," Dana said to change subjects.

"I could've, if I thought you would mind. Frankly, I told Omar he could finish the job some other time. He has enough on his mind."

"Like *what*?"

"His mother, Dana," Corrine said, her tone wiping the laugh from Dana's mouth.

"Did something happen to Mrs. Penn?" Dana's heart braced for bad news.

"She's in the hospital. Omar didn't tell you?"

As Good As Over

"Can I get you another cup of coffee?" the receptionist asked Carmen. Carmen nodded in appreciation, hoping another cup would help clear her head. If Dr. Jessup's little white pill helped to alleviate the worse anxiety attack she ever had last night, its effects returned this morning with a vengeance, punishing her for taking it when she knew better not to. She woke up feeling like she was trapped in a fog and couldn't see her way to the bathroom. When she went to hop out of bed, a massive headache walloped her. A crane slamming against her forehead repeatedly couldn't have been more painful.

"Here you go." The receptionist handed Carmen another steaming Styrofoam cup of coffee. She thanked the woman and took a sip, watching the woman walk back to her desk, and wondering if her unsociable attitude was an indicator of what she could expect from the investigator.

Gordon Matheson was his name. He was in charge of investigating sexual harassment complaints on behalf of human services. He and Carmen had played phone tag before finally connecting. Really, Carmen avoided the man's calls for as long as possible, hoping she wouldn't have to go through with this interview. She wouldn't have either, if Kendall had admitted the truth and cleared this mess up last night. Why lie?

"I swear on my dead dad's grave I did not file a complaint of any kind against you," Kendall had told her.

"You're a damn lie, Kendall! Who else would?"

"Why would I do that to you? What the fuck kind of person do you think I am?"

"You're an asshole, that's who you are! You've taken enough from me. Now you want my job too! You want to be a manager that bad, Kendall? Is that it? Or maybe you did it because I can have your illegal ass deported! I don't know why you did it, but you did!"

"You are a crazy woman, Carmen. It wasn't me that did anything to you!"

Carmen was hoping their meeting last night would be civil with Kendall admitting he filed the complaint, apologizing, agreeing to withdraw it, and nobody would get hurt. Things didn't go as planned. Kendall stuck to his lie. She fought him like a cat would a dog, not caring how hostile the situation turned. In the end, Kendall had the audacity to want to kiss and make up. Carmen pulled out of his embrace and ran off. He followed her halfway home, weaving his bike in front of her car like a mad policeman slowing traffic on the highway.

"Pull over, Carmen!" Kendall screamed at her.

Carmen skidded off the nearest highway exit she came to and lost Kendall in traffic. Thankfully, she wouldn't see him today. Francisco had given her the day off under the present circumstances.

It was a waste of her time praying Kendall would withdraw his complaint at the last minute and the interview would be cancelled. As soon as Gordon Matheson walked out his office to greet her, Carmen got the answer to her prayer. The interview would go on as scheduled.

The man's appearance alone made her nervous. She could tell by the looks of him that he had been at this job for a long time and knew how to get the truth out of her. His thinning gray hair, liver spotted hands, and slow hunched walk led her to believe he was well past retirement age. He directed her to an icy, barren room and sat her in a rigid chair behind a small table. Plainly, this wasn't meant to be a comfortable experience. Carmen sat with her hands clasped on the table to keep from wringing them or picking her teeth. She wore a black pantsuit to conceal her tattoo, and was glad she had. Gordon Matheson looked like the type to judge a book by its cover before anything else.

Before the interview got underway, Gordon Matheson warmed her up with general questioning. *"Where about are you from?" "You get back to D.C.often?" "You're married?" "I have kids myself, eight grandchildren, three great-grands. Every time I look up, they're multiplying."* He laughed at his own joke. *"Well, I don't want to take up too much of your morning. This is only a preliminary investigation. If I feel I need further clarification, you may hear from me. Answer the questions to the best of your knowledge, Mrs. Dougherty."*

During the interview, Carmen did exactly as Gordon Matheson advised her to do, *answer the questions to the best of her knowledge.*

"Would you call yourself a fair manager, Mrs. Dougherty?"

"Yes."

"Who's your favorite employee?"

"I don't have a favorite, Mr. Gordon."

"Every teacher has a pet, Mrs. Dougherty."

"I treat my staff the same across the board. My staff will tell you."

"I'll make a note to ask." He paused and made note. "Would you say the atmosphere in your department is easy going or opposite?"

"In this business, some days get hectic," Carmen answered.

Gordon Matheson's questions went on as such. *"Is there much overtime in your department?"* he asked. *"How are projects divvied between employees?" "How quickly do employees promote in your department?"* Carmen answered each question fluently, the way she did when she interviewed for a job. Maybe it was the side effects of the anxiety pill she took last night that had her so outwardly composed. Inwardly, it felt like the longest, heart-stopping hour of her life. She felt as if a lie detector machine was hooked up to her that would zap her if she answered wrong.

"How would you describe your management style?" he asked.

"That depends on what style the situation calls for," Carmen informed him coolly.

"What if the situation called for a termination?"

"My style would be direct."

"Direct in what way, Mrs. Dougherty?"

"I would directly cite the reason for termination."

"Ever had to terminate an employee, Mrs. Dougherty?"

"Yes."

"Ever threatened to terminate an employee?"

"With cause and following company protocol."

"Can you be more specific?" he asked.

"Specifically, over the years…insubordination, poor handling of clientele, excessive absences, etcetera."

"Ever threatened to terminate an employee for not performing sexual favors?"

"No. Never!"

"Ever promoted an employee for performing sexual favors?"

"Performing sexual favors for whom, Mr. Matheson?"

"That would be you, Mrs. Dougherty."

"No, I haven't." Carmen refrained from chewing her thumbnail.

"What's your method of communication with your staff?" Gordon Matheson asked.

"My method?"

"Correct."

"I communicate with my staff through different means."

"Can you name them?"

Carmen shrugged. "It could be through emails, one-on-ones, during staff meetings, landline…"

"Do you communicate more frequently with some employees than others?"

Carmen shifted in her seat, crossed and uncrossed her legs, and answered. "When necessary."

"Ever received an inappropriate email from an employee?"

"No."

"If you received an inappropriate email from an employee, how would you react?"

"Inappropriate is subjective, Mr. Matheson. Can you give me an example?"

"One that is sexually explicit."

Carmen's legs went weak. "I've never received a sexually explicit email from a member of my staff, Mr. Matheson," Carmen lied.

"You're sure of that?"

"Yes. I'm sure."

"Do you recognize these, Mrs. Dougherty?"

Carmen must have blacked out or shut her eyes at some point. When she came to, she was staring at the sleazy emails she and Kendall exchanged, a stack of them, as though Kendall saved them for this very moment to destroy her life for his own gain.

"These are very hard for me to dismiss as routine emails, Mrs. Dougherty. The details of your relationship with Kendall Diaz are well documented, if that is his name."

The pill and the coffee combined suddenly had an adverse effect. Carmen had no control of her emotions at this point, bringing her to tears one second and apologizing for her affair with Kendall the next. She gave Gordon Matheson a full confession. Hell, the man should have been a priest.

"I HAVEN'T HAD A CIGARETTE all morning. Now I need a smoke," Tan said and let out an exhale. "Well, you can always find another job because you're as good as fired."

"If that's what it comes down to, Tan."

"I don't like the way you're sounding, Carmen."

"I'm so tired of this."

"I know you are, honey."

"The investigator already interviewed my entire staff. Kendall's last on his list, and I know how that's going to turn out." Carmen blasted the air conditioner in her car to breathe, then gripped the steering wheel to keep her hands steady.

"I'd better get you and DJ's room set up. What do you think Devon's going to do when he finds out? Renew your wedding vows?"

"Tan, please! I'm shaking so bad I can't drive!"

"Are you driving now?"

"Yes!"

"Well, pull over before you get into an accident!" Tan's own paranoia wasn't helping Carmen calm down. She made a quick detour into the newest mini mall in her neighborhood to pop up and parked aslant in front of a Japanese restaurant. To breathe, Carmen lowered the car window.

"This is why you need to move back home, Carmen…"

Carmen could feel her lungs losing air.

"I'll call you back, Tan." Carmen tossed aside the phone and jumped out of the car, leaving behind her handbag, car keys, and forgetting to lock her door. She was sure she was having a nervous breakdown. Too embarrassed to make a fool out of herself by flagging someone down to call an ambulance, she took a brisk walk, taking in as much oxygen as her lungs could hold. Her breathing technique wasn't working. She was drifting further and further away from reality, her surroundings looking more like a painting she was trapped inside of than real. To get a grip, Carmen wandered into a beauty supply store and asked to use the bathroom.

"We don't have a public one," the women said. Hearing the voice of another human being brought Carmen back to life. Slowly, that feeling, as though every cell in her body was forcing the blood to her brain, passed. She wasn't crazy and she wasn't going to let Kendall drive her there. "Try next door," the woman said.

"Thank you." Carmen walked out. When she got back to her car, she found everything intact, her purse included. Tan had called her back five times. She would call Tan back later. She called Devon instead and didn't get an answer. Three of her calls to Devon had already gone unanswered today, and it wasn't because Devon was too busy at work to respond to her calls. He was ignoring them and her too. The fight they had last night would end their marriage without a doubt, this coming right behind her fight with Kendall.

Devon had met her at the front door the minute she walked into the house. "What happened to you?" he said like he didn't recognize his own wife. How could he? She was wearing wet clothes, a thorny hairdo from standing in the rain, none of which she had the strength of mind to clean up and hide from Devon before walking into the house.

"Nothing happened to me, Devon." He followed her to the bedroom where she changed out of her wet dress and into a robe. If only she had calmed her nerves under a stream of hot water, mellowed out with a glass of wine, taken a few deep breaths, maybe she wouldn't have made a bigger mess of her life than she had already made. Had she been behind the wheel of a car, she would have driven herself off a cliff. She was *that* emotionally unstable.

"Did you get my calls? Where were you?" Devon nagged. "I'm supposed to be at a dinner meeting right now." Devon may as well have been talking to air. She couldn't hear or respond to his questions teetering on the edge of a nervous breakdown. "Carmen!" Devon said, grabbing her by the shoulders so she looked at him.

"I can't deal with this right now, Devon!"

"I asked you a question. Why didn't you answer your phone when I called?"

"Because I didn't, okay?" It was too much for Carmen to handle, her fears, her guilt, her anxiety, her fight with Kendall, being under investigation and possibly losing her job, her career, her family. She slammed the bathroom door in Devon's face and locked herself in.

Devon banged on the door before jimmying the lock and letting himself in. How pitiful she must have looked, sitting in the corner, curled over her knees, her eyes bleeding black tears from mascara.

"Look at you!" Devon said. "You hear your son in there crying? You're scaring him and me too. What is wrong with you?"

"Nothing."

"It doesn't look like nothing to me."

"Just leave me alone, Devon!"

Devon was so furious he punched his fist into the bathroom door. "I'm not going through this again, Carmen! You think I don't know what's up? And don't give me that shit about having panic attacks. I can handle the truth, but I can't handle this again!"

Carmen had her chance to be honest and transparent, to save her marriage, even if she couldn't save her job. She was a coward, the words of Dr. Jessup ringing true. She was working harder at getting a divorce than avoiding one.

"The truth, Carmen, or I'm walking out of here!" Devon demanded.

"You want the truth?" Carmen said, rising to her feet and getting in Devon's face. "I want a divorce!"

"Is that what you want?"

"Yes!"

"You got one!"

"Go on! Leave me! Get the hell out and this time don't come back! I don't need this, Devon! Do me and yourself the favor!" That wasn't the half of what she said to shift her shame and guilt on Devon. The thought of her verbal lashing made Carmen want to curl up and die.

Devon left all right, and took their son with him.

IT WAS TOO EARLY IN the day for Devon to be home from work. Carmen changed out of her pantsuit into a comfortable pair of jeans and shirt, put on a baseball cap and drove to pick up DJ from daycare before Devon got to him first. Spending an afternoon with her son was what she needed to feel normal and whole again. If all else failed, she knew she was a good mother. Nobody could take that away from her.

She and DJ had lunch, played at the park, then stopped to have ice cream before going home. Carmen carried DJ into the house and put him in his bed to finish out his nap. Wanting to hold onto a piece of Devon, she curled behind their son and wrapped herself around his little body, falling asleep with a sense her life, as she knew it, was over.

Hours later, Carmen awakened in a dark room, having slept the afternoon away. She didn't need to check the house to know Devon hadn't come home from work. Her heart felt the void.

Ruined Plans

Tempest had one goal on her mind—getting to the Super Bowl. She reserved a red convertible Benz with cream leather seats, as if she could really afford to. Her bank account was so low she was thinking about moving back into one of her daddy's properties. She was only *thinking,* however. Her mind wouldn't completely go there. Besides, she could only live in the moment, and at the moment, every extra penny she had was going toward her trip. The only setback in her plans was getting Dana and Yasmine to go with her. Booking a room was another hurdle. The entire city of San Diego was already sold out. She couldn't find a room to save her life.

During her drive to her manicure and pedicure appointment, her mother called.

"Hi, baby," her mother said in a way that let Tempest know something was wrong.

"What happened, Mama?"

"Nadine is threatening to miscarry."

"Oh, no!" Tempest had to pull into the nearest gas station not to rear end someone.

"Will is on his way home to take her to emergency. They got a stranger watching the babies. Somebody in the family needs to get out there and pick the other kids up from school."

Somebody, usually meant her.

"I hate to bother you, but can you help Will out? I'm at work and Charlene's got a head this morning."

Tempest sighed inwardly. "I'll go, Mama. You think Nadine will be okay?"

"Nadine's gonna be just fine." Her mother chuckled. "Some things your Mama knows. Do you know what that Nadine had the nerve to ask me?"

"What, Mama?"

"To pray for her. She doesn't know I've already been praying—praying she stop acting like she been cursed by the devil himself when she ought to be making a joyful noise. You think I was ready for another baby? That Salia come out of nowhere, but when she got here, your daddy and me didn't waste a day not counting our blessings."

"That's right, Mama. I'm on my way to Nadine's now."

"Thank you, baby. I know I can always count on you."

Tempest rescheduled her nail appointment and was now driving to freakin' Woodland Hills in bumper-to-bumper traffic. When she got to Nadine's house, the stranger watching the babies was Nadine's friend and neighbor, Caroline, who probably had more time to babysit than she had.

"I always watch the kids for Nadine," Caroline shrilled, like her feelings were hurt that Tempest had come to take the kids off of her hands. Tempest apologized, thanked Caroline and told her she would take over from here.

Forget what she said about having kids. She might postpone having rugrats indefinitely. One-year-old Ali, who was a little 'D' linebacker himself, wouldn't let her put him down for a second without crying. And her three-year-old niece, Sonya, was a whirlwind that never stopped. For two hours, between the two of them, Tempest was worn out.

By two in the afternoon, Tempest figured out how to put Ali down for his nap. She sat his chubby butt in the swing out back and let him rock himself to sleep. Sonya, she let spin herself into a tornado on the grass until she was dizzy. As long as the girl didn't fall into the pool, Tempest figured she couldn't hurt herself.

Nadine and Will's backyard was a tropical haven, full of palm trees, birds of paradise, and other exotic leafy plant life that Nadine cultivated in the years her and Will had lived in the Hills. The weather was perfect too. Following a short bout of rain, it was warm as a spring day. Tempest reclined in a lounge chair near the pool, thumbing through one of Nadine's *Home* magazines, drifting into relaxation mode. She had been working excessive overtime, not realizing how tired she was. Maybe it wasn't the overtime that was exhausting her more than brown-nosing Linda for a promotion she wasn't going to get. If that buyer position was still open, she hadn't heard another word about it, not even through the grapevine. Tempest sighed, closed the magazine and plunged into a daydream, imagining herself at the Super Bowl.

A smile spread across Tempest's face. She couldn't *wait* for the day she saw Sterling again, at the right time and the right place. *I won't be the one in tears this time.* A big splash cut her daydream short. Tempest ripped open her eyes to find Sonya in the pool. The girl had taken off her clothes and jumped in. Good thing Nadine had gotten Sonya swimming lessons because Lord knew she couldn't jump in and save the girl, not knowing how to swim a lick.

"Sonya! You're mother's going to kill me! You come back here, little girl!" Tempest scampered from one side of the pool to the other, chasing after Sonya who thought it was funny watching her frantic aunt run around. She finally caught Sonya's arm, dangling her like a wet towel. "You're in big trouble, little girl."

Realizing the time, Tempest panicked. "Shoot! It's two forty-five!" She should have picked up the other two kids from school ten minutes ago. Tempest pulled Ali's heavy butt out of the swing, wrapped Sonya's wet behind in a bath towel and drove five blocks to the neighborhood elementary school to pick up Will Jr. and Maurice. On her way back to Nadine's, her mother called. Nadine and the baby were fine, her mother said. The hospital was keeping Nadine overnight for observation.

"Overnight!"

"Charlene's on her way to relieve you," her mother reassured her. Tempest sighed with relief.

Back at Nadine's, Tempest watched the clock, waiting for Charlene's SUV to drive up. If she took the back way home, catching the Hollywood freeway instead of the 405, she might avoid rush hour traffic and make her six o'clock hair appointment.

The moment Charlene drove up, Tempest was outside handing over Ali.

"Where're you off to so fast?" Charlene said.

"I'm late for an appointment." Tempest jumped into her car parked next to Charlene's SUV in the driveway. She couldn't back out with Charlene purposely keeping her from closing her door. Tempest purposely ignored Charlene.

"Excuse me, Charlene."

"I heard you're going to the Super Bowl."

"Who told you that?" Tempest said, like that was the biggest lie Charlene had told.

"Nadine told me. Oooo, Tempest. I wanna go," Charlene whined.

"How, Charlene? There's not enough room in the car."

"Who's going?"

"Dana, Yasmine, and me."

"You got room then."

"What about money, Charlene?"

"What about it? I can borrow money from Daddy just like you."

"We're doing a turn-around, leaving at the crack of dawn."

"And? I can hang better than you can and party all night. What're you talking about?" Charlene paused to switch Ali to her other hip, likely because he was wearing on it. "You know my thirtieth birthday is coming up."

"Your birthday is in April, Charlene."

"And? It'll be an early present. Please, baby sis. Derrick ain't gonna do shit for my birthday but take me to eat and buy me some cheap-ass flowers that die before I put 'em in water."

"What if I help Derrick throw you a big party?" Tempest said, hoping that would get Charlene off her back.

Charlene rolled her eyes. "It wouldn't be a surprise. And that's way in April, anyway. I want to do something now. I ain't had no fun lately. Please, Tempest. You never invite me places. Like the time you and Dana sneaked to Vegas without me."

"I didn't sneak, Charlene."

"I'm not gonna stand here begging you. If you don't want me to go..."

Tempest sighed loudly. "Okay, Charlene. You can go. But we're leaving on time. Be ready or you're getting left." Tempest backed out of the driveway like a mad woman. Halfway down the street, she called Dana and planned to call Yasmine next.

Dana didn't answer her phone. Yasmine did, but like she was too busy to talk. "I'm expecting a call from my agency in a minute," she said.

"Are you going, Yas?"

"Going where?"

"With me to the Super Bowl?"

"I'll find out in a minute. New York Fashion Week is coming up. I have a chance to get cast, girl!"

"Really, Yas!"

"Yeah, girl. The theme is multiculture. I heard people are ready to see some color on the stroll this year. If they want black,

I'll give them black, girl. If they want white, I'll pop in my blue eyes and put on a blonde wig. I don't care. I want this job!"

"You'll get it, Yas. I can feel it."

Yasmine suddenly screamed. "That's my agency calling. I'll call you back." She hung up.

Tempest hung up too, suppressing her tears. If she got stuck going to the Super Bowl with Charlene alone, she wasn't going, which meant she may never see Sterling again.

Guess Who's Coming to Dinner

Christmas dinner at Matthew's parents' house was less than an hour and a half away. Dana couldn't decide what to wear and wasn't in a hurry to choose. Everything in her closet was likely too ethnic or too casual. And if her clothes didn't meet Matthew's parents' approval, her sister locks would send them into shock. She felt like Sidney Poitier in "Guess Who's Coming to Dinner?"

Dana resolved, after a frustrating hour of pulling clothes on and off, that whatever she wore would get a thumb down from Matthew's parents, and she had to ask herself if she really cared.

On her way out, Dana stopped by the den to check on Devon, who had stayed at the house since walking out on Carmen, again. With Devon around, the Christmas season was as dark as Halloween, notwithstanding the small artificial Christmas tree Corrine decorated and the meager lights Dana hung outside to cheer up the house.

"You need anything before I leave, Devon?" Dana said, waking him from a nap in front of the TV. Dana couldn't help pampering her brother; neither could Corrine. Whatever his request, they catered to it.

"Can you fix me a bowl of strawberry shortcake with two scoops of vanilla ice cream?" Devon asked. Dana returned five minutes later and handed Devon his dessert.

"Let me ask you something, Dana," Devon said.

"What?"

"Have you ever wished you could do things differently?"

"Sometimes. Why? What would you do differently?"

"I don't know…be on my own for a minute. I love Carmen; don't get me wrong. I would marry her again if I had the chance, even after everything. And I'll never regret having DJ. That's my *heart, Dana.*" Devon slapped a hand over his heart with moist eyes, making Dana's eyes tear. She hated Carmen for hurting her brother, she really did.

"But sometimes I wonder," Devon concluded.

It felt as though her own hands were strangling her neck not to tell Devon the truth about Carmen. If she did, it would confirm Devon's suspicions and put him out of his misery of second-guessing his intuition. She would have told her brother by now if she could live with being directly responsible for destroying a family. Then again, if it came down to a custody battle over DJ, she would become the overprotective sister Carmen feared and didn't care who hated her for it.

"Things will work out. Give it time," Dana said, doing her best to remain neutral for the time being.

"Thanks. Have fun at the party," Devon said.

MATTHEW'S PARENTS' HOUSE HAD THIRTEEN thousand square feet of living space with a heated indoor pool, a tennis court, a full gym, a casita, and it sat off a cliff looking down at the ocean. In the center of the circular cobblestone driveway was a twenty or so foot Christmas tree decorated like those Dana saw in department stores, white lights and all the trimmings.

As if this was a normal way of life for the average person, Matthew flew his jeep through the iron gates, parked behind a line of foreign luxury cars and said, "Comparatively speaking, I was the poorest kid in the neighborhood growing up."

Now Dana was interested to know what kind of business Matthew's family owned and operated to afford a home that could be mistook for the White House. Or maybe she didn't want to know. Matthew was right. It might prejudice her against him. The yacht was one thing; the house combined took elite to new heights. Dana didn't know why excessiveness sickened her, possibly the vanity of people more fortunate than most. She didn't care how "normal" the rich and famous tried to act, it was impossible to be normal living in a palace. Normalcy to these people was living amongst their own kind and being out of touch with the kind of kids she worked with on a daily basis and families who lived paycheck to paycheck, wearing second-hand clothes and shoes, and sending their kids to school hungry.

Dana didn't pay much attention to the inside of the mansion until she was standing in the middle of a massive foyer with semicircle grand staircases on either side and marble flooring. She tagged along with Matthew, who pulled her from one grand room to the next, stopping along the way to introduce her as his "girl" to this snobby person and that snobby person. Real honest to goodness servants carried trays of food and drinks, including, caviar and champagne.

"No, thank you," was Dana's response when she was offered a taste. She couldn't stomach eating. "I thought your parents were having a small Christmas party. Who are all these people?" she whispered to Matthew.

"Neighbors, employees of the company, family, friends, the usual suspects," he said. "Let's dance."

"I think I'll sit this one out." Dana sat in an armchair near the roaring fireplace, watching Matthew, who was pulled onto the dance floor by a redhead to party to the *Black Eyed Peas.* She had never seen Matthew dance nor make an attempt at dancing. She

watched him with a big smile. He definitely wasn't a member of
the rhythm-less nation. His moves were pretty impressive.

In the grand kitchen, the width of two living rooms, Dana
met Matthew's parents. Alvita Kerry was a lean woman who
carried herself like the queen of the manor. Matthew's father,
Innis Kerry, was a balding, stocky man who acted less uptight
than Matthew's mother, but no less self-important. They greeted
Dana with more indifference than shock.

"Welcome," said Alvita Kerry in an aristocratic accent.
"You're a teacher, Matt tells us?" She shook the tips of Dana's
fingers.

"Yes, I am," Dana said, putting on a smile.

"I don't know what drove Matt here to become a teacher, but
I'm sure you have grounds, Dana," Innis Kerry said, his smile
contradicting his peeved eyes. Dana didn't know what *grounds*
she had for becoming a teacher in his mind, but felt compelled
to defend her passion, and Matthew's.

"Matthew and I both love kids, that's the main reason," she
said as respectfully as she could.

"Indeed," said Innis.

"Dana," said Alvita, "you and I must have a chat later. Matt,
introduce your friend to your grandfather. He's in his wing. Says
he's not feeling well. I don't believe the old scrooge."

"Another time, mother. We're bailing to the back," Matthew
said. Alvita stuck out her cheek for Matthew to kiss it. He obeyed
and quickly led Dana into the backyard. "Pretty painless, wasn't
it?"

"For me. What about for you?"

"A pain in my ass," he said, making Dana laugh. They walked
down a cobblestoned pathway, past the few party guests sitting
around a fire pit, through a lush garden, and over a garden bridge
with a small pond beneath. Along the way Dana learned that
Matthew's father was of Scottish, German and Irish decent, and

his mother was African. The two of them met while residents straight out of Ivy League medical school.

Interesting story. But in Dana's opinion, she looked more *African* than Alvita Kerry whose much straightened hair was worn long and down her back, and whose glittery dress was more Americanized than the black and white African print maxi sun dress she wore with a beaded choker. Okay, she had dressed to make a statement. Matthew's parents now knew who their son was sleeping with—a real black woman proud of her heritage. Speaking of which, why was she sleeping with Matthew in the first place? And why had she allowed herself to be inspected by a woman who held her head like she had something up her nose and pretended she had no roots, least of all in Africa?

"You can bet I'll get the third degree about you," Matthew continued on. "Your overall approval rating will fall somewhere between five and ten percent. They'll want to know your pedigree and if you come with a certification." Dana gave Matthew a look that made him quickly add, "That's a pun, Dana."

"What are they afraid of, that you'll marry me?"

"They should be…." Matthew smiled and squeezed her hand. If Dana was sick of anything, it was men throwing around the "M word" like women had nothing better to do than to say "I do." She refrained from rolling her eyes.

"Why do you care so much about what your parents think, Matthew? Not that you shouldn't care, but aren't you a grown man?"

"There's the matter of my trust fund," he said and smiled his tight smile.

Dana came to a stop. "Don't tell me you live off of a trust fund?"

"Mum's the word. Wouldn't want it to get out." He laughed at his own joke, having had more than three glasses of expensive champagne, that Dana counted.

"Let me guess, you also played lacrosse and went to boarding schools," she said.

"Danaaa...you're generalizing again. In my world trust funds are birth rights." Matthew opened the door to the casita, expecting her to follow him inside. Dana didn't move, staggered by the revelation that Matthew lived there.

"I thought you lived alone?" she said.

"I'd call this alone. I'm pretty self-contained back here." Matthew wrapped his arm around her waist and guided her indoors. "Come on in. This is an epic moment for me. Welcome to my humble abode."

"Looks more privileged than humble," Dana said under her breath. After she took in the cozy casita with two bedrooms, a fireplace, custom tiled bathroom and kitchen, she had to take a deep breath not to walk right back out. First, she tolerated Matthew's parents. Now, she finds out Matthew and Omar were in the same boat. *A momma's boy is a momma's boy, rich or poor.*

"I expect you're starving, since you hated everything there was to eat," Matthew said.

"Fish eggs sure aren't my favorite."

"Should I whip up something or have a tray or two delivered from up front? Never mind. I know your answer to that question." Matthew turned toward the kitchen.

"Don't bother to cook, Matthew. I have to go."

Matthew faced her with misgiving, jamming his hands deep into his pants pocket. "Do you mind if I ask why?"

"It's after midnight for one."

"You bet," he said. "But can we talk about this before you leave?"

"Talk about what?"

"Dana, I know when you're disgruntled. You're not exactly a master of disguise. Tell me, now that you've been acculturated into my ancestry, what's your impression of me?" He sat her down next to him on a sofa fit for an executive office and searched her eyes for the truth.

"Why would my impression of you change?" Dana said, keeping a straight face.

"It doesn't bother you that my family owns and operates Innis Healthcare?"

"You sound more bothered than me."

"I fucking get that way at times."

"If that's your *ancestry*," Dana said mockingly. "Why would it bother you?"

"It comes with its rewards and frustrations, you could say."

"What does?"

"Money."

"So, you wear tattered tennis shoes and go around acting like Joe Blow because you're ashamed of having money? Give me a break. I don't buy it, Matthew."

"As odd as it sounds, it's true. And let me add that it's my family's money, not mine. And I find the tattered tennis shoes comfortable."

Dana shook her head. "That's selfish to me, Matthew. Your family's money could feed a third world country, and you're complaining about it while reaping the benefits of a trust fund?"

"It gets under your skin, doesn't it? My lifestyle?"

It did get under her skin, but Dana decided to be less judgmental and more understanding of Matthew's position. He couldn't help the family he was born into and furthermore, Omar was broke and she never judged him for it.

"Tell me, if you hadn't become a teacher, I'd be talking to whom right now? A doctor, a pharmacist, a what?" she said, empathetically.

"The COO of an empire, with total reported yearly revenue in excess of twenty-two million dollars." Matthew laid his head back on the sofa as if the thought exhausted him.

"You in a suit and tie wouldn't be normal."

"My being in a classroom of third graders when I'm the only heir to my granddad's precious throne is more avant-garde, believe it or not."

"What's wrong with being a COO, if that's what you're cut out for?"

He sat up with fire in his eyes. "That's just it, Dana. I'm not cut out for it. Don't you see? I get a charge out of being in a classroom with third graders. The things they say are classic! I have this incredibly cute black girl in my class. Maya, right? Get this. She walks up to my desk one day and says to me, "How can I write about ancient Greece, Mr. Kerry, when you said they didn't have no paper back then? Now that's *classic!*" Matthew's eyes glazed from his laughter, which in turn made Dana laugh.

"Wouldn't it be great to write a book about the funny things kids say?" she said.

"When can we get started?" he said, excitedly.

Dana leaned over and kissed Matthew, taking him by surprise.

"Is there another one where that came from?" He returned her kiss, one that begged her not to leave. "You know, Dana? You might be the first girl I've had that isn't impressed with my family's capital and doesn't shop at Abercrombie and Fitch."

Dana laughed. She was impressed with Matthew for more important reasons, and for the first time saw more to this guy than meets the eye. She kissed him again, as desirably as the mood she felt coming on.

"I have something for you," he said.

Taken by surprise, Dana said, "Not a Christmas gift, I hope! We're not exchanging gifts, remember? We agreed."

"Call it a housewarming gift," he said, walking to the next room.

"I don't have a house yet!" Dana called after him.

"One day you will!" he called back. Paying her no mind, Matthew returned from the bedroom hauling a large box Dana was reluctant to open and too excited not to. "I hope you like them. Go on, open it" he urged.

"Them? What is it?" she said, smiling and unwrapping the box carefully. Dana laughed joyously at what she found. "You bought me a set of dishes, nice ones too!"

"Thought you might need a set. If you don't like them, I have the receipt —"

"I love them. I really do."

Dana never left Matthew's humble abode that night. The next day they spent the morning together at a shelter, feeding the homeless. Three days following Christmas, she and Matthew traveled to his family-owned cabin at Big Bear Lake, high in the snow-covered mountains of the San Bernardino forest, a skier's dream. Incredible couldn't effectively describe Dana's time with Matthew.

Old Habits Die Hard

Carmen was on the run. She had packed her bags and fled Los Angeles with DJ before Christmas. Per Francisco, the investigator was on vacation through the New Year, which meant the findings of the sexual harassment investigation were on hold. In the meantime, Francisco suggested she use her vacation time and relax. Marissa would act as the interim sales director, he said. Carmen knew what that meant. She also knew Marissa hoped she never came back. Well, Marissa got her wish. By New Year's Eve, Carmen made up her mind. She was divorcing Devon for his own good, and moving back to D.C. to rebuild her shattered life.

"You want lemonade or sweet tea?" Tan said, holding up her choices.

"You don't have to keep serving me, Tan. I can get it myself," Carmen said.

"The tea or the lemonade, honey?"

"The tea." Tan went back to the kitchen, poured the drinks, and came back with two tall icy glasses of sweet tea. Carmen hated to say it, but it wasn't easy to ignore; her sister's hips were as wide as the French doors she walked through. She hadn't seen Tan in over a year, and in that time, Tan had put on fifty plus pounds. Tan blamed her weight gain on the hysterectomy she had a year ago. Carmen thought it would help if Tan stopped cooking like Paula Dean. The house kept an aroma of food— today's country-style breakfast mixed with tomorrow's black eyed peas, collard greens, jambalaya, mac & cheese, broccoli casserole, fried chicken and the cakes and pies Tan had her up all night baking to celebrate the New Year.

She wouldn't have been honest with Tan about her weight gain had Tan not asked her opinion. "Can you tell I put on weight?" Tan said.

"Stevie can tell," Carmen kidded.

"Kiss my ass, Carmen. I haven't gained that much weight."

"You might gain less if you did more than watch the soaps all day."

"You see these gift baskets, honey?" Tan said, referring to the leftover Christmas baskets she handcrafted and those she started constructing to sell for Valentine's Day. "It's more than a workout to put these together, *and* make door-to-door deliveries. And how many Mary Kay reps do you know making my kind of money that sit on their ass all day?"

Her sister, Carmen thought with a laugh, was resourceful. After Tan divorced, she lived for day and nighttime soaps, while sitting back collecting hefty child support and alimony checks from Carl. Tan's purpose in life had become raising her twin boys, primarily. A single mother working outside the home, Tan believed, would set her boys up for failure, even though Tan couldn't officially call herself a "single mother." Carl had joint custody and was footing most of Tan's household bills each month, not out of court order, but purely out of guilt for his one-time affair.

Tan should never have divorced Carl under the circumstances, Carmen believed. He was a nice, soft spoken man that would give Tan the world if she wanted it. So what he had an affair? One measly one in their seven years of marriage? The man was remorseful and cried like a baby for Tan to forgive him. Tan stuck to her principles.

In many ways Carmen admired Tan's survival skills. She didn't know how she would survive, financially or emotionally, after she divorced Devon. Tan's advice was,"File for divorce first or risk losing your son." Her mother, now on her second divorce, advised her to move fast before Devon knew what hit him. If she had inherited one family talent, it was the art of a speedy divorce. At Tan's insistence, Carmen called the attorney Tan used, one that, per Tan, would get her what she deserved. What did she deserve? Did she deserve to get fired, to lose her son, to lose everything? Carmen had to wonder if she was getting exactly what she deserved.

The boys, Conrad, Cameron, and DJ, were with their mother and had been for much of her visit. Carmen was enjoying the freedom, one advantage of moving back home. Another advantage was Tan's generosity. Her sister had a heart of gold. If Carmen let herself, she would take advantage of Tan's giving spirit. Today alone Tan treated her to a fifty-minute essential massage, aroma therapy body wrap, and a pedicure at a day spa. Now they both sat like lazy old geese in overstuffed chairs on the screened-in porch, while Tan smoked her cigarettes and Carmen watched the early winter snow fall softly through the forest in the back of Tan's two-story brick Colonial. The peace and relaxation were foreign to Carmen after the emotional rollercoaster ride she had been on for the last six months to a year.

"I love Silver Springs, don't you? It's so peaceful and charming," Carmen said about the Maryland town Tan moved to with Carl two years before their divorce.

"There's a house two blocks away for sale, at a good price. Let's go look at it." Tan looked ready to call the realtor on the spot.

"You're really trying to get me to move back home, aren't you?"

"What did Devon say again, you'll move his son to D.C. over his dead body? We can have that arranged." Tan laughed. Carmen did too, despite herself.

"That wasn't funny, Tan."

"Yes it was."

"What about getting around custody laws? You're forgetting that little problem."

"Where there's a will, there's a way, honey."

Carmen's relaxed muscles tensed. "You and mom are a real trip. You really are."

"What?"

"This isn't easy for me, Tan. When you divorced Carl, the twins didn't have to move to another state, away from their father. You're not the only mother who loves her child. I have DJ to worry about and a job to find before I can think about buying a house anywhere. And you're forgetting another thing...I still love Devon!"

"Are we going to Rochelle's tonight? 'Cause, honey, you sound like you can use a party," Tan said. Her laugh was infectious; one characteristic about her sister that hadn't changed, along with her buttery smooth skin and russet eyes that sparkled like Tan couldn't be happier, weight included. They both laughed long and lazily.

"I can use a *drink,* that's what I can use," Carmen said. "I'm dried out. Can't you keep a bottle of wine or something in the house for your houseguests?"

"Not with my babies around I can't," Tan said, looking like Carmen committed a capital offense by mentioning alcohol.

"You heard of child safety locks? Hell, I'll buy you a pack."

"If you don't want your kids to become drunks, don't send them a double message by exposing them to alcohol. I'm raising presidents, honey, not alcoholics, drug addicts or drop-outs."

"A little wine never hurt anybody, as long as it's done in moderation," Carmen said.

"Your cousin Rochelle never heard of the word moderate. She'll have more than wine and men up the kazoo tonight."

Carmen lifted her head in interest. "Really?"

"Best believe it," Tan said.

Carmen leaned back and snuggled in her warm throw. "A house full of men? That scares me how lonely I feel today. I think I'll stay right here."

"You know how I feel. When you have two perfect little men to satisfy all your needs, you don't need sex," Tan said.

Carmen glided her eyes toward Tan and stared at her sister like she had lost her mind.

"You know I'm lying, don't you?" Tan said. "I was just trying to make you feel better. "

"I was about to say…" Carmen said. Again, they laughed long and lazily.

Carmen imagined if she had suffered from Endometriosis most of her life like Tan, and had been told she would never have kids, she might be satisfied too. Maybe she needed to suffer more in life. Having everything she ever wanted—a home, a great husband, a career she loved, and a beautiful son sure hadn't fulfilled her life. And going years without having sex like Tan sure wouldn't. Hell, she didn't know how she was going to survive another night without a man at her disposal.

"Let's get the hell out of here and ring in the New Year right!" Carmen said, pushing herself out of the chair.

An hour later, Carmen had on a silver satin cocktail dress, a spaghetti string number that dipped down her spine, hugged her behind, and cut off mid-thigh. She wore rhinestone jewelry, spike heeled pumps and a fox fur jacket with it. Tan couldn't decide on what to wear and changed her mind about the party.

Her clothes were the real deterrent. Tan may have hips, but she had great curves that didn't need to be hidden under a large swathe of floral print fabric unbecoming on any woman's body and should be outlawed.

"When was the last time you shopped?" Carmen said, fishing through Tan's closet.

"You know what I'm about to do, honey. Go right over to Ma's. I miss my babies anyway," Tan said in frustration. Carmen would have wrung in the New Year quietly with her mother, Tan, and the kids if she didn't suddenly need a glass of wine and men up the kazoo to cheer her up.

She left Springfield, Maryland and drove to Prince George's County. Tan told her Rochelle had married a big time business tycoon and divorced him before the ink dried on the marriage license. Now Rochelle was living in a two million dollar house too big for one person and two dogs. Upper Marlboro was beautiful from what Carmen could remember about the swanky community. Rochelle lived in a jaw-dropping estate where the party was in full swing behind the towering double paned windows. She parked Tan's big, four-door Mommy van and headed inside.

"Sexy, can I talk to you?" a man said, grabbing Carmen by the hand before she could get up the driveway. She noticed him talking on his cell phone when she was walking up. He was tall and good-looking, with that east coast look going on in his black wool trench over a suit and tie. His shadowed beard and mustache were neat as a pin, his smile, Kodak.

"I'm married," Carmen said quickly, and for her own good.

"Is that how you keep the dogs off?" he said.

Carmen laughed. "I'm married, really."

"I don't see a ring."

"Because I left it back in California with my husband." Carmen gave him a naughty grin, feeling his eyes on her hips as she swayed on like a lioness on the prowl. She knew how good she looked in her dress, adding an extra dip to her hips, and smiling at him over her shoulder. The man caught up to her before she rang the doorbell.

"Don't I know you?" he said.

Carmen faced him and chuckled. "Now, how could you know me? I haven't lived in D.C. in umpteen years.

"I never forget a pretty face."

"Hmmm…I wonder where I've heard that line before?"

She liked his laugh, raspy and baritone. "A pretty face like yours will throw any brother off his game." He snapped his fingers. "Wilson High. That's how I know you!"

Carmen cringed. "You went to Wilson?"

"I'd shake your hand and reintroduce myself if I didn't know everything about you, Carmen Hill." His eyes ran up and down her body like he had seen her nude. Carmen's face overheated in the cold. Had she had sex with him back in high school and forgotten his name and face.

"I'll give you a hint… the back seat," he said, taking her by the hand and drawing circles in her palm with his index finger, a childish signal kids had for sex back in high school.

Hell, she wound up in a back seat with a bunch of boys in high school. That didn't mean a thing, nor did it mean they had sex.

"Black Celica?" he said, throwing her another hint.

Carmen's face was blank.

"I'll tell you what," he said. "Instead of going inside, why don't we have our own *Auld Lang's Syn* at my place?"

Carmen was feeling reckless enough to agree to anything. She was virtually divorced, so what the hell? His name, Carmen found out during the ride to his place, was Jarrett Bennett, who graduated a class ahead of her and was now an attorney.

No wonder she vaguely remembered him. The sex was worth erasing from her memory bank. She hoped he learned a few tricks since high school and grew eight inches. *Quit!* Carmen thought, laughing to herself. Her mind was running in a direction it shouldn't be going. The most she planned to do tonight was have a few drinks, enjoy a nice conversation with an ex, ring in the New Year and return to Tan's dry in every way.

They entered Georgetown. Jarrett's place was a jazzy red brick condo, neat and clean like Jarrett. When they walked through the door, he slid her fur off of her shoulders and thought he knew her well enough to plant a kiss there.

"You've gotten bold since high school," she said.

"Only when I can't help myself." He planted another kiss on her left shoulder.

"You're forgetting, I'm married."

"Your husband is back in California, and your ring... How married can you be?"

"Not very, anymore," Carmen said. She strutted across the hardwood floors and took a seat on the living room sofa.

"If evidence is a predictor, I could've saved you the trouble of a divorce. You were never a one man kind of woman from what I remember." He removed his coat, suit jacket and tie, which he hung on the wood coat rack with her fur. "How about a drink?"

Carmen couldn't find her voice to speak, struck by Jarrett's impression of her character, a false one to add. "Zinfandel, if you have it," she got out.

"Whatever you want, I have, sexy." Jarrett retrieved the wine from the kitchen. His condo, with the click of the remote, turned into a readymade bachelor's retreat. Slow jams suddenly played and the lights mysteriously dimmed. Carmen took the wine goblet from Jarrett's hand and took a long swig. The spicy liquid, with a hint of fruitiness, raced through her bloodstream like a shot of warm milk.

"Take it slow. I have more where that came from and all night refills."

"I only have until midnight," Carmen made clear.

"Or what? You'll turn into a pumpkin?"

"I might."

"In that case, let's get it cranked."

Carmen extended her glass. Jarrett refilled it to the rim and sat within inches of her, leaving half the sofa unoccupied. "Here's a toast to the old school days." He clanked his glass against hers and took a gulp of his own drink, which smelled of something much stronger than wine. "Another toast to first loves." They clanked glasses again and drank. "I sure was in love with *you*," he professed. "You're the reason I'm not married to this day."

Carmen pursed her lips.

Jarrett raised his right hand. "I swear I'm telling the whole truth and nothing but the truth, so help me God." He gazed into her eyes. "Seeing you again must mean my luck is about to change for the better."

"I'll toast to that," Carmen said, raising her glass in the air then swigging more. She and Jarrett talked for a while, about the "good old days," which Jarrett remembered more about than she. Taking over the room, in a melodious drone, was *Shai's*, "If I Ever Fall in Love Again," playing through the satellite sound system.

"Awe! Remember that one?" Jarrett snapped his fingers and bobbed his head to the 90's slow groove, having a party only he was tuned into. He threw his head back and laughed. "I remember that night at the park? That's a night a young inexperienced boy would never forget. You had a brotha *whipped*. Remember that?"

"Vaguely," Carmen said.

"Remember the night after the game, you and me, in the locker room?"

Carmen shook her head.

"You forgot everything, didn't you?"

"I put those days behind me, and want to keep them there."

"I hear you. Love 'em and leave 'em Carmen, still sexy and beautiful." He caressed her thigh. Carmen shouldn't have gotten started on the wine. She was feeling loose and sexy, lonely and desperate, horny and careless. Jarrett's hand started to feel good.

"My husband has a bald head like yours," she said, raking her fingers over Jarrett's shiny skull like she did Devon's, slow and sensually. Jarrett made a gurgling sound, his eyes rolling to the back of his head.

"You know how to find my erogenous zone, don't you?" His hand traveled further up her thigh and found her zone. At first, it felt good that a man desired her. Jarrett's strong body, his delectable cologne, and his tasty mouth had her wet and ready. In the course of their foreplay, a sad and miserable feeling came over Carmen, filling her eyes with tears. She wanted this sweaty man off of her.

"What happened to taking it slow?" she said, stopping Jarrett from taking off her clothes.

"We're right on time, baby." His mouth attacked hers. He turned into a werewolf, with eyes that looked scary and unnatural. "You remember the locker room now, don't you?" he panted.

Carmen pushed him back and sat up. "I have a bad memory of those days. Don't take it personal." He took a swig of his drink, his face contorting as though he had tasted poison in his glass.

"Maybe you got me confused with them other hard dicks you got with. You did get around."

"I'll leave that one alone," she said to keep from obliterating his confidence.

"Females like you don't surprise me. Get with the whole basketball squad and pretend you can't remember."

"It's time for me to go." Carmen gulped the last of her wine and picked up her clutch bag. Jarrett pulled her back down on the couch.

"Let me get one last kiss for old time sake." His mouth covered hers as he thrust her on her back and jammed her legs back like they were in the back seat of his black Celica. This was seriously high school and this man had some serious ego issues going on. Carmen knew not to fight him off. His ego couldn't take it. What did she expect from a man packing three inches, and that was being generous. Carmen went along with the mood, letting Jarrett grope her in places that were cold as ice.

"If we're going to do this, can we do it somewhere comfortable?" she said.

"My king-sized Posturepedic is ready and waiting," he said.

"I'm right behind you. Let me pour myself another drink and tell my sister I won't be home tonight." Carmen pulled her cell phone from her clutch bag and waited for Jarrett to leave the room. "Don't fall asleep before I get there!" she called out.

"Pour me a shot too, will you!" he said. The minute his dumb ass was out of sight, Carmen grabbed her fur and saw herself out his front door. Hell, she should've stuck to Rochelle's party.

Tan was too scared to come out before the shooting started and sent Carl in her place. A block away from Jarrett's condo, Carl drove up in his Chrysler sedan, then drove Carmen back to Rochelle's to pick up Tan's van.

"How'd your sexual harassment charge turn out?" Carl said as he drove slowly along the snow sprinkled highway, straining to see the dark road ahead. Carmen shook her head. She knew Tan couldn't hold water if she tried.

"How much did Tan tell you, Carl?"

"Only what I interpreted on my own. It is my line of work."

"I don't know what kind of cases you've dealt with, but this one is open and shut."

"I've seen cases go in the complete opposite direction. The system is there to protect, but people with ulterior motives also abuse it. You have the fact you're married and have a family on your side. If this employee has harassed you, as I understand, it'll take a lot to prove motive. We can fight this all the way to the Supreme Court if we have to."

"Thanks, Carl," Carmen said and kept quiet the remainder of the ride. At least Tan held half her water and didn't tell Carl everything. Nevertheless, unless she wanted the entire country to know the sordid details of her affair with Kendall, this case wouldn't be going to the Supreme Court. Anyway, it would cost her a fortune in legal fees she didn't have to defend herself.

Carl let her out in front of Rochelle's house. "You need me to follow you home?"

"Tell Tan I'm fine, Carl," Carmen said.

"I'll see you tomorrow at Tan's New Year's party?"

"I don't have anywhere else to be," Carmen said dryly.

Carl drove off. The clock struck twelve. From Tan's van, Carmen watched the New Year celebration through Rochelle's doubled-paned windows go on without her, partiers kissing, hugging and singing as if they truly believed something supernatural happened and their lives had changed for the better at the stroke of the clock. Carmen couldn't see anything in her life changing for the better. Things were sure to get worse.

She never wanted to cry so much in her life. Her tears were stuck somewhere between her throat and her thoughts of Nicole. Each visit home she thought of visiting Nicole's family. She never made it back to her old neighborhood, fearing Nicole's mother still blamed her for Nicole's death.

At 12:05 AM, her cell phone rang. Carmen answered in a hurry, thinking Devon wouldn't let the New Year turn without calling her.

"Happy New Year! I love you, baby!" Kendall yelled. In the background, she heard ruckus and loud music.

"Don't happy new year me!" Carmen said. "What the hell do you want, Kendall?"

"I want you, baby."

"Fuck you, Kendall! Don't call me, ever again!"

Carmen hung up on Kendall, started the engine and sped off in case she ran into another ghost of boyfriends past.

Time Can't Heal All Things

*M*isery snowed Carmen under on New Year's Day. She put on a phony smile, grinning and bearing the fun Tan's houseguests were having without her, including her mother, father and his young new wife. The one person Carmen couldn't fool was DJ. He clung to her like he alone could make her smile with his funny faces and big kisses. He was the only light in Carmen's black day. When Devon finally called, wanting to talk to his son only, Carmen's mood took a nosedive. Why drive a stake through her heart, never bothering to say if or when he was coming home.

"I need to use your car," Carmen said to Tan at the turn of nightfall. Tan was pulling her lemon cream pies from the refrigerator.

"If you're going to the store, pick up another two cases of sodas. Folks will drink you out of house and home, won't they?"

"I'm not going to the store, Tan."

Tan placed the pies on the kitchen counter like they were fresh out of a hot oven, then placed her hands on her hips. "I thought you got enough of Jarrett Bennett last night."

Carmen, who wasn't up to explaining herself said, "I don't know where I'm going, but I won't be long, okay?"

Tan watched Carmen warily. "Okay, honey…My keys are in my purse."

Carmen bundled in a wool, tam neck scarf and wool trench coat, leaving DJ in her family's care.

BEFORE SHE KNEW WHERE SHE was going, she was on Interstate 66, heading for D.C. proper. Some of the houses in her old neighborhood, built in the early 1900's, were distressed; others had been upgraded with the times. Carmen's family once lived in this area of town before her parents moved to a more prosperous area, so Carmen thought that was the reason until Tan reminded her why they really moved—after the kidnapping.

Carmen passed the Glenwood Cemetery where Nicole was buried. When she passed her old house, she rolled by like she had never lived there. Down the block was Nicole's mother's house, or used to be. After so many years, Carmen was sure the whole family had moved. She parked anyway and knocked on the wood door of the small, two-story brick house. Nicole's brother, Tone, answered. He was as surprised to see Carmen as Carmen was to find out Nicole's family hadn't moved.

After they ran out of formalities, Tone invited Carmen inside the house and out of the cold. His neck was wide like his shoulders, his arms short and muscular like his legs. He didn't ask her why she had come by after all these years, and had he, Carmen couldn't have answered. Seeing Nicole's mother might be the underlying reason. She needed to know if the blame lingered in her eyes, or if time had cleared them up. Carmen would never find out. The moment she walked into the house and before she sat down on the checkered couch to catch her breath, Tone told her Nicole's mother died of cancer two years ago.

"I'm sorry, Tone," she said.

"It's cool."

"How's De-De," Carmen said, referring to Nicole's older sister.

"Living in South Carolina with her husband and kids."

"What about Mr. Glover?"

"You know that niggah disappeared years ago."

The whole Glover family went to pieces after Nicole's murder, Carmen recalled. She also remembered how Tone beat a man close to death because he drove a brown car like the kidnapper's. Not long after, De-De was strung out and Mr. Glover walked out. Carmen took direct responsibility for the tragedy, though Tan maintained the Glover family never had it together and were destined to fall apart.

From the looks of the living room, Tone had been celebrating the New Year with a six-pack of beer, a to-go plate of ribs and a football game before she arrived. Carmen felt comfortable alone with Tone in the dark, smoky house. It was like sitting next to her own brother, if she had one. Tone cracked open a fresh can of beer, took a long swig, then drew back as if getting a better look at her from afar.

"Life must be treating you good. You still look sixteen, girl," he said.

"If I look it, I sure don't feel it."

"Well, I feel and look thirty-seven. Want a brew?" Tone said.

"I'm okay."

"So, what've you been doing with yourself, besides looking good?"

Since talking about her life would only lead her to talking about Devon and thinking about Kendall, Carmen simply said. "I have a beautiful son. What about you?"

"Keeping it on the up and up after seven years in the pen."

"What were you doing in jail, Tone?" she asked for asking sake. The fact that Tone had spent time in jail didn't come as a surprise to Carmen, given Tone's notorious reputation for crime.

"Watching time go by. They let me out on good behavior, got tired of feeding a niggah," Tone said. Then, as if filling out a profile for *eHarmony*, he went on to say. "I got me a gig working for the city now. Got this house moms left me, but can't find me a good woman, though." His grin was tilted, his voice slow and lazy. What Carmen saw in Tone's eyes wasn't the desire of a sexually deprived man, but something else. Maybe he saw in her eyes what she saw in his—what was, what could have been and what turned out to be.

"I thought you were a ladies' man, Tone," Carmen teased.

"I thought I was too." They laughed and began a trip down memory lane, first talking about his family, then about hers, the old neighborhood, and eventually about Nicole. Talking to someone who actually knew Nicole as well as she did felt like a cup of warm soup to Carmen's soul.

"My little sister was beautiful, wasn't she?" Tone said.

"She had all the cutest boys in love with her," Carmen said. "I was so jealous."

"I almost killed a few niggahs for messing over her too."

"I remember," Carmen said.

At a point, Tone stopped talking and said, "What made y'all get in a car with a psychopath anyway?" It was the million-dollar question asked of Carmen by everyone—her parents, teachers, friends, investigators and anyone that heard about the kidnapping.

"Immaturity, stupidity, should've known better," Carmen answered. "It was my bright idea, you know? Not Nicole's."

"I've had a lot of bright ideas, more than the law allows," Tone said.

Following the dreaded question, Carmen sat for as long as she could on the verge of tears, before pulling her keys from her purse. "Well, I guess I'd better go."

Tone walked her to the door. "Give me some love, girl. I may never see you again." Carmen was sure Tone never would. She swayed in his embrace, holding on tight to her emotions that were at a breaking point. If hugs cured a bleeding heart and healed a wounded spirit, Tone's did both for Carmen that night.

Whatever good paying a visit to Nicole's old house did for Carmen lasted as long as her plane ride back to California. Two days later, Devon served her with divorce papers and Francisco called her to his office. The results of the investigation were in.

Sea of Fish

The condominium Dana fell in love with in Paramount fell through. By the time Reginald put in her offer, five others had come first. Every house or condo Reginald had shown her since wasn't worth looking at or buying. Disappointed, Dana agreed to waste her money on going to the Super Bowl with Tempest tomorrow. She was on her way to stay the night at Tempest's house when Omar called.

"What are you doing?" Omar said.

"Driving."

"Stop by the shop for a minute."

"Can whatever it is wait until I get back, Omar?"

"Back from where?"

"Tempest has me going with her to San Diego tomorrow. I thought I told you. How's your mother doing?"

"They released her from the rehab center yesterday. She's back at home. Pops is happy."

"That's the best news I've heard today," Dana said, feeling a warmth come over her.

"It might take years before she's back to herself, even with physical therapy and the whole nine."

"She had a stroke, Omar. Be patient with her."

"That's hard to do when you're used to seeing your moms independent. You know my mom, Dana."

"Like I know mines, always on the go," Dana said, finishing his sentence.

"I had to give her a bath yesterday. Man! She didn't like it anymore than I did, but I got through it."

"What happened to the home care nurse?"

"Pop's insurance only covers so many days."

"You need me to do anything before I leave? You know I will."

"I know you will. I appreciate it. But you've already done enough, sitting at the hospital all day, doing puzzles with moms. You know she loved that, on top of taking pops shopping once a week. Can you believe that cat never grocery shopped in his life?"

They both laughed.

"I believe it," Dana said. "You, Todd and your dad depended on your mother to do everything."

"If we did, that's over now."

"Just for now, Omar. She'll get better. Have faith," Dana said, picking up the sorrow in Omar's voice.

"I'm trying to," he said. "So, where are you now?"

"Pulling into Tempest's gate," Dana said. Actually, she was two blocks away. Had she come from home, she would have been at Tempest's place in no time. She hadn't told Omar she was coming from the Bay, where Matthew had taken her on a romantic gondola ride through the Naples Canal following their short workday.

"If you really want to do something for me, come by the shop. You're right up the street."

"When has South Gate been up the street from Fox Hills, Omar?"

"I'm managing a new shop on La Cienega."

"La Cienega and what?"

"Centinela."

"Really? That's right up the street."

"That's what I tried to tell you. You'll be here in ten minutes or less," Omar said.

Dana paused to think before answering. What if Omar had misinterpreted her compassion for something more? She loved doing whatever she could to help Omar and his family while his mother recovered, but that didn't mean they were anywhere close to back on track.

"What's the address?" Dana said, nonetheless.

"When you get here, you won't miss the sign," he said.

A "Closed" sign hung on the window of *Subway*, next to window art that read "Opening Soon." The lights were on, but the place was empty. Dana knocked several times, and would have left had Omar not come gallivanting to the door in time, wearing jeans and a white T-shirt that looked as though he had been playing in the dirt.

He spread his arms wide. "Where's my hug?" He wrapped Dana in his arms warmer than a heated blanket.

"You're getting me all dirty," Dana said, finding a reason to pull away from him.

"Sorry. I've been working since five o'clock this morning."

"You're opening a new store?" She walked around, noticing the empty beverage case, food bins, and bread compartment. "No cookies either!" she said, peering through the cookie bin. "I was looking forward to a batch for our road trip tomorrow." Dana turned around to find Omar in her face.

"Dana," he said, wearing a child-like grin."Come here. Sit down."

"Why?" she said, as he pulled her by the hand.

"You'll find out in a second." He sat her at a table in the center aisle. When Omar bent down on one knee, Dana stood up. She didn't know what he was doing, but she didn't want to sit idle and find out.

"What are you about to do, Omar?" she said, fanning her hot face, while pacing.

Omar laughed. "You can't find out if you don't come back over here and sit down."

"Tell me first."

"Can you trust me for once?" he said. Against her common sense, Dana sat. Omar took a knee before her again, and took hold of her left hand. "Dana," he began. "Remember my dream, the one I told you I've had since high school. This is it. This is my dream." He spread his arms, opening his hands like he held the world in them.

"What is, Omar?"

"The first of a chain of shops I'm opening. Everything I want or dreamed of having is in this store, including you."

"Omar - "

"Hold on. Let me finish," he said, cutting her off. "You and I, *we*, us, we're made for each other, Dana. You know it like I know it. My mom loves you, Todd, my pops..."

"Omar -"

"I know what you're about to say," he went on. "That was different. I was tripping that night, in a panic. I knew I was losing you, Dana. I'm not trying to lose you, not to another cat who can't love you like I love you, who won't take care of you like I will. So, I'm asking you again, this time the best way I know how." Omar pulled a satin ring box from his pant pocket and opened it. "Will you marry me?"

It took Dana a minute to answer with thoughtfulness. "Why are you doing this to me, Omar? I don't know what you want me to say."

"Isn't this what you wanted?"

"Yes...three years after the fact, and how long after we broke up? You're not being fair." Now that the numbness in her legs had worn off, Dana walked to the counter. Omar followed. She didn't know how to tell him she was in love with another man because she wasn't sure whom she loved anymore.

"Are you saying no?" he said, sounding hurt.

"I'm saying I don't know."

"In three years, did I ever do you wrong?"

"No."

"Did I treat you like you were the most important lady in my life?"

"That's debatable."

"You know what I mean, Dana."

To a degree, Dana couldn't argue with Omar's point. He never treated her "wrong." He just didn't treat her as right as he should have treated her.

"So, is it yes or no?"

"I don't know, Omar. I just don't." Dana walked to the front window and stared out at the shopping center parking lot. The people and cars moving about appeared on another planet from her thoughts. Omar's proposal had hit her harder than a freight truck coming out of nowhere. She had to have a serious talk with herself to keep things in perspective. How could he do this when she was finally transitioning to the next phase of her life, without him? This was classic Omar, always about what he wanted, when he wanted it. What about what she wanted, when she wanted it? Why should she marry a man who doesn't get that marriage is a joint venture, a partnership in which both parties are affected by important decisions? She was the other party he forgot to include in his decision to buy a franchise, not that she couldn't be more proud of his accomplishment and happier for him. But what about trusting her with his dreams? Three years and he never once shared his dreams with her. Trust goes both ways.

"We're made for each other," he says. She could dispute that argument too. There was a big difference between saying they were soul mates and believing it. Okay, so the sex was great between them, and they could talk about anything for hours on end, and laugh over the silliest jokes, and she never felt freer to be herself than when she was with him. But that didn't necessarily make them marriage bound. She could name as much compatibility with Matthew. She would admit the sex wasn't the greatest with Matthew and she wasn't always herself around him or his family, but the sex was coming along, and both of them loved teaching, loved kids, loved the sea, and spontaneous adventures. Maybe Matthew was her true soul mate.

Omar turned her around and studied her as he often had, as though her every feature was admirable. His sleepy eyes drew her in like a warm fireplace, his lips were like fire and ice against hers, bringing her to chills while setting her afire.

"I love you, Dana Dougherty," he said, after their smoldering kiss ended. "We can have a litter of babies if you want, just say yes."

"Can I take a day or two to think about it?"

"Take as much time as you need. I'm not going nowhere." He cupped her face in his warm hands and kissed her again, leaving Dana dazed and confused.

"DID HE REALLY, DANA?" TEMPEST said when Dana made her announcement coming through the front door. "You look shocked."

"I am." Dana shook her head and flopped down on Tempest's red sectional.

"How did he ask this time? Like what did he say?" Clearly more excited than Dana, Tempest sat next to her, her face caked in a green cleansing mask spooking Dana out.

"He actually proposed on one knee with a beautiful ring included."

Tempest grabbed hold of her hand. "Where is it?"

"I couldn't take the ring, Tempest. That would be accepting his proposal, which I haven't accepted and don't know if I will, if I should, or if I want to."

"Because of Matthew, huh, Dana?"

Dana whimpered in false tears. "I hate Omar for doing this to me. Three years I waited and *now* he proposes, at the worse time."

"Omar loves you, girl."

"That's what he says," Dana replied and pinched her lips.

"Matthew is really nice, but I'm sorry, I love Omar. That's my boy! Him and I are like this." Tempest held up her crossed fingers, grinning animatedly. "You two are made for each other, I think."

Dana covered her face and shook her head. "Please don't say that."

"I'm sorry, but you are…like Sterling and I were." Tempest jumped up. "I'll be right back. I need to wash off this mask." She fled the room. When Tempest returned, her face was radiant, but her eyes were red from her obvious tears. At first, Dana regretted that she agreed to this trip with Tempest tomorrow. Nothing about Super Bowl weekend excited her. Now she was happy to go, if only to support her best friend and play cousin. Maybe after this weekend Tempest could finally put her love for Sterling to rest. It was obvious to Dana Tempest's self-confidence was down. She had never seen Tempest work so hard to appeal to men, handing out her number to guys she wouldn't normally look at once. Dana wouldn't be as concerned if Tempest's behavior was typical of her vanity. But after what happened between Sterling and Diamond, Tempest hadn't been herself.

For the rest of the night, Dana avoided the subject of proposals and marriage, ignoring Tempest when she tried to push the issue. "I'm done talking about Omar, Temp," Dana said, and turned off the light to get some sleep.

They were packed and ready to leave the house at the first sign of daylight in the morning. Dana packed a simple overnight bag, which held two changes of clothes, one change of shoes and a toiletry bag. Tempest packed enough clothes to fly to Paris for a week. Within ten minutes of curling up on the couch and closing her eyes, Matthew called.

"Hi, Matt," she said, her voice crackling with sorrow already.

"Hey there, just calling to say goodnight. Are you sleeping?"

"On my way."

"Call me and let me know you made it."

"I'll try to remember."

"Danaaa…" He sang her name in a way that sent chills though her body.

Smiling with closed eyes, Dana said, "I'm here."

"I'm in love with you," Matthew said.

Dana's eyes shot open. She said nothing for moment, hoping Matthew's silence didn't mean he was waiting for her to return his sentiment.

"You don't love me, Matthew," she said.

"Great way to escape a comeback," he said sarcastically.

"Can we talk about this when I get back?"

"You bet." Matthew hung up quickly. Dana knew what that meant. His feelings were hurt, and they should be. Omar infiltrates her heart again and suddenly Matthew can't gain access? She could have at least said she loved everything about him, which couldn't be truer.

Dana closed her eyes and thought about Carmen. She hated to give Carmen credit for anything, but Carmen was right about one thing, there were plenty of fish in the sea, and hers were jumping. The only problem was deciding which fish to throw back and which to keep; the hardest decision she had to make in her life.

Dana groaned into the pillow. She had enough to sleep on to last the weekend.

Mission Impossible

A million or more out-of-town fans were expected to pack the San Diego streets for Super Bowl weekend. They all must have decided to drive—on the 405 south. They could crawl to San Diego faster than they were moving. In one hour, they were barely outside of L.A. County. Tempest blamed Charlene. They were supposed to leave at 6:00 AM. Charlene came knocking on the door after nine o'clock, saying Derrick had her car and she didn't have a ride. "I would've been on time if you had picked me up," Charlene said, blaming her. Tempest accepted the blame without argument. She could have picked up Charlene, if she wasn't secretly praying Charlene never showed up.

To keep entertained on the road, Tempest tried to guess which celebrities were hiding behind the tinted windows of the stretch limos and town cars.

Another two hours went by and they were only halfway to San Diego. Tempest felt a major headache coming on. Charlene kept telling her how to drive, and getting those freakin' polly-seed shells everywhere, and Dana was complaining about the bumper-to-bumper traffic. *Stay positive*, Tempest told herself.

Five hours on the road for what should've been a two-hour drive and they finally made it to San Diego. It was sad she didn't know or care which teams were in the Super Bowl this year. Tempest was just happy to be on the scene. The smell of excitement in the air gave her an immediate adrenaline rush.

She heard functions were poppin' all weekend. Tonight was the exclusive Player's Ball. If Sterling was in town by now, she might run into him there. Then there was the "NFL Experience." It was a must tomorrow, especially if she didn't run into Sterling tonight. Also, after the game, Jamie Foxx was throwing a function, plus there was a Player's Gala, which might be her last chance to run into Sterling.

In case Dana and Charlene didn't pack enough clothes, Tempest over-packed. Unbeknownst to them, she planned to stay the entire weekend. And she sure wasn't going to tell Dana they didn't have a place to change or shower, let alone sleep. Dana would probably catch the bus home, sticking her with Charlene for the weekend. Maybe Dana would have so much fun tonight she would change her mind about doing a turn-around, although, exciting Dana about anything usually took a miracle. Tempest knew she was wrong, but she was desperately seeking Sterling and would stop at nothing to find him. Out of a million or more people, however, her chances of running into him were slim to none.

As they exited the freeway into downtown San Diego, Tempest rolled back the convertible top to check the weather. It was picture perfect.

"What are we doing first, Tempest?" Dana sounded somewhat excited—finally.

"I printed out the agenda on the net. Functions are poppin' all over town."

"I'm hungry, I know that," Charlene said.

"Me too," Dana agreed.

"Where're we eating at, Tempest?"

"I don't know, Charlene."

"Have you talked to your co-worker about the room? I can't go anywhere tonight without taking a shower after that long ride," Dana said.

"I know that's right. Where're we changing at, Tempest?"

"How do I know, Charlene!"

Dana frowned up. "I thought we had a room we could use."

Tempest wore a sheepish grin. "Oh, I meant to tell you. My co-worker's not coming. But we'll find somewhere to change, girl. I'm hardly worried."

"You're joking, right?" From the corner of her eye, Tempest could see Dana giving her that *I'm gonna kill you, Tempest* look. Tempest kept her eyes on the road.

"I'll change at a gas station. I don't care. I'm ready to party!" Charlene said.

"I'm ready to go home," Dana said.

Charlene and Dana had Tempest's nerves so bad she was driving as if she knew where they were going. They drove in circles like three blind mice, trying to find their way through a maze of one-way streets.

"Turn right, right here!" Charlene ordered, causing Tempest's foot to accelerate. They all tilted to the side when she made a sharp right turn. Charlene's backseat driving was driving her crazy! She couldn't take directions from everybody. She was already driving like an old lady, scared to death she might wreck the Benz she could barely afford to rent.

"Where should I go next, Dana?" Tempest said, ignoring Charlene.

"Turn into this McDonald's," Dana said. "I have to eat before I pass out."

"I know that's right," Charlene said.

Maybe it was a good thing Charlene came along. Tempest nor Dana were bold enough to approach two strangers at McDonalds, ask if they had a room, and then have the nerve to ask if they could borrow it. Dana offered to buy the guys something to eat for their generosity.

"You don't owe us nothing," the one named Elgin said. "We wouldn't leave you sistahs out in the cold like that."

"Don't clean us out while y'all in 'nare," the other one named Leo joked, in a sluggish drawl. They were in their late twenties and full of hospitality all the way from Mississippi. During the ride to Elgin and Leo's hotel, they took a wrong turn and ran into a mob. It looked like the New Orleans Mardi Gras; wall-to-wall people traipsing up and down the middle of the road, car horns tooting, stereos blasting, and women howling from sunroofs.

"If you'd listen to me, Tempest, we wouldn't be stuck in this shit."

"It's *fine*, Charlene."

"Stop!" Charlene yelled, this time causing Tempest's heart to leap forward in her chest. Her foot slammed on the brake, bringing the car to a jerking stop.

"Charlene! You scared me!"

"Is that who I think it is?" Charlene was looking back.

"Where?" Dana said, twisting her neck around. Tempest looked back too, thinking she would see one of the celebrities she read would be in town this weekend. When she saw Sterling a million bees buzzed in her ears and a flood of white lights splotched her sight. She could recognize his bowed legs, broad shoulders, and football neck from across the continent.

"Sterling!" Charlene yelled at the top of her lungs, hanging out of the freakin' car like a ghetto queen. Tempest's whole body cringed. Thank goodness Sterling didn't hear Charlene's big mouth above the street noise.

"Roll up the windows! Hurry up!" Tempest slouched down in her seat. Remembering that the controls were at her fingertips, she sealed the windows and raised the convertible rooftop. They were at a standstill, right where Sterling and his friend, Trey, were strolling down the middle of the street. Tempest kept her head down and didn't let out a breath until Sterling disappeared into the crowd.

Dana looked at her as if to say, "I thought you wanted to see Sterling?" But Dana knew not to mention Sterling in front of Charlene. They both agreed it was best not to, knowing what Charlene's reaction would be.

"Forget Sterling's cheatin' ass," Charlene said.

"I'm not thinking about Sterling, Charlene," Tempest said.

"I know you *ain't*. He better hope I don't see him again tonight. If I do, he'll get cussed out. Ain't that right, Dana?"

"I'm not in it," Dana said.

Tempest kept quiet.

THE ODOR IN ELGIN AND Leo's room on the first floor of a Motel 6 was a combination of stale tobacco and skunkweed. From the looks of it, Elgin and Leo hadn't been back since the maid's visit. The double beds were made up, suitcases were neatly stacked against the wall, and the bathroom had clean towels. Tempest was glad, leery about showering behind strangers and catching a deadly foot fungus.

They agreed on thirty minutes to shower, dress, apply make-up and get out of Elgin and Leo's hair as fast as possible. While Dana showered, Tempest applied her make-up, and Charlene kept watch at the window to make sure Elgin and Leo didn't barge in while they were dressing. They rotated watch. Charlene, the last to come out of the bathroom, was fully dressed, her make-up beautifully applied. Tempest gave Charlene a once-over and turned up her lip.

Dana laughed. "Here comes the fashion police."

"You're wearing that, Charlene?" Tempest said.

"And I look damn good too." Charlene was obviously proud of her get up, so Tempest left the subject alone. By the time

Tempest lined and colored her lips, there was a knock on the door. When Charlene answered, Elgin and Leo's tongues fell out of their mouths, practically. Their salivation had little to do with Dana who hadn't dressed like she wanted to attract attention in Tempest's opinion. She wore basic black jeans, square-heeled boots and a sheer white bell-sleeved blouse with that African beaded choker Dana loved to wear with everything. What Dana wore couldn't compare to Charlene's black halter cat suit that lay on her body like new skin, and Tempest's scarlet red mini dress that exposed skin at the waistline and worked her long legs like stilts in platform pumps.

"Where you going looking like *that*, Momma?" Leo said to Charlene.

"To have me some fun. My man ain't acting right either. Humph."

Leo spread his arms like wings. "I'm taking applications. I'll be your man for the night."

"I bet you will," Charlene said, laughing flirtatiously.

"I'm lovin' Ca-li-forn-i-eh!" Elgin exclaimed. Tempest smiled and slid into the driver's seat. Charlene sat in the back, and Dana sat on the passenger's side. Leo and Elgin leaned over the converted top to keep them from backing out.

Leo looked like Charlene's type—tall, lean, lazy-eyed, sagging low, with teeth that *blinged* when his mouth opened. Elgin was clean cut and had his eyes on Tempest, looking her over like a tall drink of water that would quench his thirst.

"Y'all know y'all fine, don't y'all? You fine too, Little Momma," Leo said to Dana. Tempest wanted to laugh when Dana looked at her crossed eyed.

"Thanks for being so nice," Tempest said, sincerely.

"Can we get a number or something? We did let y'all use our room." Leo looked all sorrowful. Dana and Tempest exchanged glances. *Nothing came without a price*, Tempest thought. One of them would have to give up a number for the favor. Tempest sure wasn't. Neither was Dana.

"Give me your number," Charlene said to Leo, quickly programming Leo's number into her cell phone before Tempest skidded out of the parking lot.

A CLAUSTROPHOBIC WOULDN'T SURVIVE maneuvering through the bodies packed in downtown San Diego. Any hint of mayhem and Tempest feared she would be trampled to death. Since certain downtown streets were blocked off to cars, Tempest had to park the Benz and walk. She could've saved her money. On foot, she was catching eyes left and right, men hollering at her, grabbing at her, and stuffing party flyers in her hands. Dana was forced to take quick baby steps to keep up with her and Charlene's long legs weaving around bodies to get through the crowd. Tempest kept up her pace, anxious to get to the Player's Ball before she missed Sterling, if by chance he was there.

"Where we going now, Tempest?" Charlene barked. "My feet hurt!"

Tempest paid Charlene no mind, moving like a woman on a mission.

"I hope we're going somewhere where I can sit down," Dana said.

They were so close to the Player's Ball, Tempest could almost smell Sterling's cologne. She kept walking.

To enter the Player's Ball guests must have an invitation or an NFL Player's card. They had neither. The red carpet was rolled out for this function too. It led from the sidewalk to the entrance of the building and had a makeshift grand archway swathed with black velvet, guarded by two beefy doormen. They couldn't even get that close. Hired security was patrolling the checkpoint at the foot of the sidewalk and the perimeter of the courtyard. When a limousine pulled to the curb and Reggie Bush stepped out, Tempest's jaw dropped. Now she was dying to get in.

Tempest nudged Charlene and whispered. "That's Reggie Bush."

"Can he get us in?"

"No, Charlene."

"Then why do I care?"

"Let's find another club, Temp," Dana said, sounding fed up with the whole trip. "We're not getting in and I don't know if I want to."

"We'll get in. I already prayed about it, girl," Tempest said confidently. She had no idea how they would get in, but she was desperate enough to try anything.

"Eh!" this guy standing a few feet away said. He motioned with his head for Tempest to step his way. She almost ignored him before she realized he was a baller. His body was so broad and solid that she could see his muscles rippling under his silk shirt. Tempest stepped right to him. Even in heels, she had to look up to see his eyes. He had to be six-seven and weigh three hundred or more pounds. They stared eye-to-eye. Tempest didn't bat hers. She knew she had him when he blushed.

"You trying to get in?" he asked her.

"Can you get us in?" Her voice was baby sweet.

"I got two tickets. How many do you need?"

Tempest held up three fingers, smiling sweetly. He thought for a minute; then entwined his arm around hers. "Come on. I'll get everybody in," he said. They walked arm and arm in the line designated for invitees and players only. Charlene kept nudging her in the side, showing all thirty-two teeth. Dana's lips were still poked out. Tempest figured Dana would get over it once they got inside.

Tempest found out the guy's name was Adrienne Thomas. He played defensive lineman for the Cleveland Browns. A rookie, Tempest guessed, who was picked up in the last round. He walked with his chest out and chin up, but he didn't have that air of confidence the *big ballers* carry. Adrienne reminded Tempest of Sterling when he first signed, afraid his NFL career wouldn't last past one season.

"What's your name?" he asked her. When she told him her name, he said with a grin, "Are you a *temptress*?"

"I can be," Tempest said, flirting with him all the way to the entrance.

"I like you already." He gripped her arm tighter, like he was taking her to his hotel room tonight. When they reached the archway, Adrienne flashed his NFL player ID and talked security into letting her in gratis. Dana and Charlene handed over the invitations he had given them.

They were in! Tempest couldn't believe it. Her eyes panned the spacious building in one sweep. There wasn't anything lavish about the inside, other than the lounge furniture draped in white linen. Guys stood around checking out the ladies and the ladies were checking out each other, especially those wearing outfits as eye-catching as hers. When Tempest didn't see Sterling in the crowd, she breathed a sigh of relief. Timing meant everything.

Charlene and Dana said they were going to the bathroom. The bathroom was always Tempest's first stop, but Adrienne was holding onto her as if she were his lifeline. If she ditched him now, he would know she used him to get in, which would be outright wrong. She let him lead her through the crowd and into the ballroom.

She and Adrienne worked up a sweat on the dance floor, partying to song after song. When the last fast song ended, a slow song played. Adrienne pulled her close before she could leave, rotating his pelvis against hers like Elvis Presley. To put some distance between the two of them, Tempest laid the palms of her hands on his expansive chest, and leaned back against his vice grip. He pulled her closer, cutting off her circulation.

"You mind buying me a drink, Adrienne? I'm kinda thirsty," Tempest said.

"I'll buy you anything you want—Diamonds and pearls —if you come to my room tonight."

Tempest laughed off his invitation.

"I'm serious, Temptress."

"Tempest," she corrected.

"Tempest the Temptress." He licked his lips. "You got these long legs too, full of *thickness.*" His large hands slid up the back of her thighs. "I can do a lot with you tonight."

Tempest laughed nervously. "You're cute, Adrienne." She moved his hands from her behind and placed them back on the small of her back where she hoped they stayed. Her eyes scurried around the room for Dana or Charlene—and met Sterling's head on. He was standing with Trey, near the foot of the dance floor, staring right at her. Two hundred degrees of heat consumed her like a steam bath. Pretending she hadn't noticed Sterling, Tempest twirled Adrienne clockwise so her back was to Sterling. Her heart was beating so hard against Adrienne's chest he must have thought he had excited her. He pulled her closer, shoving his ham hock of a thigh between hers.

"You're coming with me tonight."

"I am?"

"I want you to," he said, all breathy and smelling of rum and coke. Tempest half heard whatever else Adrienne said over the blood rushing into her ears. It was hard to believe Sterling was standing behind her, with a front row seat to the show she was putting on for his benefit. Adrienne's hands found the back of her thighs again and moved halfway up her dress. She hoped Sterling was so jealous his face was green. *God is good!* She couldn't have prayed for better timing.

"Let's go, Adrienne," she said, entwining her arm with his and heading in Sterling's direction.

"If you're hungry, you can order room service," Adrienne said, so sweet Tempest felt awful for using him to get back at Sterling. This wasn't in her plans. She really didn't have a plan anymore. She was acting on pure emotion and adrenaline. Walking alongside Adrienne hid her from Sterling's sight better than a large tree trunk. She stayed poised, as if she was on a runway at New York Fashion Week with Yasmine. She hoped Sterling got a good look at her behind, because he could kiss it good-bye in this lifetime.

"Tee!" Tempest heard Sterling call out behind her. She froze and almost cried.

"What's up, Sterling?" Adrienne said like Sterling's biggest fan. Tempest wanted to dissolve on the spot.

"It's you, man," Sterling said and gave Adrienne dap.

"I'm trying to be like you, brody."

"Naw, it's you, man," Sterling insisted.

Adrienne slumped his broad shoulders. "We drafted in the same round, at the same time; man, I need your same kinda break. You're big ballin'.'"

"Your day will come," Sterling replied, then glanced Tempest's way. The reservation in his eyes told Tempest he didn't know whether she would slap him or hug him if he spoke to her. Tempest wanted to do both. She would storm off and leave Sterling and Adrienne to rekindle their friendship if she could put one foot in front of the other. She was paralyzed inside, more than a star-struck fan ecstatic to be in Sterling's space. Adrienne was so star-struck himself he didn't detect the energy sparking between her and Sterling.

"What's up, Tee?" Sterling's question came at her from another country.

"You know Temptress?" Adrienne said.

"It's Tempest, bro," Sterling corrected, as though his own name had been butchered.

"Tempest the Temptress." Adrienne pulled her close to him like a trophy he had won. "I'm taking this one home with me tonight."

Sterling's eyes seized hers. His nostrils flared. His face turned rock hard. "That's my wife you're holding onto." Sterling said this like she was the trophy he had lost and wanted back. Tempest couldn't stand there another second. She smacked her lips, rolled my eyes, and walked off with major attitude. Now, if she could find Dana and Charlene, she was going home! Her mission had been accomplished. Sterling was out of his mind with jealousy and now knew how it felt to have your heart crushed.

The ventilated air in the lounge was refreshing. Tempest took it in and exhaled. When she spotted Dana and Charlene walking toward her, she flew to meet them halfway.

"I've been looking everywhere for you guys," she said.

"We were with Elgin and Leo, girl," Charlene answered. "They're about to take us where the real black people party at down here." Dana's incensed eyes said she wasn't going anywhere with Elgin and Leo.

"You see Sterling back there anywhere?" Tempest whispered.

"We been seen Sterling. I'm the one who told him you were in here."

"Charlene!" Tempest screamed.

"What? He said he was sorry. I broke his ass down, told him the next time he messes over my baby sister, he's gonna wish he hadn't. Anyway, he's hooking me up when he signs his new contract!" Charlene laughed rowdily and tried to high-five Dana who ignored the gesture. Of all the times for Charlene's sweet side to come out, when she wanted Charlene to act ugly.

"If you want to kiss up to Sterling for his money, go ahead, Charlene. I'm leaving."

"Not without me," Dana said, following along.

Tempest didn't make it outside the building before Sterling caught up to her.

Matthew 6:14

A limo drove Tempest and Sterling to Sterling's luxury hotel. His room was pure chic heaven, with a king size white linen bed, leather headboard and six fluffy pillows. Tempest didn't go near the bed. She sat in one of the elegant chairs near the arched windows and picked up the hotel magazine, pretending to ignore Sterling.

Agreeing to leave with Sterling may not have been a good idea, not from Dana's viewpoint for sure. Dana's face turned into a pomegranate when she told Dana she was leaving with Sterling for an hour or two, sticking Dana with Charlene, Elgin, and Leo. *Poor Dana.* Tempest knew she was wrong, but she couldn't help herself. When Sterling stared at her with his heartbreaking eyes, and asked if they could please go somewhere and talk things out, it took everything in her to stop her tears from falling.

So far, Sterling hadn't talked much. She remembered when they would've had a week's worth of conversation no matter how long they had been apart. Those times were over. In the limo, Sterling stared at her pitifully, while she stared out of the window, purposely giving him her coldest shoulder.

Tempest peeked over the magazine. A stranger checking Sterling out on the sly would think he was born with a silver spoon in his mouth. He certainly looked more polished and at ease these days. He had on designer jeans, a black premium leather jacket, a spandex tee, and $400.00 dress shoes, Cole

Haans to be exact. If she had picked out his outfit, she would've suggested a raspberry or baby blue tee instead of sage, which didn't do anything for a cool tone person like Sterling, except make him look washed out. But playing his personal shopper was over too.

Tempest fidgeted in her seat and flipped through the magazine a second time. It was close to midnight and she had been sitting longer than planned, waiting for Sterling to say whatever he wanted to say to her. He was taking his sweet time hanging the clothes on his bed neatly in the closet. It wasn't until he hung up his jacket, sat on the bed, removed the gold chain from around his neck, detached his cell phone from his belt, and methodically laid them on the nightstand that he spoke:

"What're you wearing?" he said. His eyes poured over her outfit like hot liquid, causing her heart to thump. Knowing how Sterling hated her to show too much skin, she crossed her legs and leaned to the side, hoping he didn't miss the full length of her leg and half of her butt. Why should she care what he thinks?

"Clothes, Sterling," she finally answered. Tempest set aside the magazine and stared at him like he wasn't anyone important.

"What made you wear that dress?"

"Not because I wanted to catch a cold."

"Is that why you came to the Bowl, to catch something?" His tone was infused with anger. His eyes dug into hers, chipping away at her nerve.

"Maybe I was invited, Sterling," she said, and uncrossed her legs, pulling down the hem of her dress.

"Who invited you, that rookie Adrienne?"

"Maybe he did, maybe he didn't."

"When did you hook up with him?"

"Adrienne and I just met, Sterling," Tempest said before she could think. Sterling was good at that, storming her with questions, knowing she couldn't think fast enough. Shouldn't it be the other way around, her giving him the third degree?

"His hands were all on your ass and you just met him?"

"Even if I didn't, it's not your business."

"You'll always be my business." He grinned in jest. Tempest didn't blink or smile.

"Why, Sterling?"

"Because I love you."

Don't cry.

"You don't know what love is."

"I know what love is, Tee. If you had moved with me when I asked you to, I would've showed you how much I love you."

Tempest almost jumped up in a rage. "Don't freakin' try to blame me for what you did, Sterling! If you really loved me, it wouldn't have made a difference!"

Sterling dropped his head and rubbed the back of his neck. "You're right…it shouldn't have," he mumbled. They both knew Adrienne was out of the picture and Diamond had entered it. If Tempest so much as whispered Diamond's name, she would drown in her own tears. She didn't want to cry. She had to stay strong. She took a deep breath and swallowed the snag in her throat.

"She didn't mean anything to me. I can't tell you more than that," Sterling went on.

"I didn't mean that much to you either."

"You mean everything to me, Tee."

Please, do not cry. Tempest rolled her eyes instead.

"You don't believe me?"

"Why should I, Sterling?"

"Because I called you every day, and told you how much you mean to me before you changed your numbers. Why would you do that, knowing I was in the middle of the biggest season of my career and couldn't get to you?" Sterling's voice actually cracked as if he would cry.

Outwardly, Tempest stayed strong. Inwardly, her tears rumbled in her chest like a brewing storm ready to downpour. Her head felt light while her heart weighed heavy. What should she say or do next? Much of her wanted to wrap herself in Sterling's arms and pretend Diamond never came between them. But really, what had Sterling said or done to convince her to forgive him, other than to blame her for hurting *him*? He hadn't thought to fly home and see her when his season ended, to move heaven and earth to win her back. Nothing should have stood in his way if he really loved her.

"If you don't know why I changed my numbers, Sterling, I don't know why I'm here." Tempest headed for the door, feeling as if she was pushing against a gust of wind with each step she took. She pushed harder, taking long strides.

She made it into the hotel's corridor, then waited anxiously for the elevator to arrive. The faster the doors opened, the faster she could leave Sterling behind, with all the groupies for him to choose from. The elevator took an eternity to arrive, it seemed. When the elevator doors finally parted, Tempest flew inside and frantically pressed the lobby button. She was so done with Sterling.

Before the doors could close, Sterling bolted inside the elevator, startling her. Without a word, he laid his head on her shoulder and slumped.

"I love you like mad, Tee," he said. "I don't know what else to do to show you. If you want me to get on my knees right here and beg you to come back, I'll man up. Whatever you want me to do, …just don't leave me again." Tempest never heard Sterling sound so defeated. She got the sense that if a light wind blew through the elevator shaft, all two hundred forty pounds of him would tumble like a weed. Here was her opportunity to stampede his heart like he had hers, wipe her feet on him like a doormat, make him feel as small and worthless as he made her feel that night. Yet, what did she do? She stood there crying, with weak legs and limp arms, ready to tumble with Sterling if a wind happened to blow them both over. When you love someone as deeply as she loved Sterling, it's easier said than done to walk away. She could go on pretending she didn't love him, fooling her family, her friends, and herself, even trying to fool God, and the truth would outlive her.

In that moment, Tempest believed God spoke to her heart. *"For if you forgive people their trespasses (their reckless and willful sins, leaving them, letting them go, and giving up resentment), your heavenly Father will also forgive you." Matthew 6:14.*

The elevator sailed down twenty floors before stopping. Tempest took Sterling's hand in hers, telling him without words she forgave him. He pressed his lips in the hollow of her neck, folded his arms around her waist and squeezed her with all his might.

"Will you stay with me tonight?" he asked.

Sterling didn't have to ask her twice. "Yes," Tempest said without hesitation.

Family Ties

It was Monday. The gym wouldn't be seeing Dana today. She went directly home from work, intending to do nothing more than vegetate in front of the TV. Her body was still recovering from that nutty trip. She could've killed Tempest, and should have. By the time she saw Tempest again, Tempest had stars in her eyes.

Tempest tried to talk Dana into staying the weekend. Not even Sterling's offer to fly her home Sunday night convinced Dana to stay. She retrieved the keys to the Benz from Tempest and hit the road. Her eyelids were heavy as sandbags. Only the radio blasting, the AC gusting, and bumpy white lines kept her from landing into a ditch. She made it home in two hours flat— leaving Tempest and Charlene in 'la-la' land.

When Dana pulled up to the house after work, Devon, Carmen, and Corrine's cars were parked out front. The divorce mediation was today. Ignoring her tired legs, Dana hurried inside. The living room, now painted a soothing taupe by Omar, was peaceful and quiet. Corrine sat on the living room sofa reading a book as though nothing was amiss.

"What's going on, Mom? Where's Devon?"

"In the den with Carmen, talking," was all Corrine said, without looking up. Dana stood over her mother waiting for details. Corrine offered none.

"Talking about what?"

"I'll explain it to you later."

"So how did the mediation go?"

"Later, Dana," Corrine insisted. Her tone suggested that everything was fine, that Dana should calm down and stay out of it. That would be her mother's tone if the roof were on fire, so there wasn't any telling what went on at Family Court today.

In her room, Dana changed out of her work clothes and into something comfortable, pausing to tune into the silence. Not that she was trying to eavesdrop, but she couldn't hear a peep coming from the den. That was a good indication the mediation went better than she thought. Hopefully, Devon and Carmen came to a reasonable agreement about where DJ would live. If Carmen thought she was taking her nephew back East, Dana would personally contact the judge in protest.

Dana was preparing to sit down at the dining table with her plate of leftovers when Devon and Carmen emerged from the den. Carmen didn't give Dana a chance to speak. She said, "Hey, Dana. Momma Corrine, I'll see you later," kissed Corrine on the cheek and hurried out of the house.

Devon meandered toward her and sat down at the table.

"How did it go?" Dana said immediately.

"We came to an agreement," was all Devon said, teetering on two legs of the chair and staring off like Dana wasn't in his direct sight. A child who had wandered too far away from home couldn't have looked more lost than her brother. Maybe the mediation didn't go well.

"What kind of agreement?" she asked.

Devon explained what happened at the hearing, taking time to defend his position along the way. When he finished talking there wasn't enough testosterone in the world to make Dana understand how men think. How could Devon let Carmen move without contesting? So what if it was too emotionally difficult.

So what if the legal process to keep DJ in state was lengthy and expensive. Devon takes the cheap way out? Gives up on his son without a fight?

A lump developed in Dana's chest. She massaged it with her fingers. "You're saying I won't see my nephew anymore?"

"That's not what he's saying," Corrine chimed in, sounding like she was appeasing her own doubts more than Dana's.

"I'd like to know when I'll see him. Once a year, every other summer? When, Devon?"

"You weren't listening, Dana. The court's giving us thirty days to reconcile our differences. We're working things out, if we can."

Dana hiked her brow. "Did I hear you right?"

"Don't get excited."

Trust me, I'm not. "Are you sure you want to reconcile with Carmen?"

"I'm not sure of anything right now, but you're about to have another niece or nephew to babysit." A box of cigars and birth announcements couldn't boast the glee of a proud father to be more than Devon's smile. Dana almost said, *"Who's the daddy?"*

"I guess I should congratulate you," she said instead.

Devon laughed. "You guess? You're tripping, Dana." If only her brother knew how hard she was tripping. Dana covered her mouth with the palm of her hand to keep from telling him if he reconciled with Carmen, he would be in the company of three—him, his wife and her man. It was time she said something to Devon about his trifling wife.

"Did Carmen say anything to you?"

"Say anything to me about what?" Devon walked to the kitchen, opened the refrigerator, and grabbed an apple from the fruit bin. He returned to the dining room, leaned against the doorframe and chomped on his apple. "Say anything about what?" he pressed.

How could she put this?

"Did she say anything about why she's been acting the way she's been acting lately?" Dana said.

He took another bite of his apple. "I know why."

"You don't, Devon. If you did, your divorce would be final."

"Dana, you're talking to your brother," Devon said. Devon had a way of looking at her. When they were kids, and he did something Corrine disapproved of (like sneaking girls into his room), he would look at her in that same way and say, "Dana, did I do it?" She instinctively got his meaning. If he did, act as if he hadn't. "I know enough. Let's leave it at that," Devon added.

Dana nodded with understanding, never saying a bad word about Carmen to Devon. Blood might be thicker than water, but she had DJ and her new niece or nephew's interests at heart.

That night Dana couldn't get a decent night's sleep. Omar and Matthew were playing phone tag, one calling her after the other. Then Tempest called to give her an exhaustive report of her weekend with Sterling, going on and on about all the pro ballers and stars she met, throwing in how drunk and crazy Charlene had gotten, and how far Sterling had gone to make up. "He took me shopping and let me clean out the stores, girl!" Tempest boasted.

All Dana wanted to do was sleep.

THE NEXT DAY, DANA PAID a visit to Carmen, and not a friendly one. When Carmen opened the door, she looked as if Dana was the last person she wanted to see. Dana pointed a finger in Carmen's face before she knew it.

"I need to talk to you," she said and barged inside the house. When Dana turned around to face Carmen, Carmen's hands were at her hips.

"Have you gone crazy, Dana?" Carmen said.

"No, but I will if you cheat on my brother again."

Carmen's face went through a number of emotions and got stuck on stupid. "I don't know what you're talking about?"

Dana thought about DJ and said, "Who's here?"

"Nobody," Carmen said. "But let's get back to why you walked in here like you lost your mind, pointing your finger in my face. Ask me the whole story before you make accusations you know nothing about."

"I know everything I need to know." Dana held up her cell phone and pressed play, letting the video presentation of Carmen do the talking for her. Carmen's face and posturing changed, but not as Dana expected. She didn't know what she expected really, Carmen to break down in tears and show a fraction of remorse at minimum.

"You're spying on me now, Dana?" Carmen said coolly. "Don't you have anything better to do?" Carmen walked to the dining room, took a seat at the table, and sipped her glass of wine. Her leg jittered, the only indication that she was visibly shaken up.

Dana pressed the end button on her phone. Carmen had gotten the picture. Her lying, cheating ass was caught.

"Does my brother know about this man?" Dana didn't give Carmen a chance to answer. "You know he doesn't!"

"You don't know what Devon knows, Dana."

"If he doesn't know, it's because I haven't told him for my nephew's benefit, not yours," Dana ranted on. "Do you really think Devon doesn't know? My brother's not stupid, Carmen; he's just stupid enough to take you back. How could you do this to him? Devon treated you like you walked on water."

Finally, Carmen's eyes shone with remorse. "Does Momma Corrine know?"

"Know what? That you're trifling or that you're pregnant?"

Carmen stood up and got in her face. "Look, Dana. You don't know what I've been through, so don't come in here passing judgment on me."

"What Devon has been through, you must mean," Dana said. "And is this baby Devon's or your side action's?" Carmen walked to the kitchen, gazed out of the kitchen window and nursed her wine. Dana was right behind her. "Well, is it?"

"It's Devon's, don't worry," Carmen said.

"How do I know that for sure?"

Carmen whipped around to face Dana. "I guess you'll have to wait to find out, won't you." Carmen took another sip of her wine.

"You think you should be drinking in your condition?"

"I think you should leave before one of us gets our feelings hurt." Carmen's stare was intense. Dana's eyes pierced right back. They squared off, possibly about to fight over her brother for the first time in ten years, a fight that would surpass the physical and do irreparable damage to their friendship.

"What kills me the most is that I looked up to you, Carmen," Dana said, backing down. "I wanted to be just like you, if and when I get married, and now I find this out." Dana shook her head. "Are you still screwing around on my brother while you're trying to reconcile your marriage?"

"What do you think?"

"I don't know what to think anymore. I don't even think you're sorry for what you did, to tell the truth."

"What do you want me to say, Dana? Whatever I feel, you'll never understand."

"Maybe not, but if you ever cheat on my brother again, it won't be Devon that'll get hurt." Dana's gaze stayed on Carmen before she walked out of the house.

Driving home, Dana wondered if the look on Carmen's face said, "*You don't have to worry about me hurting your brother again,*" or "*I'd like to see you try to hurt me.*" Carmen was so good at concealing her true feelings, Dana wasn't sure what was running through her sister-in-laws mind. Dana was just proud she spoke up for her brother, if he never spoke up for himself.

Luck of the Draw

Everything in Carmen's office was packed and gone, including photos, employee awards, books, DJ's drawings, coffee mugs and other personals items she didn't want to leave behind. From her office window, Carmen stared off, seeing beyond the LAX traffic control tower. Behind it, dark clouds hung over the ocean, the rain making impressions of dewdrops on the window. Carmen didn't much notice, however. Her thoughts were clear into the future. She saw her family, happy and whole again, the new baby, and the events of present being a distant memory. But her future remained cloudy. No prayer or wish in her heart could reassure her that her marriage would survive another day. Was that her deepest fear, that everything she loved she was sure to lose?

To add, she had to deal with her sister-in-law along the way. Carmen shook her head, thinking back on the day Dana came to the house to "tell her off," she supposed. She should have expected it. Sweet little Dana, no older than sixteen when she and Devon met, had actually threatened to kick her ass, in so many words. If she wasn't in shock, she may have said something. But it wouldn't have mattered what she said to Dana. No one would understand how deeply her sorrow ran for what she had done; no one but she and God, and at the end of the day, that mattered most.

All things said, Carmen knew whatever ultimately happened between her and Devon, she and Dana would always be sisters.

Only a true sister would withhold the evidence Dana had on her and not use it against her. Three months had gone by and so far Dana had kept her incriminating evidence to herself.

Carmen thought back on her visit to Nicole's house and the one thing Tone said that stayed on her mind. "Take a lesson from me, Carmen. I was locked up for a long time, not in a six by eight foot cell, but in my mind, reliving what I couldn't go back and do over. You can't change destiny, baby, you can only live through it."

And with any luck, survive it, Carmen thought.

"Carmen, my friend. I will miss you."

Carmen turned around as Francisco ambled up to her, his arms outstretched for a hug. It might take years before she lucked up on another boss as great as Francisco. Carmen expressed her sadness and appreciation in a long embrace with Francisco, apologizing for wetting his suit with her tears.

"Aye! It's okay." He snapped a handkerchief from his lapel pocket to dry off, then smiled at her fatherly, his eyes saying she was making a big mistake.

"You don't have to do this, Carmen. The job is still yours if you want it."

"Francisco, you and I both know it's time for me to leave, for everybody's good." Francisco's nod told her he got her meaning. She might kill those women she worked with if she stayed. "You have a good replacement. I like him. He caught on fast."

"But he's a guy. Who will I flirt with?" They swapped flirtatious glances for the last time and smiled. "If you need another reference, you know who to call." He laid a hand on her shoulder. "Eh, it happens, Carmen. But if someone asks, it didn't. Comprende?"

"Comprende."

Carrying the bouquet of flowers the catering department had given her, she and Francisco walked through the cubicle area of the sales department that led to the hotel's corridor. The only one of her sales associates to wish her a farewell was Brian. Now that she was leaving, Carmen understood Brian's lukewarm personality toward her. It wasn't that Brian didn't want to be bossed around by a black woman; he wanted to do his job and stay out of the office drama. Carmen couldn't say the same for Marissa and Lillian. They knew not to look her way when she passed. Lillian's head was down, her fingers pretending to dial a number on the phone, and Marissa's back was to her. When Carmen passed Kendall's cubicle, it was empty. She didn't have to worry about seeing him again. If by chance he looked her up or called, she only had one thing to say to him. "I'm sorry for everything."

It turned out Kendall was an innocent bystander in Lillian and Marissa's scheme to get her fired. It didn't matter whose bright idea it was, they both stood to gain by getting rid of her. Marissa could take over the sales director's seat she thought would automatically become hers, and Lillian could have Kendall to herself, which didn't happen either. Had they asked, Carmen could have told them that life wasn't always fair, even if you play by the rules.

Lillian and Marissa would have gotten away with their dirty little scheme had Kendall played along. Francisco, being more than a great boss, but also a great friend, filled her in on aspects of the investigation she wasn't privy to. Per Francisco, Kendall told the investigator their sexual encounters were strictly consensual, denying Lillian's claim that he was scared to come forward on his own, fearing termination. That meant it had to be Lillian's ass that hacked into Kendall's computer and printed out those emails the investigator got a hold of.

To support Lillian's lie, Marissa played the offended eyewitness, saying she was "distressed and couldn't work while her boss made open and public advances toward male employees." It was all bullshit. Yet, in the end, Lillian and Marissa got their just reward. Here she was saying her final farewells and there they sat, going about their daily work schedule.

Kendall, on the other hand, didn't have to worry about being out of a job. He lost his when immigration handcuffed him and hauled him to jail for falsifying his employment records. Carmen hoped like hell he was back in the Dominican Republic, and like her, trying to put the pieces of his life back together after a tumultuous year.

Carmen said good-bye to Francisco at the front door of the hotel and backed out of her designated parking space for the last time.

Instead of going home, as she intended, Carmen headed south on the 710 freeway and exited Willow Street, wondering how would it feel to drive into the lot of a new property, not as a sales director, but as an event coordinator? She drove slowly by her new place of employment, feeling no drama connected to the one-story, basic building, with ten elaborate banquet rooms. The facility was two stars down from the Tower West Hotel and didn't host the exclusive clientele Carmen was accustomed to, but she was willing to take the demotion. She was in no hurry to manage employees, least of all of the opposite sex. She was keeping life simple from here out.

The baby reminded Carmen that it was time to eat. She didn't let her reservations or fear of rejection stop her from calling Devon.

"Are you up for lunch in thirty minutes?" she said when he answered.

"That's a coincidence. I had my phone in my hand, ready to call you," Devon said, with a smile in his voice. "How was your last day on the job?"

Heart of the Matter

Nobody had to tell Tempest she was a fool for forgiving Sterling. She heard it enough times from everybody. She knew there was a chance a million more chicks would entice him to be unfaithful again. There was also an equal chance that he learned from his mistake. If, for instance, she chose not to forgive Sterling, to dismiss the love and friendship they shared before Diamond came along, what guarantee was there the next man she loved wouldn't hurt her too? There wasn't a guarantee. So, why not take a chance with the man she already loved?

Nadine, who supported her decision from the start, said that was the most logical thing she had ever said. "To each his own, baby," her mother said. Her Daddy only shook his head and went back to watching TV. Tempest found out later that he said what he had to say directly to Sterling, loud and clear. Whatever Charlene said, Tempest wasn't trying to hear.

Some people would never understand the heart and how one person could fill each of its chambers and keep it beating. Maybe it came with age when you stop caring what people think or maybe it came with maturity. What Tempest experienced did more to mature her than time itself. If she could handle falling from a skyscraper and hitting rock bottom, she could handle most anything. And now, for the first time in her life, she was moving away from her family and friends, a true test of her growth.

Last night was her going away party, or more so her eating, dancing, singing and celebrating party. It started at seven o'clock in the evening and ended at three this morning. Today, Tempest couldn't hide her sadness. She stood in the living room, looking at the moving boxes stacked and ready to be shipped, and cried. Moving so far away from home wasn't easy for her. Well, it wasn't *so* far away, only nine hours by car and an hour or so by plane. The biggest plus about Sterling signing with the Oakland Raiders was that San Francisco was one of Nordstrom's buying headquarters and Linda thought there was a good chance she would land that buyer position she applied for. Tempest thought so too. She nailed the interview. Her knowledge of merchandising and fashion was beyond the panel's expectations.

God had poured His blessing on everyone it seemed. Back in March, Sterling signed a nine-million-dollar contract over four years, with a three-point-four-million-dollar signing bonus and was in the process of buying his mother a beautiful house in a better neighborhood. Dana bought a house too, if it could be called one. Carmen and Devon were having a baby; Nadine and Will had a beautiful baby girl, and on the first day of summer she married Sterling in a fantasy wedding.

Who said money couldn't buy happiness? Sterling paid Don Lou enough money to put her dress at the top of his calendar, with no hassle or fuss. It was an exquisite crisp beauty, with one thousand pearls embroidered onto silk and satin, and one unique *T. Perry Design* touch—crimson color. It took Sterling's breath away.

That night, Sterling took hers away, again and again. Their honeymoon started at the Beverly Wilshire Four Seasons Hotel and ended on an exotic island in Tahiti, in an over-the-water bungalow, with a flower petal adorned Jacuzzi. Their seven days of heaven were worth every day of their wait!

Tempest hadn't mentioned Diamond's name once since she and Sterling reunited. She pushed what happened between

Sterling and that chick so far back in her memory sometimes she forgot it ever happened. On the days when it popped back into her mind, taking hold of her heart and squeezing it, Tempest recited *Matthew 6:14* and kept her thoughts positive. When she decided to forgive Sterling, she did it with her whole heart and soul.

New Phases

Dana relaxed on the aft deck of her thirty-four foot yacht, sunning in the warm Santa Ana winds. The afternoon sun cast a beautiful light on the water, making it sparkle like a fine cut diamond for miles ahead. Dana was spellbound by the reflection. She would happily sit there until sunset if she weren't meeting Matthew for breakfast in an hour. She rationalized that she deserved a few minutes longer to enjoy the moment. After all, she was surviving on little sleep following Tempest's going away party last night.

Tempest had actually gone through with it, married Sterling in spite of everything. Dana supposed the half million-dollar engagement ring Sterling gave her didn't dissuade Tempest from saying "I do." How many women would turn that down? Not Tempest. Dana laughed to herself. She was happy for her best friend, and meant it from the bottom of her heart. After all, Tempest supported her decision to make the most unconventional move she could imagine making in her life.

"That's so romantic, Dana," Tempest said when Dana gave up looking for a house and started looking at yachts. Dana didn't consider her decision romantic, but it was definitely adventurous, exciting and *daring*.

Her yacht couldn't compare to Matthew's family yacht in any way, shape or form. It was half the size and about fifteen years older, but it was a pearl white beauty, and as economical as living in a two-bedroom condo in Paramount. Her largest expense was her monthly live-aboard slip fee at Long Beach Marina. Otherwise, the only downside to living aboard, so far, was doing her wash at a Laundromat, bumping her head mornings on the low ceiling in her modest stateroom, and the long hike it took to get to her car at the marina. The inconvenience, however, was not a great sacrifice to behold a breathtaking waterfront each morning, dreamy sunsets each night, and shops, boutiques, and fine dining a deck away.

Corrine would likely never get used to the idea of her daughter living aboard a "boat." Dana hadn't quite gotten used to it either. She took a crash course on yachting, but there was so much more she had to learn. Thanks to Matthew, her learning curve was cut in half. She had a great deal to thank Matthew for, when she thought about it. It was Matthew who helped her nab the boat at an affordable price. It was also Matthew who was giving her lessons on how to operate a power yacht. Matthew turned out to be a great friend, one who Dana would cherish for years to come. His kindheartedness forced her to reevaluate her intentions. She had to ask herself if whenever Matthew fell outside the boundaries of her expectations, would she jump back into Omar's bed—the man she felt most akin to, who would love her into old age and be by her side until the day she died. Omar was that kind of man, unquestionably.

But whether either relationship transitioned to the next phase of her life was no longer that important to Dana. She was keeping her options open. Next weekend, she made plans to cruise to Catalina Island with Matthew, her first trip out on her very own cruiser. The following weekend she had a date with Omar. They were flying to Vegas for a franchise convention Omar wanted to attend. Not exactly her idea of a romantic getaway, but at least Omar was venturing out more these days.

Dana also had her volunteer work to keep her busy. Omar talked her into joining him at the Boys and Girls Club. Now she was playing big sister to teen girls. Her job was to counsel these girls, to be a friend, and to act as a role model, putting her perceived parenting skills to the test. Volunteering with the girls made a room of twenty-two second graders feel like a vacation. On the one hand, these strong willed girls needed her advice and guidance. On the other hand, they were more certain of themselves and the direction of their lives than she.

It took Dana back. At that age she wasn't much different. Somewhere along the way she found herself feeling around in the dark, letting life direct her instead of directing it. Hopefully, she could teach these girls half of what they had taught her—to laugh without reason, cry in the open, view boys as cute but not so important, and should she stumble and fall, laugh at herself because as they love to say, "It ain't that serious."

Mostly, these girls, from the poorest neighborhoods by the standards of most, reminded her to hold onto her dreams. One day she would marry, buy a house with a large backyard and fill it with six kids. In the mean time, purchasing her very own yacht was the best 27th birthday gift she could have given herself.

Dana finally thought of the perfect name for it. She named it simply "*Rose.*"

About the Author

SHERYL MALLORY-JOHNSON is the author of two previous books. She holds a Bachelors Degree in Business Administration from Texas Southern University, and a Master Degree in Social Work from San Diego State University. Along with being a full-time novelist, Sheryl works as an adjunct professor teaching literature. She also provides book coaching and writing services to aspiring authors. She resides in Southern California with her family.

Visit Sheryl's website at www.sherylmallory-johnson.com

CPSIA information can be obtained at www.ICGtesting.com
Printed in the USA
LVOW100036210312

273977LV00010B/3/P